ABOUT THE AUTHOR

Elizabeth O'Roark spent many years as a medical writer before publishing her first novel in 2013. She holds bachelor's degrees in journalism and arts from the University of Texas, and a master's degree in counseling psychology from the University of Notre Dame. She lives in Washington, D.C. with her three children. *A Deal With The Devil* is her ninth book.

ALSO BY ELIZABETH O'ROARK

The Devil Series:
A Deal with the Devil
The Devil and the Deep Blue Sea
The Devil You Know
The Devil Gets His Due

The Summer Series:
The Summer We Fell
The Summer I Saved You

A DEAL WITH THE DEVIL

ELIZABETH O'ROARK

PIATKUS

PIATKUS

First published in Great Britain in 2023 by Piatkus

1 3 5 7 9 10 8 6 4 2

A CIP catalogue record for this book
is available from the British Library.

ISBN: 978-0-349-44066-8

Printed and bound in Great Britain by Clays Ltd, Elcograf S.p.A.

Papers used by Piatkus are from well-managed forests
and other responsible sources.

Piatkus
An imprint of
Little, Brown Book Group
Carmelite House
50 Victoria Embankment
London EC4Y 0DZ

An Hachette UK Company
www.hachette.co.uk

www.littlebrown.co.uk

This is dedicated to my crew,
the Badass Middle-Aged Elven Assassins,
without whom I wouldn't have published
a single book.

❧ 1 ❧

Good versus evil.

Comic books make it look so easy. One guy wants to destroy the world. Another wants to save it. The bad guy has a scar and is cruel to his girlfriend. The good guy has a jawline that could cut glass and gives half his dinner to the stray dog in the alley.

Real life is more complex. Sometimes the bad guy is hiding a heart of gold under that scarred exterior. Sometimes they *both* have a nice jawline and you often don't know what you've signed on for until it's too late.

Except when you're invited to work for Satan...then it's fairly clear what you're in for.

The offer has come over coffee with my friend Jonathan, on a pleasant patio where palms overhead filter Santa Monica's bright morning sun. "Let me tell you how much it pays before you say no," he adds, which is exactly the sort of suggestion you'd expect from Satan's head of personnel.

I should clarify that Hayes Flynn, Jonathan's boss, isn't *technically* Satan—as in, he does not rule the underworld or have horns. While he might own a pitchfork, I assume based on those custom Tom Ford suits he wears that he has a *guy* for all his pitchfork-related needs.

And Satan is my nickname for him, not Jonathan's, but still an apt one. First, because he's a plastic surgeon to the stars, which is exactly the kind of job you'd expect of Satan, were Satan for some reason unable to practice law.

Second, because he's British. It's common knowledge that any extra-suave British male who is not James Bond is a bad guy, or so I assume based on Jane Austen novels and the one James Bond movie I've watched.

And finally, because he's slightly too perfect, which points to some kind of black magic at work. Too tall, too fit...square-jawed and dark-eyed and lush-mouthed in a way that makes him a danger to others. Just ask all these poor actresses he takes out once or twice, leaving them behind to post sad pics and vague quotes about loneliness on Instagram. I can't guarantee they're about him, but he's certainly pretty enough to inspire plenty of self-pity in his wake.

Not that it's a problem for me. My superpower, acquired over the course of this very difficult year, is that I'm immune to beautiful men. My sister would say *broken*, not immune, but she's been with the same guy since she was fourteen, so what does she know?

"What would I be doing?" I ask, leaning back in my seat. The question is mostly a formality. Given my financial situation, I'm not in the position to say no to much at present. "I assume since it's Hayes we're discussing, it must involve some human trafficking or heroin."

He laughs, leaning back in his chair, weary and amused in the same moment. "Nothing quite that bad. I want you to replace me while Jason and I are in Manila."

I set my coffee down with a thud. The hunt for Jonathan's temporary replacement began months ago, the second he and Jason got the heads-up their adoption was approved. "What happened?" I ask. "I thought you found someone."

He shakes his head. "It wasn't a good fit." Which I assume is code for *Hayes is being an asshole*, or *Hayes slept with her during the interview*. Though Jonathan's never said a bad word about his boss, thanks to *TMZ* and *DeuxMoi*, I know better. He makes my ex look like a choirboy. "Anyway," he concludes, "it occurred to me I should just hire you. He needs an assistant. You need money. It's perfect."

Jonathan deals with demands: celebrities expecting to be slid into Hayes's packed schedule on a moment's notice, or Hayes requesting sought-after reservations and exotic foods. The job calls for tact, diplomacy, and the ability to make the impossible happen. Saying I'm the perfect choice is like setting up a sixteen-year-old boy with a ninety-year-old female and insisting it's perfect because they're both straight.

"So you're desperate and can't get anyone else to take the job."

He looks up from his egg-white omelet, his mouth twitching. "No, Tali. You're discreet and I think you'd be good for each other. Also, it pays four grand a week."

My eyes go wide. I knew he did well—certainly better than I do working at Topside, a bar specializing in Jimmy Buffett and bandannas worn as headgear—but not *that* well. Four grand times the six weeks he'll be gone won't solve my problems, but it will make them a hell of a lot smaller.

"You probably should have led with that," I tell him, and he breaks into my favorite Jonathan smile, sweet and surprised, like a child who's been paid an unexpected compliment.

"That was easier than expected, given how you feel about Hayes," he says, pushing his glasses up the bridge of his nose. "And I want you to know...I still think you're going to finish the book. But I thought if you could stop panicking about paying back the advance, it might take some of the pressure off."

He has more faith in me than I have in myself, then. The book—for which I received a hefty advance I've already spent—has remained only half done for the past year and is due in a matter of months. If selling my soul to the devil was an option at this point, I'd probably take it, so I'm not going to turn down merely being on his payroll.

But it all feels too easy. This is *Hayes* we're discussing, after all. "So that's it? I mean, don't I need to interview or something?"

A shadow passes over his face, a tiny curl of worry. "You'll need to sign a contract and a non-disclosure agreement, but that's about it. Hayes trusts my decisions. It'll be fine."

I'm not so certain about that, I think, remembering the one and only time Hayes and I have stood in the same room. I still don't know why he was in Topside, sticking out like a sore thumb in his expensive suit, or why—for one long moment—he was watching me with something that seemed like interest. But he hadn't even reached the bar before that thing in his face changed, turned cold and resigned, and the next time I looked up he was gone. Perhaps it had nothing to do with me, but it doesn't seem like the most auspicious start to our working relationship.

"I just have one request..." Jonathan says. He leans forward, arms of his suit pressed to the table, hands flat. "Don't sleep with him. Please. If you jump into bed with him the day I leave, I'll have to come straight home."

I laugh loudly enough to draw stares from the neighboring tables. It's appalling that Jonathan, my oldest friend, would even suggest it.

"Give me some credit. I would never have sex with someone like Hayes. I'm done with untrustworthy men."

His shoulders sag as he scratches his forehead. "I worry you've got an idea about Hayes created entirely by some bullshit gossip and your vivid imagination." His eyes fall on me, full of sympathy now. "And Matt never seemed untrustworthy. We were all as surprised as you when that went south."

My chest tightens. There's nothing reassuring about what Jonathan just said. I'd prefer to hear where I'd gone wrong, to have him point out the signs Matt was going to fail me the way he did, but even now all anyone can say about my ex is *but he was such a great guy*.

Jonathan reaches across the table and squeezes my hand. "It's gonna get better, Tali. When the right guy comes along, your walls will recede."

I sort of doubt that, given my plan is just to avoid men altogether.

But either way, Hayes Flynn won't be touching my walls, or anything else.

❧ 2 ❧

I pull into the circular drive and glance over the schedule Jonathan gave me:

- *7:30 Arrive at the Starbucks on Highland. Order one venti latte (whole milk) three sugars.*
- *7:45 Let yourself in using code. Disable alarm. Place coffee and papers on kitchen counter.*
- *If Hayes is not downstairs by 8 AM, text him. If that fails, you'll need to go wake him up. Warning: he may have company.*

I'm worried I'm missing something, and in truth I'm not even sure I've gotten those first few instructions right. The latte has already sloshed on my skirt and I don't know if I'm supposed to add the sugars myself or if The Dark Lord can actually do that much on his own.

I could check with Jonathan if I really had to, but he's currently in route to Manila, and I should probably save harassing him for the bigger questions. God knows they're likely as the day unfolds—if I even last that long. Sitting here in front of Hayes's Hollywood Hills mansion, I'm starting to feel a little uncertain on that front.

First, because I already hate my boss, which is always a bad sign.

Second, because I *really* hate his house. I'd expected something more like Hayes himself: clean lines and beautiful angles with pops of lush, unexpected beauty. Instead, it's the house you'd buy if, perhaps, you got famous off a YouTube song about farting—large enough to house a sizable village and replete with far too many tacky flourishes: fountains, columns, arching windows, *turrets*. And in a climate where flowering trees and bougainvillea flourish, his only landscaping involves some neatly trimmed hedges and a single, stocky palm, which hints at the exact sort of soullessness I'd expect from someone with his tabloid history.

I put my shoulders back and take one deep breath before I exit the car. Whether I like him or his house is irrelevant. This job is a means to an end for me, the first decent break I've had in a very hard year, and I'm not going to mess it up.

No matter how awful he clearly is, I don't have to like him to hold my tongue and do his bidding. It's only six weeks, after all.

Juggling the papers and the coffee and my bag, I manage to open the door and silence the alarm. My heels echo against the floor as I walk through, deeming the interior every bit as disappointing as the exterior: marble floors, lots of huge wood furniture, two winding grand staircases leading to separate wings of the house. I'm lonely sleeping by myself in a studio, so I can't imagine how I'd feel in a space this vast. Then again, Hayes undoubtedly doesn't sleep alone often.

I pull out the two cell phones I've inherited from Jonathan—one for Hayes's normal calls and one for emergencies—and am about to arrange the newspapers when I hear him coming down the stairs. My heart begins to beat—overfast, nearly audible. Dealing with patients and running errands will be the bulk of my job. *That* I can handle. The one thing I'm not prepared for is meeting the man himself.

I glance in the mirror across from me, confirming that the new silk blouse is still tucked in and the spilled coffee stain on my skirt isn't too obvious. Everything about me screams "pocket-sized and nonthreatening"—hair pulled back in a high ponytail, mascara and lip balm on my face and nothing more—aside from my eyes, which remain a trifle, *um*, defiant. I need them to say *I'm here to serve*, and at present they say something more like *I'm carrying pepper spray*, or *I know gang members*.

Before I can correct it, he appears, dressed in a crisp white shirt and black suit, even taller than I'd realized—and even prettier. Dark hair gleaming, damp and pushed off his face, a slight flush to his sharp cheekbones, still warm from the shower.

It's a face that would force you to look a second and then a third time. A face that makes you brace for the sound of his voice...undoubtedly low and rough as gravel, the kind of voice that plucks a chord at the base of your stomach, makes you squeeze your thighs together in anticipation. Or would, were he not looking at me as if I'd just broken into his home.

"Is this a joke?" he demands. His voice is exactly as I imagined. Too bad he had to ruin it by being him. He must have known I was coming, and I haven't done anything wrong *yet*.

"No," I say, suddenly grateful the counter separates us. "I'm Tali. Jonathan asked me to fill in for him while he was gone. I assumed you knew."

A muscle flickers in his jaw. "He told me my replacement was named Natalia," he says, blowing out a tight breath. "Not his friend, the *bartender*."

He says "bartender" as if it's synonymous with *racist* or *pedophile*. I'd think a guy who drinks as much as he does would have a great deal of respect for my profession.

"Is there a problem?" I ask. My voice is probably more threatening and less conciliatory than is called for—no bad situation I can't make worse. But I quit my job for this, so I'm not going down without a fight.

"I need to speak to Jonathan when he lands," he says, pressing the bridge of his nose between thumb and forefinger. "There's obviously been a misunderstanding. I mean, do you even have any experience?"

Do I have experience answering the phone and picking up dry cleaning? Yes. Loads. I truly can't believe Jonathan worried I'd sleep with this guy. Granted, I'd like to do plenty of things to him, but they mostly involve spit, and not in a sexy way.

"Yes," I reply, folding my arms beneath my chest. "Last I checked, answering phones didn't require an MBA from Harvard."

"Which you clearly don't have," he says.

I could counter that I've attended grad school, but referencing something I *quit* probably won't help my case.

He grabs the coffee, sighing as he glances at the sugars. Apparently, he *is* too busy and important to tear his own sugar packets. Lesson learned for tomorrow, not that it appears there will be a tomorrow.

"I'm calling Jonathan," he says, already walking away. "Don't get comfortable."

The door slams and my breath leaves me, slowly and thoroughly. What the hell even happened? I'd understand if he disliked me after getting to know me—he wouldn't be the first—but he was being a jerk before I even opened my mouth.

I lean against the marble counter and press my face to my hands, the disappointment sinking in at last. I've already quit at Topside and on very little notice. They won't be hiring me back, which means unless I find something else quickly, I'm heading home to Kansas with my tail between my legs, just the way my ex-boyfriend predicted I would.

What's hardest is that this job felt like a *sign*—that things would be fine, that I was going to be able to dig my way out of this hole I'm in. But every bit of luck I ever had evaporated the minute I accepted that advance. Why would this be different?

❧

EVENTUALLY I MAKE MY WAY TO JONATHAN'S OFFICE, JUST TO the right of the kitchen. It's small and sunny and Zen-like in its austerity. Aside from the desk and chair, the only décor is a single bright green fern and two framed photos—one of Jason and one of the three of us, laughing in the breeze with the Santa Monica pier lit up behind us.

I sip my cold coffee and begin to take down the weekend's messages, waiting to be fired. I've almost, *almost*, accepted the idea, by the time he calls midday. But my stomach still drops. I've never been fired before. Nor have I ever lost this much money in one fell swoop.

"This morning," he begins stiffly, "I was...surprised. I just want to be sure you know what you're in for here. It's not an easy job."

Relief hisses through my blood, like steam escaping a valve. I'm not sure what changed his mind, and I don't really care. "That's okay."

"You'll be working long hours," he says, "and you'll have to do...other things as well."

I sink into my chair. "That sounds like the sort of vague thing Harvey Weinstein would suggest," I say with an awkward laugh.

This is greeted with utter silence. Apparently, I've once again derailed a conversation with one of my misplaced attempts at humor.

"No," he finally says. "But there may be things about my lifestyle you find distasteful."

"You mean the turrets?" It just comes out. I internally cringe at my lack of filter. I need a muzzle. "Never mind. I don't care about the distasteful stuff. It's fine."

"Okay," he says on a heavy, disappointed exhale. Clearly, he was hoping I'd walk away on my own. "You can stay on until Jonathan gets back. And I'm sure he told you this, but let me reemphasize: *no one* gets my personal number. No one."

Jonathan already explained this to me, with the urgency of someone discussing nuclear codes. I'm to take messages if anyone calls, and forward any texts that seem pertinent, personal or otherwise. But the only people who actually have Hayes's number are his friend Ben, Jonathan, and now me...so he'll know who's to blame if it gets out.

"Make sure people leave you alone. Jonathan told me."

"Exactly," he replies. "Yourself included." And then he hangs up without another word.

I heave a deep sigh and close my eyes. It's going to be a really, really long six weeks.

There is, I've discovered, no day so bad that passing my ex-boyfriend's new billboard can't make it worse. As I weave past hipster coffee shops and organic grocers on the way to work, Matt's pretty face smiles down at me from the side of a ten-story building, conveniently positioned so I can't avoid it without taking my eyes off the road entirely.

Matt's first big break was in this Vietnam-era movie, *Write Home*, playing a young soldier whose death had viewers weeping. His pretty face is what first caught people's attention—the lush lips, the blue eyes, the perfect features. But I think what won people over is that he'd basically played a version of himself: sweet, earnest, well-intentioned. A simple guy who cared about those around him and just wanted to return to his girl back home.

It's the face I still see when I look at that billboard: The high school sophomore who fell, inexplicably, for a bookish fourteen-year-old. The sweet boy who took me to prom, who got almost every "first." Shouldn't I see the lie in him when I look up and see his face now? I really hate that I don't. Because if I still don't know where I went wrong with Matt, how will I ever know with anyone else?

I arrive at Hayes's house. Newspapers are gathered, the alarm is turned off. I'm not letting Matt ruin my day.

Hayes's coffee is placed on the counter with the sugar already added. Wouldn't want him to tear and stir it on his own, like an asshole.

I brace myself when I hear him coming down the stairs, anticipating more of that sour attitude I got the day before, but he barely glances at me when he enters the kitchen. In spite of his obvious exhaustion, he is hard to look away from and I respect myself less because of it. Those broad shoulders and pouty mouth of his don't make him a decent human being.

He takes a sip of coffee and closes his eyes. "Advil," he demands. "Drawer to the left." He speaks at half-volume, his voice raspy.

Once upon a time, I might have felt some pity for him. But I'm a little focused on keeping my pity for myself at present, and he's old enough to know what happens when you drink yourself into a stupor.

I find the bottle and slide it to him. "How did you get home?" I ask.

His eyes narrow. "Unqualified *and* judgmental. Such a winning combination," he mutters, pouring way more pills in his hand than he should. "There's a service that will bring your car home if you've been drinking. Where's the schedule?"

I cross the room to pull it off the printer. Though Hayes generally has one surgery day and one in-office consult day a week, his claim to fame—the part not involving his dick, anyhow —is what occupies every weekend and any free weekday: house calls. Celebrities don't want to risk getting photographed with a bruised and bloody face, so Hayes goes to them, making home visits like some pioneer doctor, albeit one who focuses more on inflating lips than amputating limbs.

He frowns when I hand it to him. I have no idea if that frown is my fault or the schedule's, but Jonathan did warn me Hayes is extra cranky on house call days.

Which are almost every day of his week, so Jonathan could have just said *he's always extra cranky*, for the sake of efficiency.

He rises. "There's a woman upstairs. Make sure she leaves after she gets up."

My jaw falls open. I suppose this is one of the *things* he referred to so obliquely yesterday. "You don't want to, you know, say *goodbye* to her?"

He raises a single, imperious brow as he reaches for his coffee. "Why would I, when I've got you to take care of it for me?"

"And how exactly am I supposed to get her out of your house? Is there a firearm available, perchance?"

I hear a soft grumbly noise which may be a laugh or is perhaps his way of saying *shut the fuck up* without actual speech. "Just take her to breakfast," he replies, like a man who's done this a thousand times before. "It's best to never end things on the property, in case they refuse to leave. Oh, and send her some flowers."

My eyes roll so far back I'm worried they'll get stuck that way. "What should the note say?"

He shrugs, rising. "I don't know. You'll come up with something, I'm sure."

"*Don't expect a call*," I suggest.

He rubs his forehead. "How silly of me, thinking you might be able to handle that *one* detail without guidance. Just thank her for a lovely evening or something."

"Fine. What's her name?"

He stops in place, staring at me while he thinks, as if he expects the answer to appear on my forehead. "Lauren?" he suggests. "Or Eva?"

"Are you seriously telling me you don't even know the name of the woman you inserted your penis in last night?"

His gaze lands on my mouth for one long moment and then flicks away as he releases a slow, controlled breath. "Are you seriously telling me I can't ask you to do one goddamn thing without hearing your opinion about it?"

I guess he has a point, but I can't seem to let it go. "I just can't imagine you don't actually know her name."

"I only date women who know to expect nothing from me," he says, turning to leave. "Learning their names would create false expectations."

"I'll make sure she's gone," I reply, frowning as he walks away. It's exactly the kind of bullshit I'd expect him to say. I just didn't expect him to sound quite so...unhappy about it.

❧

THE HOUSEKEEPER, MARTA, ARRIVES AN HOUR LATER. WE MET yesterday but didn't have the lengthiest conversation, given my knowledge of Spanish is entirely gleaned from watching *Dora the Explorer* with my niece, which isn't particularly useful in my current situation. I don't recall a single episode where Dora has to tell Boots the Monkey there's a naked woman upstairs.

"Senorita," I say, pointing toward the second floor before I mime sleep, pressing my face to a pretend pillow. "Dormir." She seems to understand. Odds are, it's par for the course around here.

I give Lauren/Eva a few hours to sleep, hoping she might leave the house all by herself, but when that fails, I give up and go to Hayes's room. Unlike the rest of the house, his bedroom looks pretty lived in right now, between all the clothes on the floor and the completely naked blonde in his bed. I step carefully in her direction—I really don't know what I'd do if I stepped on a used condom. Amputate my foot, most likely.

"Hey," I say when I reach her. "Lauren? Eva?"

There is no response.

"Abby? Gwyneth? Dame Judy Dench?"

I clap my hands. There is still nothing. I start to wonder if she's dead, which is when my writer's brain runs away from me. I see it all flash before my eyes: realizing she's stiff, reaching for the phone to dial 911 and having Hayes's voice answer on the other end. "*I knew you couldn't be trusted,*" he'd say, as a gate comes down, locking me in. "*I warned Jonathan you'd fail the test.*"

I reach out and shake her shoulder, increasing my volume until I'm practically yelling.

She finally raises her head. Makeup is smeared all over her face and Hayes's expensive sheets.

"Why are you yelling at me?" she murmurs.

Her head starts to sink into the pillow again. Who the hell sleeps *this* hard in a complete stranger's home? "I'm sorry," I reply. "The cleaning lady needs to get in here. It's ten thirty."

Her eyes go wide and suddenly she's springing out of bed, snatching her bra off the ground. "Shit, shit, shit. I'm due in court. I don't have time to get home."

She picks up the tiny red dress on the floor. "I'm trying a sexual assault case today. Oh, Jesus, this is bad."

I'm still processing my shock—I'd assumed anyone who came home with Hayes would be on the *wrong* side of the law—when her eyes flicker to my brand-new, purchased-for-this-job outfit.

Please don't ask, I think. Yes, I'll earn twenty-four grand if I make it the full six weeks, but even that won't quite cover what I owe if I don't finish the book.

"Can we trade?" she pleads. "I'm begging you. Please trade clothes with me."

"I can't wear, uh, *that* all day," I reply, flinching. "I just started this job and—"

"But isn't he at work?" she asks. "He'll have no idea."

I want to say no. I'm never getting my clothes back, especially once Hayes fails to call her again. But she looks so worried —and I've had enough times in my life where a small mistake felt like the end of the world—that I reach for the red dress.

It's not like anyone's going to see me anyway.

❧

"I NEED YOU TO MEET ME IN MALIBU," HAYES SAYS EXACTLY fifteen minutes later.

It's a plot turn I should have absolutely predicted, given the way my year has gone.

"Umm...okay?" I look down at the red dress, which barely meets my thighs.

"Is there a problem?" he asks. We haven't exchanged ten words and he's already put out. "Or the better question might be *is there any part of this job with which you won't have a problem?*'"

"No problem at all." *Unless you have an employee dress code.* "I'm on my way."

I gather the supplies he's requested and get in my car, wondering as I weave through the city how the hell I'm going to explain why I'm wearing what amounts to a sexy nightgown.

Despite the coming humiliation, something eases in my chest as I turn north on the Pacific Coast Highway. How could it not with the ocean to my left and the cliffside jutting toward the sea ahead of me? With my windows down and a warm breeze blowing in the scent of salt water and sage scrub, all feels right with the world, even if it's a world in which I am mostly naked.

I meet him in front of a beach house that probably costs more per year than I'll earn in my lifetime. I pull the requested cooler of filler and Botox from the back and turn to find him standing rigidly beside his car, staring at me.

"Are you...are you wearing my date's *dress?*" he asks, horrified.

The silver lining to having nothing left to lose is that...I have nothing left to lose.

"Do you like it?" I whisper, raising nervous, hopeful eyes to him. "I disposed of her, just like you asked."

He's frozen. There's confusion in his gaze, and the tiniest seed of dawning terror.

"*What?*" he barks.

I bite my lip and clasp my hands together like a penitent child. "I thought you'd like it. Now we can be together forever."

His mouth hangs open and I can read his thoughts so clearly —*This can't be happening. Oh my God, what has she done?*

I want to keep it going but I sit back against the hood of my car and start to laugh instead. "Holy shit. I wish you could see your face. Your guest was late for court and asked to wear my clothes."

A low breath escapes him. "*Bloody hell.*" He runs his hands through all that pretty hair, making a mess of it. Man, I'd love to do that to his hair just once. "Wait. She asked to borrow your clothes, and you said *yes?*"

I shrug. "She was really freaked out."

He stares at me as if he's awaiting further explanation, and when it doesn't come, he reaches between us to grab the cooler. "That was nice of you," he says, his face tight with displeasure as he walks away.

Weirdly, he seemed more comfortable back when he thought I might be a murderer.

❄ 4 ❄

I like to think of myself as someone who puts family first, but when my older sister's name appears on my phone, I consider letting it go to voice mail. Until my father's death last summer, Liddie was my closest friend. Now, however, it feels like the impasse between us is so wide it can't be breached, and the last thing I need after a long day at work is one of her inevitable lectures about Matt.

"Everyone makes mistakes," she says each time we speak, because to her, Matt is family—her husband's best friend, a fixture of our adolescence. She says it feels like something's missing when we're all together, minus Matt. I wonder if it's ever occurred to her that it might feel like something's missing for me too. That when I watch her and Alex together, playing happy family with their daughter, I'm seeing where ten years with someone was *supposed* to wind up.

I've barely said hello before she launches into her latest ovulation/pregnancy update, yet another source of irritation for me. Not that I mind her trying to get pregnant, but her single-minded obsession with it irks me. Sometimes it seems like she didn't even mourn our father—the funeral was barely over before she was flipping through a book of baby names, as if she'd simply washed her hands of the whole thing.

"I thought I was ovulating but I did this test and it says I'm not," she tells me. I climb onto my bed with a cup of ramen noodles. Matt thought he was being generous, letting me keep all our shitty old furniture, but I had to downsize after he left. Our king-size bed takes up so much of the room there isn't space for anything else, and therefore serves as couch, desk, and dining room table all in one. "But you know, they say when your cervical mucus gets thick—"

"Liddie, I'm eating," I say. "And you know how I feel about the words *cervical mucus*. Have you talked to Charlotte?"

Our youngest sister, now in her fourth month at a residential care facility, claims she isn't lonely there. Liddie tends to take her at her word, for reasons I can't begin to understand. Charlotte is the same kid who told us she was fine, again and again, before swallowing an entire bottle of aspirin.

"Not this week. I'm so busy with Kaitlin during the day, and it's hard to catch her at night. How's the new job?"

Because she insisted this job was a terrible idea, I've got no choice but to claim it's going well, though that may be a bit of a stretch—Hayes clearly didn't think today's stunt was quite as funny as I did. "I'm seriously being paid four grand a week to answer phones."

"With the mouth on you, I wouldn't count on it lasting," she says. "I still don't see why you had to give Mom your entire advance."

My eyes close tight. Liddie isn't able to help ease my family's financial woes in any way, but she sure doesn't mind criticizing me for trying. "I didn't realize I wasn't going to be able to write the book," I reply, the words clipped. I gave my mother the advance to pay her mortgage. If I'd known I'd wind up putting all of Charlotte's treatment on credit cards I can't pay off, I might have thought better of it.

"You'd still have time to finish the book if you hadn't taken the stupid job," she says. I hear the clink of flatware in the background. "And you wouldn't need to if you'd just ask Matt for the money. Talk to him. He's family."

My teeth grind so hard she can probably hear it all the way in Minnesota. "No. He's not."

And even if I were poisoned and Matt was the only one with the antidote, I wouldn't take his help. If I were drowning and he threw me a flotation device, I'd use the last of my energy to give him the finger. That half of what he said at the end appears to be *true* doesn't lessen my rage. I remember the fire that burned through me after we split up—*I'll show him*, I said a hundred times a day. That fire is still there, but whenever I see him in a magazine or being gossiped about online, it feels as if he's already won.

"Let him try to fix things," she begs.

"The things he broke can't be fixed." Not by him, anyway. Probably not by anyone. I'll be damned if I'm going to let him throw money at the rest of it to absolve himself of guilt.

❧ 5 ❧

H ayes is just getting downstairs when I arrive the next morning. It's his in-office day: consult, filler, consult, Botox, consult...all day long, in fifteen-minute increments. He appears to have prepared for it by drinking large quantities of alcohol and getting little sleep. I'm only three days in, but I already expected nothing more.

"You look terrible," I tell him.

"Was judging me on the list of your job duties?" he asks, pressing his fingers to his temples as he slides onto a barstool. "I can't quite recall."

I set two Advil next to his coffee and slide him the schedule. One of these days I'm going to attach a pamphlet on functional alcoholism.

"You saw the message from your, uh, new lady friend? Keeley?" I ask.

His eyes remain on the schedule, but he nods. I still can't believe he gives these women his assistant's number. It's wrong in so many ways.

"So, there's really no one who gets *your* number?" I probably sound more exasperated than I should, given that he's called me judgmental every single time we've spoken.

"No one," he says, "and I mean no one. Not the President. Not the Pope. Not even my own mother."

A startled laugh escapes me. "You're not serious? About your mom?"

He lifts one tired brow at me. *You're being judgmental again*, that brow says. "If she calls, just pass me the message. But have a nice little chat with her if it bothers you."

"Excellent. I'll use that time to work on my British accent," I reply. "*Top o' the morning to you, guv'ner.*"

My accent could use some work. I sound like a pirate on a children's cartoon.

"No one has said that in England for, roughly, a century."

"*Throw another shrimp on the barbie. Oy, the quidditch pitch is in a right state, innit?*" I cock my arm and swing it jauntily, as if I'm Captain Jack Sparrow, leading the boys in song.

There's a small twitch of his mouth, a flicker of that dimple I've seen in photos. "I hope you're not auditioning for the part of a Brit anytime soon."

"I'm not auditioning for any part, obviously. I was living the dream as a bartender, and now I'm living the dream kicking women out of your bed and, I hope, conversing at length with your mom." He's already gathering his stuff, preparing to forget me for the day. I wish I hadn't derailed the conversation about his mother with my juvenile attempts to make him laugh.

"I know it's none of my business—" I begin.

He sighs heavily. "That seems unlikely to stop you."

"What happened with your mom?"

He regards me long enough that I'm certain he's about to tell me to fuck off, but shrugs instead. "She threatened to cut me out of her will if I didn't break up with my girlfriend," he says. "I failed to comply. Clearly, an error of judgment on my end, as my mother turned out to be right." The word *girlfriend* hits me like a hammer. I never dreamed I'd hear him utter it, unless in jest.

"*You* had a girlfriend."

I'm waiting for the punchline, but instead he sighs and runs a hand through his hair. "Believe it or not, I was a serial monogamist most of my life. I have, obviously, seen the light on that one." I hear a hint of regret in his tone, see it in the lost look in his eyes, blinked away as soon as it appears.

How do you go from being a serial monogamist to being...*Hayes*? What has to happen to change someone that dramatically?

"And she really cut you off?" I ask.

He shrugs again, as if it was meaningless.

"I was already out of med school at that point and didn't need her money. But then I moved here, near my father, and she never forgave me for it."

I kind of hate his mom a bit too, now. "I guess I don't have to ask which parent you're closer to, then."

A shadow passes over his face. "You'd think so," he says, rising to leave, "but that's because I haven't told you what my dad did."

He walks out and I find myself left with a small ache in the center of my chest. To look at him, you'd think he has every last thing a man could want: looks, wealth, women throwing themselves at him right and left.

But he also has a despicable mother, a father who may actually be worse, no siblings I know of, and a girlfriend he gave everything up for...one who is no longer around. Who does he turn to when things go wrong? Where does he spend holidays? He seems to keep himself so busy there's barely even time for him to wonder if his life feels a little empty without any family. If he was anyone but *Hayes Flynn*, seducer of a thousand shattered actresses, I'd wonder if that wasn't the entire point.

❀

THE SMALL, SUNNY OFFICE NEXT TO HAYES'S KITCHEN IS MY happy place. Or might be, if I didn't have to do my job.

Today, as always, I sit with the schedule open on the laptop in front of me, sinking further and further into my chair as I listen to rich, beautiful women list their flaws. It's disheartening at best. Money, in my view, only seems to have bought them more time to discover what they hate about themselves, leading them to call in near tears lamenting crow's feet and lines above their upper lips. There's nothing wrong with plastic surgery, but what bothers me is their desperation, their sense of urgency, as if nothing else matters. I make their appointments wishing I could instead say *look, it's gorgeous outside, you can do anything you want. Stop weeping to a stranger about the symmetry of your nostrils.*

When the calls are complete, I print invoices, then rush out to make his purchases for the day: a razor sold at a ridiculously overpriced store on Melrose, crisps and Marmite from a shop in the San Fernando Valley.

By the time I get back to my studio—which is a glamorous name for a room the size of a storage unit, and with about as much natural light—I'm exhausted.

I make a cup of ramen and finally settle down to what I consider my *real* job. The one I appear to be incapable of.

The first hundred pages of the book flew from my fingers. Aisling and Ewan are young lovers who've climbed through a hole in the wall separating fae from humans. It's supposed to be temporary, because Aisling has a younger brother to care for, but the wealth and opulence of the fae kingdom is more compelling than they expected. When Ewan refuses to leave—having changed in ways he doesn't recognize—Aisling has to save him from himself and get back through the hole before it closes for good.

I didn't realize, at the time, that I was writing about me and Matt, that the small ways he changed when we got to New York bothered me far more than I was willing to admit. I was too busy being horrified by the fact I was writing it at all. In my masters of fine arts program, we were expected to pen things that were dreary and very *real*, like a day in the life of a secretary thinking of killing herself, or five people stuck on an elevator together, slowly unraveling. Writing a fantasy romance at night was my most shameful secret for a long time, and the thing I enjoyed most. Now that I'm *supposed* to write it, I no longer want to.

When the words fail to come, when I find myself thinking *just give up*, I close the laptop and change into running clothes. I don't love running at night in LA, but it's necessary. My frustration with the book is often too much to bear, and running is the only method I've got to shove it away.

I take the winding beach path leading from Santa Monica to Venice, dodging panhandlers and drunk tourists the entire way as I mull over the story. Why can't I finish it? The book dies at the point where Aisling is supposed to step up and save Ewan from himself, and I can't seem to move past it.

I increase my pace until my lungs burn and my legs are heavy. Would things have been different if I'd stayed behind to finish my degree? Would the book have come easily? Would Matt have taken me for granted a little less than he did?

Except Matt had his first big role in LA and wanted me here with him, and I'd just gotten the book deal and needed time off anyway. The choice seemed obvious to me at the time.

Like Hayes, I moved here to be close to someone who didn't deserve me, and I gave up things that mattered for a person who's no longer around. I guess it makes sense that he leads his life as if nothing in it truly matters.

I'm starting to feel the same way about my own.

❧ 6 ❧

On the way to work the next morning, I call Liddie to remind her about the Zoom birthday party that evening for Charlotte.

Liddie groans. "Why are we doing it so late? That's right at Kaitlin's bedtime, plus I'm ovulating, so, uh, Alex and I have plans."

"Because it *isn't* late where I am, and one of us has to work. Also, *gross*."

I pull into Hayes's circular drive just as a woman who looks a lot like my sister walks out his front door.

"Your doppelganger is leaving Hayes's house," I tell her.

"Is it *you?*" she asks with a laugh. I suppose I set myself up for that one. All three of us Bell girls do look a fair bit alike. "Maybe you should ask yourself why he's fucking someone who looks just like his assistant."

"Given how many women Hayes sleeps with, it was bound to happen eventually," I reply as I hang up.

Hayes is already at the counter, waiting. "Your date looked just like my sister," I say, placing his coffee in front of him. "Except my sister would still be here telling you what you're doing wrong."

He takes his coffee and sniffs it, as if assessing for poison. "It doesn't surprise me at all to learn a relative of yours is full of unsolicited advice. But if I did to your sister what I just did to the woman who left, she'd be too exhausted to talk."

A rusty muscle in my stomach clenches, but it's been nearly a year since Matt and I broke up, and pretty much that long since I had sex, so I refuse to feel any guilt about my body's innate response to Hayes...as long as I never act on it.

"I can see where a night with you would indeed be exhausting," I reply as he rises. "I bet you don't say *please* or *thank you* once."

"Yes, because men who say *please* and *thank you* during sex are generally referred to as *customers*."

I fight hard not to laugh. A hint of a smile slips forth but I snatch it back quickly.

He hands me a Post-It note. "I need this taken care of."

He walks out—no *please*, no *thank you*, not even a goodbye. I go to the office, drop my bag on the floor, and ignore the ringing phone long enough to read the Post-It he handed me.

Much to my relief, he doesn't ask me to remove a naked female from his bed, but he does want a reservation for Friday at a restaurant that books out a month in advance, needs me to fix the car he just drove away in, and asks about "brochures" without giving me any hint what brochures he's referring to.

I give in at last and call Jonathan. I've been trying to give him his space, but I have no idea how to proceed here, and I've been dying to hear about the ten-month-old girl they've already named Gemma. He promised me photos when he left and I haven't gotten a thing.

"Have you met her?" I demand immediately, bypassing all niceties.

"Not yet," he says with a frustrated sigh. "The orphanage is putting up one road block after another."

Poor Jonathan. He and his partner waited on an adoption list for years before this came through. "I'm so sorry. Is there anything I can do?"

"No," he says, "but we may end up here longer than planned. I hope that's not a problem on your end?"

I laugh ruefully, leaning back in the office chair and propping my feet on the desk. "It might be a problem on your boss's end. He hates me. Every time I speak, he has this look of utter contempt on his face. It's seriously making me wonder why we helped England out during World War Two."

"Well, there was the whole bit about the Holocaust, and Hitler dominating Europe," he says. "Maybe he's like a boy with a crush, pulling your pigtails."

"A guy who's slept with half the actresses in LA isn't *that* awkward with women, nor would he be interested in me in the first place."

"Don't sell yourself short, Tali," he says softly. "You're beautiful and smart and different from what he's used to. And I think Hayes is a lot lonelier than he would ever admit, even to himself. Just don't sleep with him."

I've only slept with two people in my entire life. I seriously don't understand why this keeps coming up. "Apparently you've missed the part about me hating Hayes, and Hayes hating me."

"I haven't missed it," he says with a small laugh. "I'm just not sure I entirely believe it."

❦

WITH JONATHAN'S GUIDANCE, I MANAGE TO ACQUIRE THE sought-after reservation and locate the missing brochures. The car must be dealt with later, on a surgery day when Hayes won't need to leave the office.

From there, it's a million phone calls about lips that don't "turn out" enough and uneven skin, and it's six by the time I leave. This whole Zoom party, suggested by my sister's psychologist, is feeling less likely to work out by the second. *You can do it late*, Dr. Shriner said, *so you won't have to rush home from work.* Little does she know seven PM is not late when you work for Hayes Flynn.

I drive home, cursing the traffic and Matt's billboard, and am only ten minutes from my apartment when the work phone buzzes.

Need tux, Hayes writes. **Black not navy. Bring to office.**

I groan aloud. Who the fuck decides he needs a tux this late in the day? I don't even know if he means a tux he already owns. That he potentially has tuxes in navy *and* black seems excessive, but minimalism isn't exactly Hayes's style. And surely he can't expect me to rent one this late.

Is the tux in your closet? I ask, but obviously he can't be bothered to reply. What skin is it off his nose if I have to waste twenty minutes driving to his house to check?

With a heavy foot on the accelerator, I race back to his house and take the stairs two at a time to get to his room, which seems oppressively cold now that it's free of clothes on the floor and women in the bed—no photos, no papers, no books, no TV. Jonathan said Hayes is not home much, but seriously...the guy has to relax at some point, doesn't he? Other than his daily workouts with Ben and the hours he spends drinking, he takes no time for himself at all. Why is he working so hard if he's never going to kick back and enjoy the spoils of war?

I find the tux in the back corner of his ridiculously large walk-in closet, hanging in a garment bag next to the navy blue and two others in varying shades of black, and take my best guess which pair of shoes he wants with it.

It's only once my task is done that I actually look around. Aside from the tuxedos and his extensive shoe collection, his wardrobe consists *entirely* of suits and button-downs. Not that I expected a lot of Hawaiian floral shirts or *Booze Crooz 2015!* tees, but I'm starting to see a theme here. If Hayes was actually a robot set on earth to do nothing but inject filler and fuck, this is pretty much what his life would look like. And I know I have places to be, and he's a million-aire with a closet larger than my entire apartment, but I stand for a second looking at it all. And feeling the tiniest bit...sad for him.

※

Hayes's office is a bit more of what I expected from his house: brilliantly modern, all gleaming ebony wood floors, white furniture, enormous windows.

And coldly imperious staff.

"Sign in," says the girl behind the desk without looking up. "We'll be with you shortly."

"I'm not a patient," I say. "I'm just dropping off Hayes's tux. Can I leave it with you?"

She finally deigns to meet my eye and then frowns. "Wait," she commands.

She hustles somewhere back in the office and a moment later returns with Hayes himself. In a navy dress shirt, top two buttons undone, he looks too hot to be real. Even if he were playing a doctor on a soap opera, I'd still be yelling, *"No doctor is that good-looking!"* at the TV.

I hand him the tux, which he accepts while his eyes flicker over me, head to foot. For once he doesn't seem to find me lacking.

"Is that everything?" I ask.

He cocks his head. "In a rush? Certainly, you've got time to give us a bit of that amazing British accent of yours."

I'd laugh if I wasn't so anxious to get home. My glance cuts over to the dour receptionist. "That's for your ears only."

"No accent. No pretending you've disposed of my date," he says. "I'm quite disappointed in this little exchange, Tali." His voice is so low and seductive my stomach clenches in response. I'm growing accustomed to the unfriendly, hungover version of Hayes...but this one is a whole new ball game.

The receptionist watches him walk away with her brow furrowed, like she isn't sure what she just saw.

I guess I'm not sure either. Hayes, briefly, didn't seem satanic at all.

৩৫৯

I HAVE TO CALL INTO MY SISTER'S PARTY FROM HAYES'S parking garage and am still late. My mother and Charlotte sit in an office at The Fairfield Center and Liddie's in her living room in Minnesota. Dr. Shriner said this would help "normalize" birthdays without my father, but there's absolutely nothing normal about seeing my pale, miserable sister and tired mother in an almost empty room while I fake good cheer from a parking garage.

"I got the gift card and the books," Charlotte tells me. "Thanks a lot." She's been there for months but she's still faking her happiness. I can tell.

"When I come home, we'll go shopping," I promise. "With what I'm earning at this job, it won't even have to be on sale."

"I still can't believe he's paying you that much," Charlotte says, shaking her head. "Like, what do you even *do*?"

Liddie rolls her eyes. "Look at her. She's got no body fat and a mouth made for blow jobs. I'm pretty sure we all know what he's *hoping* she'll do."

"Lydia, that's inappropriate," my mother scolds, with a hint of a *I'm on my third glass of wine* slur, which wouldn't be an issue if she were a little closer to home than she is at present.

"I'm not saying she'll *do* it," Liddie says. "Though I probably would if I were her. Have you seen the guy?"

"Liddie!" my mother and I shout at the same time. My mother reaches over to cover Charlotte's ears, as if she's still a toddler who might have missed what's already been said.

"Mom, I'm seventeen," Charlotte protests. "I know what a blow job is."

"Well, you shouldn't," my mother replies stonily, folding her arms across her chest. "Can we please try to make keep this conversation decent? Tell us about your day, Charlotte. Dr. Shriner says there was a party."

Charlotte's shoulders hitch and she doesn't meet anyone's eye as she runs her fingers through hair the same color as mine—golden brown, streaked with hints of caramel and strawberry blonde. "There was a cake," she says, her voice flat. "After art. But it was chocolate."

Charlotte hates chocolate. A minor thing, but my throat swells, unexpectedly. Holidays and birthdays were always a big deal in our house, especially for Charlotte, the baby of the family. She's too young to already be learning the way life narrows down to nothing as you grow up.

My niece launches herself in front of the camera and conversation turns from Charlotte to Kaitlin—at age three, the new baby of the family. "I'd better go," sighs Liddie. "I've got to put Kaitlin to bed."

I suspect she's holding me responsible for the hour and feel a pinch of irritation. "Can't Alex do it?"

"She only wants me," Liddie says.

"She's spoiled," my mother replies. "That's why you need to have another kid."

It's the wrong thing to say to Liddie right now. "Wow, Mom," she says. "Any other sage advice?"

I watch as Charlotte sinks further into her chair. Has this Zoom call made her feel less alone or *more* alone? She's supposed to be going home at the end of August. I'd like to tell myself life will improve for her there, but as I listen to Liddie and my mother argue—the guest of honor forgotten completely—it's hard to believe it's true.

7

Hayes is already up and waiting when I arrive the next day. His eyes skim over me—lingering unhappily on my perfectly unobjectionable gray sheath and black heels.

"You'll need to come with me this morning," he says, his misery obvious.

I set the coffee down with an unhappy thud. "On *house calls?*"

I laid awake for hours last night, worrying about Charlotte. Time with him is the last thing I need today.

He points at the first name on the schedule. "That star right there means I need an assistant. Jonathan booked them back-to-back."

"Unless you'd like me to use the ample medical knowledge I've gleaned from watching *Grey's Anatomy*," I reply, leaning against the counter, "I'm not sure how I'd be useful."

"It goes without saying that you won't be especially useful," he replies, his mouth twisting, "but I still need you there. Let's go."

He starts heading out. Apparently, I'm to follow like a dog—which I do, grabbing my bag as I race to catch up.

He holds the door of his BMW open for me, a surprising bit

of chivalry for a man who can't even bother to tell me goodbye in the morning. He gets into the driver's seat and glances at me. "You might want to fix your dress," he says, his tone half growl, half disgust. His gaze flickers to my legs and his jaw sets.

"Is it suddenly 1800?" I ask, twisting as I fasten the seat belt. "Will my reputation be destroyed because you caught a glimpse of my porcelain thighs?"

"You really have to argue about everything, don't you?" he asks. He hits the accelerator, taking off at a speed I generally associate with roller coasters and space shuttle launches.

"Yes," I reply. "And if you crash at this speed, you will ruin your pretty face. Good luck surviving in the real world without your looks."

He shrugs. "I'll still have lots of money, which matters far more to women."

Nice attitude, I think, but I no longer have the energy to bicker with him. Instead, I stare out the window, hoping the view will improve my mood. It usually does. Though there have been times when I've missed things about home—feeling safe when I walk down a street at night, the change of seasons—southern California makes me happy in a way Kansas never did. Ocean, mountains, perfect weather. Even here in the city, there are sprightly pineapple palms lining the boulevard, and every house we pass is dotted with color: bougainvillea or the spectacular haze of purple jacaranda. I feel whole again, looking at it, so wouldn't Charlotte as well? Wouldn't she be far better off here with the views and beach and endless sunshine than she would back home, subject to my mother's haphazard care?

If she weren't going into her senior year of high school, I'd seriously consider it. I still can't believe my mother couldn't even stay sober for Charlotte's birthday. I know my father's death hit her hard, but surely, she realizes it's time to put on her big-girl pants for my sister's sake?

"You're surprisingly quiet," Hayes says. I'd almost forgotten he was here, which was nice while it lasted. "It's been at least ten minutes since you've nagged me or delivered unsolicited advice."

"I thought you'd prefer it." I don't take my eyes off the land-scape as I respond.

"Yes," he says, turning into a small cul-de-sac. "I wasn't *complaining*. Just curious."

We pull up to the gate of a Spanish-style villa, from which purple flowering vines hang heavy, and a huge orange tree dotted with fruit stands in the courtyard's center. I'm not sure how long I'll have to live here before I stop being thrilled by all the things that can grow in a warm climate.

"So, what will I be doing?" I ask as he pulls into the driveway. "I watched a doctor on *ER* perform a tracheotomy using only a ballpoint pen and a kitchen knife. I feel like I could pull it off."

"Perfect." He shuts off the engine. "Any tracheotomies are yours. Your job *here*, however, is to stay put. Anywhere I am, you are, even if she asks you to leave."

He's out of the car before I can ask why the hell she'd *want* me to leave.

A maid in uniform opens the door and leads us through empty rooms to the back porch, where a redhead in a nightgown waits, already sipping a glass of wine though it's not quite nine in the morning. She looks up at Hayes like he's the most delicious candy she's ever seen, and when she envelops him in her arms, I suspect I know my role: designated cockblocker.

"Hello, Shannen," he says smoothly, detaching himself. "Let me introduce you to Natalia, my assistant."

It's only when she turns to frown at me that I recognize her. She plays someone's rich wife on a soap opera my mom watches, one of those characters that's always faking pregnancies and buying people off to get her way. In real life, she seems more pathetic than evil.

"I thought it might just be the two of us," she says, as Hayes applies numbing cream all over her face. "This is kind of a private thing."

I can only assume, based on how brazen she's being, that he slept with her at some point and she's refusing to take a hint.

"Natalia is here to assist me," he replies firmly. He casts a quick, uncomfortable glance my way. "And she's signed an NDA."

He refuses the glass of wine she offers and begins to fill syringes from several different vials. I'm not sure how he can tell them all apart, but he's reassuringly confident as he draws them up.

"I'll start with the Botox," he tells her, "and give your lips a chance to get numb. Frown for me."

He makes small marks with a pen—between her brows and above them—and then begins the injections.

I'm...not great with needles. I have to stifle my desire to shudder, but she's so busy flirting with Hayes she barely seems to notice. Tiny dots of blood speckle her face, but she's still hitting on Hayes as hard as she possibly can.

He finally gets to her lips. Even with the numbing cream, it's clearly uncomfortable for her. I busy myself with an empty notepad, unable to watch. When he's done, she looks at herself in the mirror. "Can't you make them bigger?" she asks. Her gaze brushes over him and settles on his crotch. "Bigger is better, as they say."

He gives her a tight smile as he begins packing his bag. "Not where lips are concerned, I assure you."

"Come upstairs with me a sec," she says, running a hand over his forearm. I feel an unexpected spike of irritation. How many times does he need to rebuff this woman's advances for God's sake?

"I'm sorry," I interject, addressing Hayes, "but you're already behind schedule."

I see a hint of relief in his eyes and weariness as well. He apologizes to Shannen, and with his hand on the small of my back, guides me to the door.

"So, I guess she's...an ex?" I ask once we're back in the car. I feel proud of myself for calling her an "ex" rather than something a little more derogatory.

"I don't ever sleep with patients," he replies. "And I don't ever treat people I've slept with."

It's a slightly more principled stance than I'd have expected of him.

"Then why do you accept patients like her at all?" I ask. "I'm guessing you make enough without them."

"That you think there's such a thing as *enough*," he says, "explains a great deal."

My lips purse as I fold my arms across my chest. "So does the fact that you think there *isn't*."

He shoots me a narrow-eyed glance before he turns back to the road. "Look, you continue to do your struggling actor thing and I'll continue to make millions of dollars a year, and if our situations somehow reverse, *then* you can feel free to judge me."

"I'm not an actress, struggling or otherwise," I reply. "But I'm sorry if you felt like I was judging you."

He says nothing to that, and I guess maybe he was right. I *was* judging him. And aside from the fact that he drinks more than he should and appears to enjoy sex with almost-strangers...I can't say my criticism seems especially justified anymore. I'm not exactly thriving doing things my way either.

The next few patients he sees are spread inconveniently all over the city—Holmby Hills to Bel Air to Pacific Palisades and down to Manhattan Beach. They aren't exactly like Shannen, but share with her a complete lack of boundaries and self-respect: husbands yelling at their wives as if we aren't there, rambunctious children screaming and throwing a football overhead while their mother has a needle pressed mere centimeters from her eye, patients making out with their boyfriends as if we aren't even there.

At our final stop of the day, before I meet the patient...I meet her dogs. They come charging out of the house just as I climb from the car, so fast and so much larger than me on their hind feet that I'm thrown backward before I even have time to process what's happened, my head smacking the window with an audible *thwap*.

And just as fast, Hayes is there, shielding me with his large frame like some kind of avenging angel. I blink up at him as he helps me right myself. We've never stood this close before, and I find myself staring at his eyes—at the tiny green flecks there. At his lovely mouth. At the crease where a dimple sometimes, rarely, appears.

"Are you okay?" he asks, jaw tight with concern. Probably just concern that I'm going to file an unsafe workplace complaint, but concern nonetheless.

I nod. It's probably adrenaline that's got me feeling warm and slightly light-headed.

He turns toward the patient. A muscle in his cheek flexes. "Genevieve, can you make sure they stay out of the room this time?" he asks. "I really don't want to miss when I'm injecting you."

"Oh, I *try*," she says, "but they just want to be near their mama."

Which sounds like *no* to me, and certainly seems like it when she leads us into the house, making no effort to keep the dogs from following. Hayes stays close to my side the entire way in, his hand on my back as if prepared to leap into action once more, and his jaw locked so tight I'm worried he's about to break a molar.

When everything is ready, Hayes tips her chin upward. Just as he presses the needle to her right cheekbone, the largest of the dogs comes charging into the room toward the two of them. Panicking, I leap in his path, only to find myself knocked to the floor.

"You should have brought Jonathan," Genevieve chides, as Hayes leans down to help me up. I thought I'd seen him angry before, but that was a pale imitation of what I'm seeing now. His eyes are dark as night, and more ominous.

"I'm not going to be able to do this unless you close the door," Hayes says, his voice so clipped it's barely civil.

"But I can't," Genevieve says. "They're sad if they can't see me."

Hayes begins packing his things. "I'm not putting my assistant through this," he says. "And it isn't safe for you either."

Hayes places a hand on my back as he marches us out of the house. I'm not sure if he's angry with her, with me, with the dogs...or perhaps all three. But as he climbs in the driver's seat, it's obvious he's very angry about something.

"I'm sorry," I tell him.

"I'm not mad at you," he says, his teeth grinding. "I'm mad at myself. I should never have put you in that position. You're half Jonathan's size."

It unsettles me, these small moments when he fails to be as awful as I thought he'd be. I force a laugh. "I'm dumbfounded you're concerned about anyone's discomfort but your own."

His shoulders sag a little, and I feel like I just took a cheap shot. Before I can apologize, he shrugs. "It surprises me as well."

We are silent most of the ride home. It's only when I stiffen at the sight of Matt's face stories above us that he seems to notice me again.

"Are you alright?" Hayes asks, glancing over at me.

"Yes," I say, though I'm not sure it's true. It's not about missing Matt, or even regretting it's over. It's just that the sight of him reminds me that trusting anyone other than yourself is a bad idea—and I'm finding myself with this bizarre urge to trust Hayes, of all people.

When I finally collapse in bed that night, exhausted, I dream about the book, but none of my characters are there. It's me, standing in a ballroom in the castle. The walls are draped with burgundy velvet, candelabras hang from the ceiling, and the feast laid out on the table is unlike anything I've seen in real life.

A man stands behind me. I can't really see him, but I know he's tall—and dangerous. "Look around," he says. His voice is low and seductive. My nipples pinch and goose bumps crawl up my arms at the sound of it. "Pick out anything you want and it's yours."

I know exactly what he is, and that anything he offers will come at a price, yet I don't move away from him the way I should. He's indecently close now—the lapels of his jacket brushing against my bare back, his breath on my neck—but I remain perfectly still, daring him to stay right where he is...or move even closer.

When I wake, my tank is damp, stuck to my skin. I'm painfully turned-on, in a way I'd almost forgotten was possible. And I hate that, because the man in the dream was, quite obviously, Hayes.

I roll to my stomach and bury my face in my pillow. It's just the stupid incident at Genevieve's worming its way into my brain when it really shouldn't. Yes, it was kind of hot, the way he tried to protect me from the dogs. Being shielded by someone a head taller and a foot wider held a primitive kind of appeal. But I'm not going to turn into yet another pathetic female fetishizing the Hayes Flynn experience. If nothing else, because I know how short-lived it would be.

❧ 8 ❧

I enter the weekend with dread worming its way through my stomach. Writing used to be my favorite thing in the world, and now it's the bane of my existence, the thing I put off with crossword puzzles and gossip about celebrities I've never heard of in *The Daily Mail*. I now know more about Hamish and Delia from a show called *Seduction Island* than any adult really should.

There are two calls from Hayes about scheduling issues on Saturday morning, but given I'd expected far worse (**House destroyed. Build new one. Also, need more tuxes**), I feel like I've gotten off easy.

Eventually, I force myself to sit down at my laptop. The story leaves off when things have really gone awry—Aisling discovers the hole they climbed through is shrinking, but when she goes to the castle to get Ewan, the doors are locked. She will need to acquire some magic of her own or they'll both remain trapped there forever.

It should be exciting...but I'm bored. I've tried to write the chapter where Aisling acquires magic. I've tried to map out her attack on the castle. I've tried skipping ahead to the epilogue, which finds her and Ewan married and settled back home.

But no matter how many words I spit out, I can't make the book something I would want to read. So, what happens in September when the manuscript is due? Do I turn in a steaming pile of dogshit and hope they don't notice, or do I return what I can of the advance and spend the rest of my life paying off Charlotte's stay at Fairfield? These are the questions that keep me up at night, that have me sliding on my running shoes after dark, knowing sleep will be impossible otherwise.

There was a time when inspiration came after I fell asleep, but this weekend my dreams bring no answers. It's just me, standing in a ballroom, with a dangerous man whispering in my ear.

THAT DREAM IS STILL IN MY HEAD on MONDAY MORNING, when I arrive to find Hayes playing the whole Satan thing to the hilt in a black shirt and pants. The dangerous look suits him—no surprises there. I run my eyes over his chest—his shirt is fitted enough to mold to his very sculpted upper body, and for a moment I picture it all over again—his hands on my arms, his breath in my ear. Warmth spreads over my skin and my bones seem to go loose before I stop myself. *What am I doing?* I mentally lock that deranged dream down and send it scuttling off to some dark corner of my brain. Never to be seen or heard again, I hope.

Shaking my head, I lift my eyes from his chest to his face. He seems rested and not hungover for once. Jonathan warned me he takes surgery days seriously. I guess I just couldn't quite imagine Hayes taking anything seriously, other than himself.

"Someone named Piper texted," I tell him. "She said she wanted to see for herself 'if it's as big as everyone says'."

"My dick," he says, as if this was unclear. "And it is."

"I'll let you inform her yourself," I reply, sliding him the phone.

He ignores it, tipping his head to observe me. "If you're not an actress," he says, "why are you in LA? Modeling?"

I laugh. "Model? I'm five-four. Who would I model for?"

"Children's clothes?" he suggests. "Or a fashion line for pygmies?"

A smile flickers over my face. "If pygmy fashion model is really a thing, I will tender my resignation immediately."

He leans back in his seat, watching me. "You still haven't answered my question."

Nor do I want to. I look over his schedule to avoid his gaze. It's all too depressing, the way nothing I hoped for is coming true.

"Why can't I just want to be an assistant?" I ask. "Or a bartender?"

"Because you seem like someone destined for more," he says quietly.

My head jerks up. I scan his face for sarcasm and find something else instead...interest, intrigue. If he knew me better, I imagine any intrigue would die a quick death. Because I once thought I was destined for more too, thanks to the writing contests and accolades in college, and time is definitely proving otherwise.

I paste an indifferent smile on my face. "I came out of the womb wanting to bartend. Which makes us well-suited, since you probably came out of the womb asking for a good scotch."

"Macallan," he agrees pleasantly. "It was my first word, actually. Coffee was second."

I grin. "I've got a few guesses what the third word was. It starts with a p."

He laughs as he rises from his chair, the sound low and warm and unexpected. It makes me feel like I've won something. He's taken two steps toward the door when he stops and turns back toward me.

"Whatever it is you really wanted to do...you're a little young to have already given up on it. And it seems unlike you to go down without a fight."

"You've known me for a week. How would you know if I fight for things or not?"

"Well," he says, "you're fighting with me now, aren't you?"

As he walks away, I admit to myself he might have a point. I've had Matt's words in my head for too long, telling me I only got the book deal because of him. Telling me I'm never going to finish.

But Matt's been gone for a year. Even if he's still talking, perhaps it's time I stopped listening.

❧❦

I SINK INTO THE PLUSH WHITE CHAIR IN MY OFFICE AND TURN on the computer, ignoring, for now, the Post-It note Hayes has left asking me to fix the hot tub and bedroom mirror. I return the weekend's messages and adjust the schedule and it's only when I've completed every last task that I wrinkle my nose and head upstairs to survey the damage.

If there's a clog in that hot tub, I bet it's something that rhymes with...fizz.

Marta hasn't come in yet, so his room still looks like a crime scene. There are clothes on the floor, chairs overturned, and a bright red stiletto is wedged dead in the center of the massive mirror. Like, how does that even happen? Was it a strip tease run amuck? Were they *trying* to break the mirror? Either seems a possibility with Hayes and his, uh, *friends*.

I move past it to the deck off Hayes's bedroom, where I find the water in the sunken hot tub alarmingly discolored and full of champagne bottles, one of which appears to be stuck in the filter. I could probably "fix" the issue simply by reaching in and plucking the bottle out, but fuck that. There's not enough chlorine in the world for me to brave immersing my hand in that much bacteria.

I call repair guys for both, and while I wait for them, my mind returns to the book and what Hayes said this morning. What happens when I admit to the publisher I can't finish it and have spent the advance? Even with what I earn at this job, I won't have enough to repay it in full. My credit cards are nearly maxed out and Charlotte's still got three months of treatment at Fairfield to pay for.

Maybe I've just gone off course and need a second opinion, but who can I ask for advice? Not my editor, as it would mean admitting the book is only half finished. Not my professors at NYU, nor my former classmates—I can just imagine all the snickering about a *fantasy romance* while they wield quietly brilliant prose about the mundane.

I'm in the middle of grocery shopping for Hayes—a list which mostly involves alcohol, mixers, and garnishes—when it comes to me: *Sam*. My old buddy from undergrad, who remained at Kansas State to get his PhD in English. He loved fantasy novels, but he was also a sharp and brutally honest critic.

And brutally honest is what I need, even if it kills me.

I get home that night and dial his number. Sam answers on the first ring. "Tali?" he asks. "Is it really you?"

I guess his surprise makes sense. Aside from the occasional email, I mostly fell out of touch when we graduated. Matt was always bothered by our friendship. It seemed best, when we left Kansas, to let it fade.

"It's really me," I reply, trying to inject some enthusiasm into my voice. "How's school?" He must be nearly done, which just makes me feel worse. I'd have my graduate degree by now if I'd stayed.

"Good. Working on my dissertation. What about you? I saw...online," he says haltingly. "About you and Matt."

Ugh. The one thing worse than breaking up with someone you've dated for most of your life is having his exploits broadcast nationwide. Everyone assumes I was the one who got dumped, and that I'm sitting back in my squalid apartment weeping over what I've lost. Which wouldn't be entirely false, I guess, though not for the reasons they'd think.

I give him the barest details about the breakup, we discuss his dissertation and summer plans and my visit back home at the end of August.

"How's the book coming?" he asks at last. Sam's so easy to talk to, I'd almost forgotten the whole reason I called.

"I'm glad you brought it up," I reply, flopping onto my mattress and arranging the pillows under my head. "I'm completely stuck at the midpoint and was hoping you could take a look at it. As I recall, you were always a voracious reader of fantasy novels."

"So hot, isn't it? The ladies love a guy who can discuss George RR Martin in detail. If I knew how to play Dungeons and Dragons, the package would be complete."

Sam has never understood his appeal, no matter how many women throw themselves at him. "Stop. You seemed to find plenty of girls willing to ignore your nerd side."

"I was kind of holding out for a girl who wouldn't *need* to ignore it," he replies.

Matt always claimed the girl Sam was holding out for was *me*, and the truth is if I hadn't already had a boyfriend, I'd have been interested. He's cute, and we probably had far more in common than I ever did with Matt.

"I'm sure there are plenty of those too," I reply. It's only after the words are out that I hear how potentially flirtatious they sound. *Am* I flirting? I don't even know.

He tells me he'd be happy to read what I've got and we make tentative plans to meet up when I'm home at the end of August.

"Hey, Tali?" he says, catching me before I hang up. "It'll be good to see you again. And I'm so glad you finally dumped Matt."

The call ends, and I sit staring at the phone in my hand. I've told myself Sam is only a friend for so long that it's a little surreal to consider any other possibility. And while the idea of dating again terrifies me, *he'd* be a little less terrifying than anyone else.

I'm still holding the phone when it chimes with an incoming text...this time from my boss. I'm less irritated than I should be that Hayes is now texting at midnight.

Hayes: **Are you awake?**

Me: **Let me guess...unresponsive female in your home and you need me to come dig a shallow grave.**

Hayes: **No, that's more of a 3 AM text. The bartender here is a twat. What's the most irritating drink we can order?**

Me: **It's called The Hayes. At least that's what irritates me personally**.

Hayes: **Always so sharp-tongued**.

Me: **Yes. Like a snake. And you're Satan, so it's perfect for you.**

Hayes: **Your tongue is perfect for me? Say more.**

Why Hayes is texting me while on a date with another woman is beyond me. What's even more puzzling is...I like it.

9

He looks worse than I've ever seen him when he gets downstairs. That's really saying something, under the circumstances.

He presses his fingers to his temples. "Take your daily vitamins," I say, pushing Advil toward him.

"You're judging me again."

"Not at all," I reply pleasantly, leaning both elbows on the counter to face him as he slides onto a stool. "Though the text you sent in the middle of the night saying 'send these girls Florida' was unclear. Did you want me to send them *to* Florida or somehow gift them the *state* of Florida?"

"Sorry," he groans. "Fucking autocorrect. That was probably supposed to be flowers. I don't really remember."

I take a sip of my coffee, looking over his schedule. "So, I spent my entire shower trying to figure out how to gift them Florida for nothing." I smile and shove the schedule toward him.

"You thought about me in the shower," he says, mouth barely twitching. "Does that happen a lot?"

"Sometimes I wonder if my soap is strong enough to kill off the bacteria from your home. Is that the kind of thing you mean?"

He winces, pressing his fingers to his temples. "Ouch. I'm too hungover for your mouth this morning."

I bet he doesn't say *that* to many women.

"You currently have nothing from noon to two if you're in need of a nap."

His lip curls. "I don't nap."

"You should," I reply with a sigh. Hayes has clearly brought this all on himself, but I feel bad for him anyway. The way he lives is untenable for anyone under normal circumstances, even without all the booze and the sleepless nights.

He holds his forehead up with his hand. "Can you get the girls upstairs out of the house after I leave?" he asks.

Girls. Plural. Any sympathy I might have felt vanishes. My arms fold across my chest. "What girls?"

"The ones *upstairs.* I thought I made that clear. Three of them."

Three women? That's the stuff of pornography and letters to *Penthouse*, not real life. And I seriously doubt any human, even him, has the agility to service more than two women simultaneously. "Can't you just be content with a run-of-the-mill threesome like the rest of the world?"

His mouth lifts. I get a hint of a dimple. "Are you saying threesomes are run-of-the-mill for you? I don't even see you having twosomes."

He's pretty much nailed it, not that I'd ever admit it to him.

"I would not be interested in a threesome because most men are barely capable of pleasing a single woman without doubling the workload."

His eyes gleam. "Maybe you've been with the wrong men."

"Maybe you've been with women who do a lot of faking."

He laughs, so certain of his *talents* he isn't even going to reply. "Don't forget to send them flowers, yeah?"

I roll my eyes. "Fine. Today's note shall read: *Sorry I came so fast and left you all unsatisfied.*"

"You seem very certain of yourself for someone who is, in

fact, having sex with no one," he replies. "And don't try to tell me I'm wrong. You're far too chipper and well-rested to be doing anything *interesting* at night."

"Maybe I'm just capable of enjoying my leisure time without letting it destroy me the next day."

"Tali," he says, rubbing his brow as he stands, "any man sleeping with you would keep you up all night long whether it was in his best interest or not. He wouldn't be able to help himself." Without even looking at me, Hayes picks up the schedule and walks out, not even realizing what his comment has done to my insides. Because something in the almost-reluctant way he said it...made it seem like he might have been talking about himself.

❧

THAT NIGHT, I GO BACK TO THE FIRST BALL AISLING AND Ewan attend in Edinad. It's the crème de la crème of fae society in attendance—all of them charming and beautiful, constantly inebriated and consumed with sex—a bit like my new boss, actually. I haven't fleshed them out much, aside from the evil queen, but suddenly, I want more. I picture a man there, just like the one in my dream. *Julian.* He's beautiful and darkly intimidating, and when he steps up behind Aisling at the ball, sliding his hands over her bare arms, she's not sure how to react.

"Name anything and it's yours," he tells her.

I don't even know where it would go in the book, but for the first time in a year, the words come easily.

❧ 10 ❧

"**H**i. This is Drew Wilson," says the voice on the other end of the line. "I'm interested in getting some work done."

"You're *the* Drew Wilson." This has to be a prank. Drew Wilson is way too famous to be making her own appointments. She's also way too young and gorgeous to be in need of cosmetic enhancement.

She sounds amused. "Are you always this suspicious?"

"World-famous singers don't usually place their own calls."

"Yeah, I'm definitely not trusting my assistant with this. She'd probably call *TMZ* before she called you. I mean, this is confidential, right?"

"Of course," I reply, though I'm really thinking what she needs is a new assistant, not plastic surgery.

She tells me her manager wants her to get a nose job and a boob job, but she needs it to be so top secret that no one but her knows. "Mostly, I don't want my boyfriend—well, I guess I can't call him my boyfriend, but let's just say the guy I'd like as a boyfriend—to know. Can you guys do that?"

My teeth sink into my lip. Drew Wilson has the kind of face other women go to surgeons waving photos of. Why the hell does she think she needs to change it? "I...yes, it's possible, but you know, you're going to have a lot of swelling after a nose job and black eyes, possibly. Your boyfriend is going to notice."

"If I did it while he's on tour, though..." she muses.

I'm not sure how she thinks her boyfriend won't notice new breasts, but it's not even the point.

"Look," I reply, "I could probably get fired for this but I'm going to say it anyway: you're gorgeous. There's nothing wrong with your nose or anything else. Are you sure you want to do this?"

She blows out a long breath. "I don't even know. Maybe it's a bad idea. My manager's been on me and this guy...have you been with a guy who's, like, fucking perfect? You get along so well, and then he just, like, doesn't call for weeks at a time?"

The question sounds rhetorical, as if it's a given. But Matt's the only person I've ever dated. I have no experience with most of the awful boyfriend/fuck buddy scenarios other women seem to have had. "I've had one boyfriend my entire life so I really wouldn't know."

"*One*," she repeats.

"It's shocking, I know. But you're stunning, Drew," I say flatly. "Don't change yourself for anyone else."

"Spoken like a girl dating the rare guy who's actually one of the good ones."

Yeah, I thought so too. I didn't have a clue until he showed me exactly who he really was.

I'M IN THE OFFICE GOING OVER THE INVENTORY WHEN I HEAR the front door open. Hayes has just reached the kitchen when I step into the room, surprise on my face though there's no reason for it—this is his home, after all. "Hey. Did you need something?"

He shakes his head, and even that small gesture is weary. "I'm going to try your nap idea from yesterday."

I smile. He's made it sound as if napping is something I personally invented.

"It sounds like you'll need it," I tell him. "Nicole texted with some interesting commentary about the other night and how she'd like to repeat it. Her text began with '*It's so big*' and had multiple exclamation points."

He barely seems to register the comment as he passes me, heading toward the living area, but I suppose he's gotten quite a few texts like that in the past. He strips off his button-down and I get a nice look at his shockingly defined biceps as he tosses the shirt onto a chair and lies down on the nearest couch, his long frame eating up every inch of space as he arranges a pillow under his head.

"I don't see women more than once," he says, with his eyes closed. "That way no one gets hurt."

He's asleep in mere seconds. I hesitate for a moment, then cross the room and lay a throw blanket over him. There's something sweet and unexpectedly boyish about his face at rest, and it creates this strange ache in the center of my rib cage. He's every bit as bad as I'd imagined at the start, and yet...he isn't.

Anyone who's ever met Matt would tell you he's "one of the good ones", while I doubt anyone would say that of Hayes. But Matt is not nearly what he appeared, while I suspect—under that beautiful, callous exterior—Hayes might be a little more.

FOR TWO HOURS, HE SLEEPS LIKE THE DEAD.

When it's time for him to get up, I call his name, and he doesn't move a muscle. He's a heavy sleeper, like my dad was. My hand looks like a child's as it presses to his broad back, warm under the T-shirt. "Hey," I say softly, "wake up."

"Half a syringe," he murmurs, eyes still closed. The man works so much he's there even in his dreams.

"Hayes," I say more firmly, kneeling beside him and shaking his shoulder, "wake up."

His eyes open, and for a moment he just takes in my face— not as if I'm a stranger or his annoying assistant, but as if I'm someone he's known his entire life, someone he absolutely trusts. It's...unexpected. By the time I've recovered, the look is gone, replaced by his standard suspicion and disdain.

"I couldn't wake you," I say briskly, rising to my feet. "I made you some lunch."

"Lunch?" he asks, placing his head in his hands as he tries to rouse himself.

"Yes, it's a form of sustenance taken midday, one universal through cultures across the world."

"I don't eat lunch," he says.

"Come on. It'll help you get through the rest of the day," I tell him, going to the refrigerator to get the salad I made him.

Hayes shrugs on his button-down as he walks to the counter, briefly revealing a wedge of taut stomach. "You sound like a mother. Not mine, obviously, but the good kind who doesn't outsource all her parenting."

"I wouldn't know about that," I reply, placing his salad on the counter. "I don't have the greatest mom either."

He cocks his head as he sits. "Interesting. I pictured you as a beloved only child, cosseted and fawned over daily."

I laugh outright. Nothing could be further from the truth. "Hardly. I'm in the middle of three girls."

"Three daughters?" he asks, pinching the bridge of his nose. "Jesus. That would drive a man to an early grave."

My heart tightens into a clenched fist. Even now, even after waking up three hundred days in a row with the same set of facts, it still doesn't seem real. Sometimes I dream the past months were a mistake, and I wake stunned anew.

I carry the cutting board to the sink, feeling fragile as blown glass. *Don't think about it. Not here.*

"Tali?" Hayes says, eyes open now and worried. "Shit. I'm sorry. You're so young. I just assumed..."

I force a smile. "Well, three daughters, early grave...you kind of called it. He died last summer."

"Jonathan told me you'd had a rough year," he admits, looking away.

I frown. Jonathan isn't the type to go around spilling other people's drama unnecessarily, so I can't imagine what led him to spill mine.

"Well, I hope he didn't tell you too much. I'd like to sustain the illusion of having my shit together a little longer."

"Have you seen the car you drive?" he asks. "I never thought you had your shit together."

I laugh. He's awful, and I like that about him.

"If it makes you feel any better," he adds, "I think half of adulthood is pretending to have your shit together when you clearly don't."

My gaze flickers to his, briefly. There is something bleak in his eyes, something alarmingly honest, and suddenly I ache for him. Hayes, on the surface, seems to have everything he wants. Too much of everything he wants. I've been judging him for the way he lives, assuming it's a reckless disregard for what he has.

But maybe it's just a reckless attempt at being content with it.

❧ 11 ❧

I'm bent over the dishwasher when Hayes enters the kitchen the next morning. I glance up in time to catch his eyes on my ass, and there's something so dirty, so deeply *male* in that look, that I feel a stab of unwelcome desire in response.

I close the dishwasher and go to the Vitamix, pouring the contents into a glass, which I place before him.

He stares at it. "This is the worst-looking daiquiri I've ever seen."

"They're called vegetables. I'm surprised you didn't hear about them in medical school, but I guess that would have taken valuable time away from learning about breast implants."

"I was actually aware of vegetables before medical school," he says, lifting the glass and regarding it with suspicion. "I was precocious in that way. I just don't know why you're giving them to *me*."

"Because you eat like shit, you drink like a fish, and you get almost no sunlight, You're like a vampire, only one who's ambivalent about his survival." I turn to rinse the blender. "And speaking of bad habits, someone named Angela texted and asked if you're still on for dinner."

"Angela?" he repeats blankly. The name clearly does not ring a bell. "Go through the texts. Is there a photo of her? I need to know what I'm getting into."

My eyes roll so hard I'm scared they'll get stuck that way. I dry my hands but don't reach for the phone. "Do you actually want me to scroll through your exchange with Angela to find out? Because I'm worried there will be dick pics."

"I seriously doubt Angela sent me a dick pic, but if she did, you can go ahead and cancel."

My mouth twitches. "I meant *your* dick, Hayes."

"Mine? You should be so lucky." He reaches across the counter and grabs the phone for himself, thank God.

"You know," I say, wiping down the counter while he swipes through texts, "a great deal of what you need me for could be solved by not drinking yourself into a stupor."

"Please, by all means, keep telling me ways to make *your* job easier." He stops swiping—I assume he's found her picture—and then returns the phone to me with an especially weary sigh. "Get us a reservation at Perch at seven and let her know for me?"

I grab the phone and pretend to type. "*Top o' the morning, Angela!*" I say aloud. "*Bloody good show, getting a free meal out of our exchange of bodily fluids. I normally just buy ladies a drink and wait for the roofies to kick in. Toodles, for now!*" I look up to see if he finds me as amusing as I find myself.

"Honestly, the hangover is bad, but your British accent is now the most painful thing about my day."

Then, despite his hangover, he smiles, and it feels as if the sun's just come out after a long winter. It makes me far happier than it should.

❧

I'M IN BED THAT NIGHT, ANSWERING A QUESTION SAM ASKED about the book and ready for sleep, when Hayes's name appears on my phone. I try to summon some indignation but can't find it.

Hayes: **What was the expression you used the other day when you were pretending to be British but sounded like a chimney sweep from Mary Poppins? I'm telling the girls about it.**

I roll my eyes. *Girls*, plural. I assume that means I'll be taking them both to breakfast in the morning. And why is he texting me when he has what must be far more entertaining company?

Me: **Was it "go the fuck to sleep"?**

Hayes: **No. Keep trying.**

Me: **Was it "this is inappropriate workplace behavior"?**

Hayes: **That line must be from the off-Broadway rendition of Mary Poppins. Definitely not from the movie. Also, someone didn't read her employment contract carefully.**

Me: **Yeah, that someone is your lawyer. There's no way that contract would hold up in court.**

Hayes: **Ah. Always good to know an employee is *already* contemplating the feasibility of a lawsuit.**

I laugh as I set down the phone. If men were placed on a continuum from ideal to disastrous, Sam would fall on one end and Hayes precisely the other. So why is it Hayes, of the two, I wish would text again?

❦

"So, what happened?" I ask when he arrives in the kitchen the next morning, unusually cranky, even for him. The last text I received—at one in the morning, I might add—said the girls, *plural*, were tedious and I could probably skip the flowers. "What did your lady friends do wrong?"

"Your concern for my sexual needs is appreciated, but unnecessary," he growls. "The night ended just fine."

His mood—and the fact that neither of them is here—leads me to think otherwise.

And the strangest part is that he seems to resent *me* for it.

🎇 12 🎇

The positive side of having asked Sam to read my book is I know he will tell me the truth. The negative side is...I know he will tell me the truth.

I'm already on the cusp of giving up on it entirely, and I worry his criticism will be the death blow.

"Well, I think I've identified the first problem," he says by phone Saturday night. "Ewan is kind of a douche."

"A douche?" I repeat, somewhat incredulously. I got accustomed to harsh critiques in grad school, but I want to go to the mat over Ewan. Because he's just a sweet, kind-hearted farm boy who's been led astray.

"Yeah. I mean, he starts off okay," Sam says. I begin to pace. "He helps Aisling with stuff on the farm and he's protective of her when they first get to Edinad, but then he turns into a selfish dick."

"Well, he's swayed by the opulence," I argue.

"I get that," Sam replies. "But the way it's written, it feels more like his true colors are coming out. Also, that hole they climb through to enter the kingdom—why's it there in the first place?"

"Poor workmanship?" I ask.

He laughs. It's nice to finally get a reaction out of someone beyond a twitch of the mouth. Hayes seems determined *not* to react at all, most of the time.

"It's your book," he says. "But it'd be a cooler book if we knew why the hole was there."

The conversation moves on to other topics—to my trip back to Kansas at the end of the summer, and Sam's trip up the California coast in a few weeks. When he asks if I want to grab dinner while he's in LA, I agree. I don't know if this is a dinner between friends, or if he expects something more...but would it be so terrible? Sam is exactly the guy I should want: He's cute and kind, and we'd never run out of common interests.

Yet I'm weirdly relieved when the next text I receive is from Hayes.

જજ

I'M IN THE MIDDLE OF A RUN SUNDAY MORNING WHEN Jonathan texts.

He's sent a photo of him holding Gemma, with Jason standing behind him, and they're both beaming at her as if she is everything they hoped for and more.

I step off the path and into the sand, blinking back tears. They're so fucking proud as they stare at her. I had one amazing father and Gemma will have two.

I hit Jonathan's name on speed dial. "She's so beautiful," I tell him. My voice rasps.

"You're totally crying, aren't you?" says Jonathan.

"No." I brush a tear off my face. "I'm out on the beach completely *not* crying. She's beautiful."

"She's something, isn't she?" he asks. The utter pride in his voice hits me right in the chest and has me tearing up again.

"Dammit, Jonathan," I rasp. "I'm in public. Stop making me cry."

He laughs. "I'd better change the topic so you can get ahold of yourself. How's work?"

I dry my face on the hem of my shirt like the classy little lady I am. "Ugh," I groan, walking down toward the shore. "Well, yesterday he seemed to blame me for the fact that he didn't get laid by his *two* dates the night before, so that was fun."

"Tali," Jonathan says, with the strained patience of a father talking to an overwrought teenage girl, "I'm sure he didn't blame you."

"You didn't see him," I reply, dodging an errant volleyball. "At least I got spared the indignity of buying them flowers and taking them to breakfast afterward."

"He's had you take them to *breakfast*?" he asks. There's no way to miss the unhappy astonishment in his voice. "That's... unusual. He doesn't typically have people over often."

My tongue prods my cheek as I process my irritation. "Wait. *What?* All this bullshit is for my benefit?"

He hesitates, which means that yes, Hayes is doing all this shit intentionally, and it hurts. I sort of thought he was past wanting me to quit.

"Sometimes Hayes wants you to believe the worst of him," Jonathan says, "and it's not at all for the reason you think."

I sit in the sand, hugging my knees to my chest. There are a few guys in the water surfing. It's the kind of thing I thought I'd do a lot more of, living in California. But then, I also didn't think I'd be here alone. "What do you mean?"

He sighs. "Do you remember how annoyed I was with Hayes last summer? We were upset that we kept getting passed up on the adoption list, and he always seemed so ambivalent about it?"

I do remember, mostly because I was surprised Jonathan expected anything of Hayes in the first place. Ambivalence about an employee from Hayes seemed par for the course.

"Hayes gave them a hundred grand. That's why our adoption finally came through. The letter thanking him was submitted with his taxes. I'm not even supposed to know."

My throat swells. I've barely cried at all over the past year, and here I am about to cry for the second time in one morning —and over Hayes, no less. "That's...nice."

"It's more than nice. We'd still be sitting on the list if it weren't for him."

I clear my throat. "I guess I'll give him a pass for most of his nonsense. But he still shouldn't be texting in the middle of the night."

Jonathan *hmmm*s quietly. "Weird."

"What's weird? Aside from the obvious fact that an employer shouldn't drunk-text his staff in the middle of the night."

"What's weird," he replies, "is that he's never once drunk-texted me."

❧ 13 ❧

During the one year I was with Matt after he got really
famous, there was a specific role I was supposed to
play at events—the sexy-yet-sweet girlfriend. I was
subtly informed that any sign of my brain or personality would
be considered a turn-off to the general public. I went along with
it, trying to be supportive. It was only after our relationship
ended that I admitted how deeply I'd resented it, how sexist I
found it and how much it hurt that Matt never objected on my
behalf.

If bonfires were legal on the beach, I'd probably have burned
the entire *hot, dumb girlfriend* wardrobe from those events by
now. Instead, I've shoved it all to the back of my closet, buried
like a shameful secret...until today. I can't keep cycling through
the same four outfits every week.

I throw all the clothes on the bed, desperate to wear something different, and choose a cream-colored dress, crafted of a
stretchy fabric that skims my figure without clinging to it,
hinting at curves I normally keep hidden. It's sexier than I'd like,
but beggars can't be choosers.

I tell myself, as I wait for Hayes to come downstairs, that I
don't care what he thinks. But anticipation whispers over my

skin as I hear him approach, and he doesn't fail me. It only lasts a second, but I see it: the way he comes to a momentary stop in the middle of the kitchen, his gaze predatory before he blinks it away.

I like it far more than I should.

He picks up the small, clear pill I've placed beside his coffee, and he holds it to the light, frowning. "You realize if you successfully poison me, you no longer get paid, yes?"

"There are things in this world more satisfying than money," I reply. "It's Vitamin D."

He eyes it with suspicion a bit longer, then swallows it. "What did you do this weekend?"

I turn from the Vitamix to him. "This feels like a trick. Was I supposed to have done something for you and forgot?"

His mouth curves. His eyes are the color of autumn leaves in sunlight. "Is it that astonishing when I ask a friendly question?"

My answer is to stay silent and continue staring at him. Because yes, yes it is.

"And your reluctance to answer leads me to believe it was something illegal or controversial," he continues. "If you have a sex webcam, I'd like to be made aware of it posthaste." His tone is entirely too casual for someone who practically asked to see me naked.

"No, I do not have a *webcam*. I was, uh, working on something."

Something I do not want to discuss with *him*. Saying you're writing a book is like saying you want to be a rock star. You can plainly see the other person's desire to pat you on the head and tell you not to quit your day job. I turn on the blender, grateful the noise prevents meaningful conversation.

"It's *worse* than a webcam?" he asks the moment I turn off the blender. I should have known he wouldn't let it go. "There's nothing to be ashamed of. Everyone winds up getting fisted on Pornhub eventually."

"*Everyone?* Your dating history may have skewed your ideas of normal sexual behavior."

"Ah," he says, leaning back in his seat. "God, it's even worse, isn't it? Was it sex with a family member?"

I give up, at last, because Hayes clearly doesn't intend to— though I'm not sure how much lower he can drag this conversation. "It's a book," I reply. My face feels too warm. "I'm writing a book."

I set the smoothie in front of him, but he barely notices. He's too fascinated by my humiliating admission. "If it's a tell-all about a devastatingly handsome doctor, let me remind you of the NDA you signed. Although if he's bringing all your sexual urges to the surface, I'd still like to read it."

If he were anyone else, I'd almost think he was flirting with me. I fight the urge to encourage him, though my ego could do with a little stroking. "Any tell-all about you would focus on why I decided to quit men altogether."

"*My Life as a Lesbian* by Natalia Bell. I'd *definitely* read that one." He flashes me his filthiest smile. It's absolutely pathetic how that smile works on me, worming its way through my blood, replicating in every cell like a virus. I want to forget every principle I hold and start undressing when he looks at me that way. He tilts his head. "I'm not sure why you're acting like writing a book is a mortal sin, however."

I begin shoving fruit back into the freezer with unnecessary force. "Because I signed a contract and spent the advance, and now I can't seem to finish it. And I'm not good at anything else, so I don't know what I'll do if I can't pull this off."

"I'm sure you're good at plenty of other things. Consider the webcam, for instance. You'd be your own boss, at least."

I snicker, grateful he hasn't asked the obvious question—*how could you have been so irresponsible?* "I'll take it under advisement."

I cross the kitchen to the printer. The *clipclipclip* of my heels is all business, signaling a close to the conversation.

"Tell me about your book," he says, as I reach for his schedule, and my shoulders sag. Yep, by the end of the morning he's going to know every unfortunate fact about me. Shall I go ahead and tell him now about the time I wet my pants in kindergarten, or wait for him to ask?

"No." I turn, leaning against the printer cabinet, my arms folded across my chest. "Because you'll laugh, and then I'll be forced to poison you. Which I'm more than happy to do, but as I have both unlimited opportunity and motive, I'll be the first person the cops look at."

He gives me his most winning smile. Dimples popping and white teeth gleaming. "Lots of people want me dead. You'd be third or fourth on any list of suspects, I promise."

I look down at my necklaces, nervously wrapping one chain around my index finger. "It's a fantasy," I tell him, imagining the looks I'd get revealing this to my peers in grad school. A whole room full of twitching mouths and sidelong glances. "This young couple enters a fae kingdom, and the queen decides Ewan, the boy, is the answer to this prophecy and traps him in the castle, so the girl, Aisling, has to save him."

He isn't laughing yet. Maybe he's holding it until the end, like applause, but, you know...bad. "Through the power of her blossoming sexuality?"

I laugh and a little of my tension eases away. "No. It's not that kind of book. She saves him by learning enough magic to take on the queen."

"Which she pays for *on her back*?"

"*Again*," I say with an exasperated laugh, "not that kind of book." I glance at the clock—he should have left five minutes ago but he's acting as if he has nowhere to be.

"No offense, but that sounds extremely dull," he replies. "A good sex scene is essential to any meaningful work of fiction."

"Ah, yes. I remember the blow job in *Pride and Prejudice*. Very tastefully done."

Suddenly something seems to shift in him. His gaze lands on my mouth for one long moment, his stare so intense that my body reacts as if his hands are on me—nipples tightening, a shiver grazing my skin.

"Fuck, but I didn't expect to hear you use that word at eight in the morning," he says. His voice is hoarse. I wonder if that's the tone he'd use in bed, braced above me and that's all it takes to leave me weak-legged. To make me feel as if he could have me on my back with a single word. It's something I never felt once, in all my years with Matt, and it terrifies me. I carry the Vitamix to the sink, wondering what the hell is happening here.

I'm relieved he's gone by the time I'm done.

THAT NIGHT, WHEN I GET HOME, I DECIDE TO WRITE ABOUT Julian. I already finished the revisions Sam suggested over the weekend—Ewan's personality change will be the result of some kind of dark magic, and the hole will be related to a mysterious prophecy—but this is the part that actually excites me.

I'd meant for Julian to be uniformly evil—the embodiment of sin. But what if he was more nuanced than that? What if his flirtatious, mildly belligerent relationship with Aisling changed him? Perhaps he even catches Aisling and Ewan escaping at the end, and instead of stopping them, he helps her through the wall himself.

It feels as if I'm turning this into another story entirely, one in which Ewan matters less, and Julian matters more. I'm not sure why that feels so dangerous, but it hardly matters.

The change thrills me, and makes me remember what I've always loved about writing in the first place...it's these moments of sheer delight, when a story starts to come together in ways that are better and more exciting than anything you ever anticipated.

I just never would have imagined a character like *Julian* would make it happen.

❧ 14 ❧

In a baseball cap and sunglasses, Drew Wilson looks like half of LA—blonde, tan, perfect. I'm still not sure how I've wound up meeting her for coffee on a sunny patio café on Oak Street. She called once again to set up a consult with Hayes and I once again talked her out of it, and here we are.

"*You're* Tali?" she asks, her brown eyes wide as I walk up to the table. "Ugh. You're so little and cute. Six would just love you." Six is her sort-of guitarist boyfriend and, from what she's described, a horrible human being.

"Hard pass," I reply, dropping into the bright red chair across from hers. "As I've told you several times now, that guy is a jackass."

"Just wait until you hear what he did," she says, sliding the menu toward me. "But order first. The service here sucks."

I laugh as I look around, realizing this is a surprisingly dingy café for someone as famous as Drew. "Aren't you, like, a billionaire?" I counter. "I'd think you'd at least be frequenting places where the service is *adequate*."

Her smile is a little weary. "I kind of like that they treat me as poorly as they do everyone else. At least I know they're being genuine."

My heart goes out to her, because I've had a small taste of what her life must be like, and I absolutely hated it.

During my final year with Matt, I found myself questioning the motives of every single person who was vaguely pleasant to me, wondering if it was authentic or because they wanted access to my newly famous boyfriend.

"The best part of breaking up with Matt was that no one cared who I was anymore," I admit. "And being able to run the trash out in my pajamas without someone taking our fucking picture."

She removes her sunglasses and I see a longing in her eyes so strong it's almost palpable. "You're lucky you can walk away," she says. "There are times when I wish I could."

Because for someone as famous as Drew, there's almost nowhere in the world she can walk or run to anymore. It would take decades for anyone to let her fade away.

The waitress arrives. She is as surly as Drew hinted she might be, and takes my coffee order with the enthusiasm of a battle-weary soldier, looking at neither of us.

"Wow, you weren't lying about the service," I whisper, leaning toward her as the waitress returns to the kitchen. "Okay, now tell me what your asshole non-boyfriend said, so I can hate him more than I already do."

She leans back in her chair and blows out a breath. "He said I was *fleshy*. He grabbed my hip and said, 'getting a little fleshy, babe.'"

I groan and place a palm over my face. I don't understand how she can be as smart as she is and not see through this guy. "You should have kicked him in the balls."

"But he was just being honest," she argues. "And it's true. I've put on weight, so I feel like I can't hold it against him. I mean, it's better to know than not know, right?"

I frown. "I think it's better to be with someone who loves you so much, a little weight on your hips is irrelevant."

She sighs. "I'm not sure that exists. Ugh. If we keep talking about Six, I'm going to need to add booze to this coffee. Which is an option I'm totally open to, if you are."

I laugh. "If my pain-in-the-ass boss wasn't already hoping for a reason to fire me, I totally would."

As if I've summoned him, my cell buzzes with a call from Hayes.

"Jesus, you're like Voldemort. I say your name and you appear from the ether," I tell him, mouthing an apology to Drew. "I'm out at coffee with a friend. What's up?"

"Working hard as always, I see. It's a good thing I don't have to pay you much."

I laugh despite myself. "Consider it comp time for all the hours I've spent awake because *someone* decided to text me in the middle of the night."

"You love my middle of the night texts," he replies. "And it's not like you have anything else to do."

"I could *sleep*, Hayes. Text Miss It's-So-Big if you need to chat at three AM. So did you want something?" His chuckle is barely audible but I hear it. I'm glad my impatience amuses him.

"I was wondering if you could make me a salad today. I have an opening at two."

My teeth sink into my lip as I try not to grin. In a life with very few accomplishments of late, this feels like a huge win for me, as pathetic as that is.

"What I hear you saying is you now *crave* my salads."

"There are things I'd crave from you long before salad," he replies, and goose bumps crawl over my arms.

When I hang up, I find Drew leaning back in her chair with a knowing smile. "Well, aren't you two chummy?" she asks. "What else are you *assisting* him with?"

"Shut up. It's not like that. He just eats like shit, and I wanted him to get some vegetables."

"I thought he was a pain in the ass?" she challenges.

I shrug. "Sure, but if he dies of scurvy, I won't have an income."

She laughs and then she leans forward, her lashes lowering, smiling like a witch about to cast a spell. "You are so much more interesting than I realized, Tali. So much more. Starting with the fact that at some point over the next few weeks, you are definitely going to fuck your boss. And I want every detail when it happens."

❦

WHAT DREW SAID WAS LAUGHABLE. EVEN IF HAYES HAS managed to go for a week or two without a threesome—he hasn't brought anyone home in a while, actually—after what I went through with Matt, he's the last person I'm going to choose. But as I prepare Hayes's salad, it does give me an idea for the book. What if there was an *attraction* between Julian and Aisling? It's worry that keeps you reading a book, a fear that things won't work out or the heroine will make the wrong choice.

And Julian would be the *ultimate* wrong choice.

Hayes strides in at that very moment, undoing the first few buttons of his shirt and pushing his hair back off his face. I feel a sudden, sharp jab of desire, watching him. Yes, Julian could make a very compelling case for Aisling if he wanted to.

I push the salad toward him. "Go sit outside."

He glances at the terrace as if it's an alien landscape. "*Why?*"

"Because while I find the idea of vampires exciting, you struggling with a vitamin D deficiency is less so."

He folds his arms across his chest, frowning. Clearly, I've thrown a wrench in his plan to avoid sunlight forever. "Sit with me, then," he says after a second. "I'll be bored, and you're *marginally* entertaining."

"I'm *extremely* entertaining."

"You could be, certainly," he purrs, with the dirtiest possible lift to his mouth. It's as if that smirk of his is directly tied to my nerve endings—that's how fast my body responds. And why *him?*

Why him instead of Sam or a hundred other men who could potentially make decent boyfriends?

I grab two bottles of sparkling water from the fridge and together we walk outside. He has a lovely backyard, with a long, quiet pool and large grassy area, though in truth, I prefer LA's wildly flowering trees and vines to his neatly sculpted boxwood hedges. He eats, and I lean my head back against the chair and turn my face toward the sun. The weather, the views...I can hardly imagine a better place to live, yet I suspect Hayes works too hard to appreciate any of it.

"You're not doing the best job entertaining me," he says.

"You won't like what I have to say," I reply, turning my head toward him. "You need to schedule some downtime for yourself. A weekend, or even a day."

"Not happening." He sets the bowl on the table and folds his hands over his exceedingly flat stomach.

"Just think about it, okay?" I plead. "Today you're going from something called a Botox Baby Shower, which I really hope doesn't involve Botoxing pregnant women—"

"Just their babies." He stretches, the seams of his shirt straining at his broad shoulders as he places his hands behind his head.

"To the gym with your buddy Ben, followed by drinks at Lucent. Your life is just too busy."

"I'll think about it," he says, though his tone implies he won't.

"Honestly, I don't know how you ever had time to come drink at Topside," I tell him. "Or why you were there in the first place. You've probably never worn a bandanna in your life."

His gaze meets mine for one long moment before it drifts away. I get the feeling there's something he hasn't told me about that night. I want to know why he looked at me the way he did. And I *really* want to know why he left.

"How else would I fill an hour between the Botox baby shower and drinks with friends?"

"Reading?" I suggest. "Quiet self-reflection?"

"I'm beginning to see why you're still single."

I glance away. I don't know why his comment bothers me. It's not as if I'm sad that I'm single. I suppose it's just that—though the biggest mistakes were Matt's—there's a part of me that wonders if I should have bended more, or at least faked interest in the Hollywood scene he found so fascinating after we arrived. Matt certainly seemed to think so.

"Jesus," says Hayes. His face has fallen. "You just broke up with someone, didn't you?"

"It's fine."

He groans, leaning forward to turn toward me. "I'm sorry. You can spit in my coffee tomorrow if it'll make you feel better."

I smile. "I spit in your coffee every day. It's not as exciting as you'd think."

He continues to look troubled when he really shouldn't. It's been a year, almost, and I should be well over this by now.

"Was this recent?" he asks.

"Not really." I straighten the hem of my skirt, toying with a loose thread. "We were together for ten years and broke up last summer when my dad died."

"Ten *years*?" he asks, incredulous. That he finds ten years of monogamy unfathomable is completely unsurprising. "How's that even possible? You're in your early twenties. You couldn't have even been in the same place the whole time."

I shrug. "Same high school, same college, then he went to New York for work, and I went to grad school there." And then he begged me to leave New York with him, and I did that too. I put him first, because I thought that's what you do for someone you love. It's a mistake I won't make again. "Matt was on location when my father died, and when I got back from Kansas, he told me he'd cheated on me while I was gone." My tone is flat, factual. I refuse to let anyone think I'm still upset about what he did, especially when it wasn't the cheating that ended it—it was what he said when we fought afterward. *Just admit the fucking book isn't going to happen, and find something else to do with your life. You'd never have gotten the deal in the first place if it wasn't for me.* For years, I'd encouraged him, supported his dreams when mine were coming true and his were not. But the moment that flipped, he couldn't do the same for me.

Hayes's jaw shifts and his eyes narrow. "He's a twat then, Tali, and he never deserved you." For someone with a pretty poor track record of his own, his anger is unexpected. "I could ruin him for you, if you'd like. Give me his name. I know people."

I'm not entirely sure he's joking.

"I'm surprised, given the way you live, that you're not taking *his* side," I whisper. So many people told me I should let what Matt did go, and there's a part of me that wants Hayes to be among them. That wants to continue believing he's the charming but unrepentant douchebag I could never trust.

He swallows. "Think what you will," he says, looking away, "but I've never cheated on anyone in my life. Nor will I."

Every bone in my body wants to argue...and yet, I kind of see it. No matter how much I dislike some of Hayes's behavior, I've never seen him break a promise.

But that doesn't mean he wouldn't. How do you ever know for sure? How do you predict when it will go wrong again? There were no warning signs with Matt. I search our history for them, but there were no lingering glances at other females, no mysterious late-night texts. He didn't even lock his phone. And the words that would end it, there's no sign of them either. I really thought he believed in me until I realized with a few sharp words he never had.

If Matt could turn so false, without a single warning sign, anyone could.

I speak to Liddie that night for the first time since Charlotte's birthday. We've texted, of course, but I guess I've been avoiding her otherwise, still irked that she used what should have been a happy occasion to start a fight with my mom. I get that she and Alex aren't in a position to help with Charlotte's stay at Fairfield, but she could at least not make things worse.

"Well, I'm not pregnant," she announces, her voice flat.

"Sorry," I say, but I don't sound all that sorry. If I'm being honest, her obsession with having a second child seems self-indulgent to me, given everything else going on. It's a problem she's created and yet she seems to think it deserves equal billing. "It'll happen when it's meant to happen," I add.

"That's such bullshit," she says. "That's what someone says when they want you to shut up about it."

Precisely, I think, though I've got just enough restraint not to say it aloud. But it doesn't even make sense. The first time she got pregnant, she was a senior in college and devastated. She's spent years lamenting the fact that she didn't finish her degree, and now that Kaitlin is old enough for preschool and she has time to spare...she's pining after the opposite.

"Fine, tell me what you want me to say," I reply. "Since there's apparently a script."

"Right," she says, with a bitter laugh. "Sorry. You're probably busy with your *book deal* and your famous boss and your famous ex, and this must all seem so very *trivial* to you."

I stare at the blinking fluorescent bulb overhead, at the off-brand crackers I had for dinner and the four walls I can nearly reach while remaining in my bed. "You've absolutely nailed it, Liddie," I reply. "I'm too busy with my glamorous life."

And then, for the first time since we were teenagers, I slam down the phone.

❧ 15 ❧

"I'm having a little get-together Friday," Hayes announces as he takes his seat at the counter Monday morning. "I'll need...stuff."

"Could you be slightly more specific?" I ask. "Since I've never seen your parties, I don't know if 'stuff' means a few six packs of Coors Light, or a kilogram of cocaine."

"Could you even *get* a kilogram of cocaine?" he asks. "Is that something I should have been hitting you up for all along?"

"I have no idea. I never learned the metric system."

He rolls his eyes and mutters *bloody Americans* under his breath. "No, I don't require cocaine. Just a bar and food. And music. And a valet, I guess. Two hundred people, maybe."

I groan. A *valet*? Two *hundred* people? "That's not a 'little get-together'. That's a wedding. Did you finally find someone worthy of you? Just so we're clear, I'm not sure you can legally wed your own reflection."

He climbs to his feet. "I'm still hoping that law gets changed."

He then leaves, having dropped this bomb on me, but he takes the smoothie with him. I find I'm unable to be as irritated as I'd like.

THE NEXT FEW DAYS SEEM TO OCCUR AT WARP SPEED. I allocate most of the planning to an event company, but answering questions about trivial crap still eats up every free second—Chilean sea bass (endangered but tasty) or tilapia? Ecru linens or taupe? Curved spindles on the chairs or straight?

I find myself texting Hayes often, and though he tells me I'm a nuisance and frequently threatens to fire me for asking too many questions, he's the one who sneaks in irrelevant texts. Asking questions about my book, wanting to know more about Julian, suggesting various sexual positions Aisling might enjoy. I reply with links to websites about sexual harassment in the workplace, but the truth is those texts are the best part of my day.

By night, I'm still working on adding Julian to the book. I think I've almost got it when Sam calls with a new suggestion.

"You know," he says. "I don't love Naida."

Naida—the woodland nymph who teaches Aisling to wield magic—is vital to the plot. It's not as if Aisling can storm a castle full of dark magic without a weapon of her own.

"It would be a lot more interesting," he says, "if she had an evil motive or wanted something in return, something complicated."

"You want me to make sweet little Naida—who wants nothing more than to own her bakery outright and earn the love of a water nymph—*evil*?"

"Sure. Like maybe she's trying to lead a zombie uprising and needs Aisling to lower the wards on the castle so she can attack."

Sam always did want to add zombies to everything. I'd forgotten that about him.

Yet he's not wrong. Those scenes with Naida bore me too. And it might be fun if Aisling had to work with someone *bad* in order to get what she wanted.

I think of Hayes's latest suggestion: that Aisling could sleep with Julian to get information about the queen. He really doesn't seem to grasp the concept of a young adult novel. (*"I'm not suggesting you describe a graphic bondage scene," Hayes argued. "Just, you know, allude to one."*) While I don't intend to have my teenage heroine take up prostitution to save her boyfriend, I can admit he may be on to something. Working with Julian is like making a deal with the devil. In order to get what she needs, she'll have to risk everything.

Me: **You win. Julian is going to help Aisling break into the castle.**

Hayes: **Which she'll pay for ON HER BACK. Don't argue, just go with it.**

Hayes: **BTW, that would be a good line for Julian to use on Aisling in bed.**

৩৵৶

I ARRIVE ON FRIDAY MORNING CLAD IN SHORTS AND RUNNING shoes, ready for the long hours ahead. The work trucks pull up to the house right behind me, and the next twenty minutes are a flurry of directions and unlocking doors and answering placement questions. When I finally get back inside, Hayes is sitting at the counter.

His eyes run over me, head to toe and back to my legs. His slow perusal makes me shiver, in a good way. "Have we changed the dress code, then?" he asks, his voice lower than normal.

"I'm not running around here in heels all day. I have my dress for tonight in the car."

"I'm sure the workmen are enjoying this look." His mouth flattens. "I'll barely need to tip when they're done."

I roll my eyes and slide him his schedule while I look over my own. For once, I think I'm the busier of the two of us.

"So," he says, "I guess there's no smoothie today?"

I glance up. "Do you *want* one?" I feel like a Disney heroine who's just discovered she's got a secret power.

He runs a hand through his hair, which is what Hayes does when he feels even the tiniest pinch of vulnerability. "Only if you have time."

I don't. But it's an admission, even if he doesn't realize it: He likes to feel cared for. He likes that someone in his life wants things for him aside from what he does for them in return.

"Of course," I say, placing his vitamin D next to his coffee with an additional supplement. "But only if you take your vitamins like a good boy. And I'm not trying to poison you. The new one is zinc. It's good for the immune system."

He pops it into his mouth. "And sperm production," he adds.

☙❧

THE DAY PASSES IN A HAZE OF DECISIONS AND DILEMMAS AND petty squabbles between vendors. I'm just praying it's not a complete disaster. The biggest party I've ever thrown until now involved pizza for twenty, and even that didn't go so well.

At seven, I rush into one of the upstairs bathrooms and twist up my hair before I climb into the shower. The fancy body wash on the lip of the tub smells like Hayes—like a summer night on a beach somewhere glamorous. I stand for a moment inhaling the scent before I realize how weird that is and get on with it, washing quickly and drying off before I slip into the green silk dress I brought.

My normal makeup is lip balm and mascara, but tonight I do the full deal: I'm not half-assing things at an event full of the city's most beautiful women.

I slide on my heels and fluff my hair before I head downstairs to find Hayes wandering aimlessly, looking a little lost. He stops in place when he sees me.

"I didn't recognize you for a moment," he says, clearing his throat. "You made an effort for once."

It's not the most effusive praise I've ever received, but I shouldn't have been hoping for praise in the first place.

"It's going to be hard enough standing next to a bunch of actresses and models. I figured some makeup was necessary."

His eyes flicker over my face. "You're prettier than any of them even without makeup," he says gruffly.

I blink in surprise, my jaw unhinged. I've heard Hayes spew flattery before, but this is different. Almost as if he said it by accident. As if it was something he didn't want me to know.

"Thank you," I whisper, but I'm not sure he even hears it as he turns on his heel and walks away. I watch him go, and something begins to flutter in my chest. If I didn't know any better, I'd think it was hope.

❧

THE PARTY IS EVERY BIT AS LAVISH AND INSANE AS HAYES wanted it to be. There's a tequila luge in the shape of a woman's face, a chocolate fountain, and one full table loaded with more tiny desserts than I've ever seen in one place. Massive silver balloons and Chinese lanterns sway in the breeze, and servers pass neon green drinks on trays, narrowly dodging attendees dancing to the music that booms from the sound system.

I'm running for several hours straight, dealing with obnoxious guests demanding special food and trying to lift the tequila luge while someone's drunk spouse is snatching a bottle of Patron off the bar for a private party he wants to hold in a cabana. It's only when someone asks me where Hayes is that I stop long enough to realize I haven't seen him in a long time.

I search the lawn and then the house, eventually finding him sitting alone on one of the upstairs balconies. It's so quiet here, it would be easy to forget there's a party going on at all.

His mouth hitches up slightly, a failed attempt to smile. "You did a good job," he says. "No. Let me correct that. You did an amazing job. It would appear, therefore, that you are good at something other than writing, contrary to your claims."

I wonder, for a half second, if he threw this entire ridiculous party simply to prove that to me before I dismiss the idea. He's not *that* selfless.

"If it's amazing, why are you up here? Shouldn't you be choosing the eighteen women you're going to let stay over tonight?"

He leans back in his seat, a glass of wine held to his chest. "That would be thoughtless of me, since it would mean making you get eighteen women out of my house in the morning."

"The thoughtless part would be bringing that many women up in the first place. No way you'd satisfy all of them."

His mouth hitches up to one side. "That sounds like a challenge."

I picture him attempting it, which leaves me both irritated and titillated at once. I turn to head back downstairs and his hand encircles my wrist.

Such a small point of contact and yet, for a moment, it's all I can notice.

"Sit," he says. "You've done enough tonight, and your car's blocked in."

I take the chair across from him. It's my first time off my feet all night and I groan in relief as I sink into the cushions. He reaches across the table and pours me a glass of Malbec. I take a sip, letting it roll around in my mouth. I'd forgotten what a pleasure good wine could be. A warm breeze carries the scent of night-blooming jasmine from his side yard and I breathe deep, resting my head against the chair's soft back. He must, at some level, think a massive party like this one is fun, even if he's not enjoying it tonight. For me, the wine in my hand and him sitting across from me is enough.

"So, if you're up here alone," I say. "I can only assume that means you're busy thinking dark thoughts about the emptiness of your life."

"Is that what I'm doing?" he asks, swirling the wine in his glass.

"I don't know," I reply. "Are you?"

"Maybe." He glances at me with a rueful smile. "There's nothing like inviting over every single person you know to make you realize you don't like any of them much."

I ache for him. His life could be so much fuller if he'd just allow it to be.

"You probably need a few people you're willing to talk to sober," I say softly, curling up in my chair.

He stares into his wine glass. "At the moment, I guess that's mostly Ben and you."

My heart gives a single hard beat. I never thought I'd see the day Hayes would admit I'm something more than his less-than-stellar assistant. "I thought I might have met Ben tonight, actually."

Hayes looks toward the sea of people in the yard. "He's out of town but he wouldn't haven't approved of all this. He's nearly as judgmental as you."

I smile. "So, he's a good influence, then. I was picturing a Hayes clone."

He tips back in his chair. "It's a sad day when we agree *you're* a good influence. How did you spend the entire advance, anyway? Based on your clothes and your car, I'd assume you aren't much of a spender."

I suppress the desire to laugh. Only Hayes would take my sad, shameful admission and insult me with it. "My younger sister needed inpatient treatment after my dad died, and I've been helping my mom out with money. Apparently, my parents' finances were in worse shape than anyone knew, even my mom."

"You take care of everyone, don't you?" he asks. His eyes are soft as velvet. When he looks at me like that, it's hard to breathe. I find I can't maintain eye contact.

"Not all that well, it would seem." Liddie and I haven't spoken or even texted in a week, Charlotte still seems miserable, and the last time I called home my mother was drunk. It feels like I'm failing, but no one can tell me how to turn things around.

The party below us has quieted to a dull roar. It's probably time to send the caterers home. I rise, reluctantly slipping my shoes back on.

"I'll pay it," he says. "Your debt. I'll pay it. If you ever make it big, you can pay me back. Otherwise, consider it a gift."

My eyes sting, and suddenly I feel fragile and uncertain. Under that beautiful, careless exterior of his lies a heart far larger than anyone out back realizes, and it's been a very long time since someone has offered to take care of me, hasn't simply assumed I'd figure it out. I'm not sure why it makes me so happy and sad at once that he's the exception.

"Thank you." It comes out as a whisper, barely audible around the lump in my throat. *God, am I really about to cry over this?* "I can't accept, but thank you."

His nostrils flare. "Why the fuck not?" he demands. "I can make all your problems disappear in the blink of an eye, with very little effort. Why not let me?"

Why not indeed? That money is nothing to him. He could earn it back in a week, while it would take me years, if not for this job.

"Because," I say, unable to meet his eyes, "everyone in your life seems to take something from you, and that's not what friends do. I guess I'd rather be your friend."

It feels too intimate, too earnest. I want to make a joke, find a way to lighten things up. But I see something in his face that hasn't been there before—as if he really sees me, as if he might even trust me—and I can't stand to ruin it. For once, I keep all the awkward jokes inside me. And then I walk away, wishing, more than anything, I could stay.

☙❧

I WAKE AT NOON. IT WAS FOUR IN THE MORNING BY THE TIME I left, and I was relieved to see Hayes had rejoined the party, smiling his lopsided grin and charming the shit out of everyone.

I assume he found some lovely, willing young model and took her upstairs with him eventually.

I need to get started on the next section of the book, but I don't know where it should go. Julian has told Aisling he'll help her, but he's not the kind of guy who's going to give away his assistance for free. He'll demand something of her—the question is what he'd even want, other than sex. He already has far more money, power, and clout than she does.

I go for a run, hoping the answer will come to me. It's a beautiful day; the sky tinted rosy-gold, the ocean so blue against the white sand it seems more like a photo than real life.

I increase my pace as I pass the pier and all the mansions I'd kill to borrow for a day. My favorite is dark brown, with four levels of decks facing the ocean. I've never once seen a sign of life there. I imagine the owner is some Hollywood exec, working slavishly toward goals that will prove empty in the end, just like Hayes. He'll be an old man before he ever steps outside to appreciate this view he's had all along, and when it happens, he won't feel proud of what he's accomplished. He'll simply realize what it is he missed with his eyes on the wrong prize.

Julian is a bit like that, but there's lingering humanity there too. Maybe the beauty of him is that he's good in ways he'd prefer no one see, ways he almost won't acknowledge to himself.

As my feet pound against the pavement, I ponder once more the tasks Julian's sending Aisling on, and then I think of Hayes last night, saying *it would appear you're good at something other than writing*.

And I run all the way home with the answer I needed bursting from me.

Aisling arrives in Julian's study to discover the wishflower—which she risked her life to acquire—is something he already has in abundance. He tells her she can keep the one she found and she's enraged.

"Why did you ask me to risk my life if you didn't even want it?" I demand.

"Perhaps, my sweet, it wasn't for me at all," he says. *"You think you need your Ewan so desperately, but look what you accomplished entirely on your own."*

I send the new pages to Sam, and he writes back an hour later telling me he loves them. "I actually like Julian a lot more than I like Ewan," he adds.

That I agree terrifies me.

❧ 16 ❧

On Monday afternoon, Hayes asks me to meet him at a bar near his office to go over the schedule. "A bar, rather than your office?" I ask. "How professional."

"I need a stiff drink to handle the inevitable nagging that seems to accompany any conversation with you," he replies. I smile to myself. I do actually have some nagging in store, it's true.

I reach the bar just after five. The place is dark and cozy—chestnut paneled walls and wood floors, charcoal velvet chairs, low lighting. I'd think it was romantic if I was meeting someone else.

He watches me as I approach, eyes brushing over me from head to toe like I'm something to eat.

"I got you a gin and tonic," he says.

I sling my purse over the back of the chair and take a seat. "I'm driving."

"You appear to be sitting, actually," he says, his eyes flickering over me once again, "and I didn't order you a *hundred* gin and tonics."

"Maybe I have a date tonight," I say, though in truth, all I've got scheduled for the whole evening is a bowl of cereal and a phone call to my mom. "I know it's shocking, but I do have some small life outside of serving your every need."

His tongue taps his lip. "I wouldn't say you serve *every one* of my needs," he counters, his voice low and filthy. I squirm in my seat. "And you don't have a date because you're still mooning over Farm Boy."

"I'm not mooning over anyone," I argue, squeezing the wedge of lime into my drink. "I'm just licking my wounds, and please don't make some gross joke about letting someone else lick my wounds...I know that's where you were headed."

He sets his drink down. "As a doctor, I doubt I'd suggest either option. But it's time for your self-pity to stop. Let me make you a Tinder profile."

He snatches up my phone and I snatch it back. "I can make my own profile, thank you very much. Anything you did would probably reference how many working holes I have."

His teeth sink into his lip as he tries not to laugh. I picture them sinking into my skin instead and feel goose bumps rise along the back of my arms.

"Okay, well, let me help," he says. "How about '*Argumentative redhead seeks—*'"

"I'm not a redhead."

He shakes his head. "Brown is too plain and I can't believe you're *already* arguing with me. As I was saying, '*Argumentative redhead seeks extremely handsome male to nag. I have three working holes.*'"

I smile against my will. "Thanks, that's perfect. I'll definitely find Mr. Right with that."

"I can tell you're going to be tedious about this. Fine." He looks over one shoulder and then the other, surveying the room. "Then who here do you find attractive? Aside from me, of course. Obviously, in a perfect world, I'd be your first choice."

"Obviously," I say, my lips humming along the lip of my glass. "It's so hard to find a man who will buy me drinks, fuck me and never call again."

His gaze sharpens, grows feral. "God, what a filthy little mouth you have," he says. His voice is pure gravel, and I feel a hard kick of want in my stomach. Or maybe that kick was a little lower if I'm going to be honest.

I imagine hearing him say that while braced over me, flushed and desperate. Or pushing me to my knees with his hands in my hair.

Which is not something I should be picturing about my *boss*.

My voice is embarrassingly breathless as I change the subject to the schedule. "You're already booking into July," I tell him. "I thought you might want some time off."

He raises a brow. "This again?"

I take a very long sip of my gin and tonic. "Yes. This again. Which reminds me..."

I pull my laptop from my bag and open the calendar, which I then turn toward him. The blank spot on Friday is as glaring as a neon sign. It seemed like a good idea at the time and seems like less of one now that I'm telling him about it. My ideas are often like that.

"You sort of agreed to take some time off." I sound like a child explaining a lie to an unforgiving parent.

"I said I'd think about it, Tali. That doesn't mean I *agreed*." His eyes are stormy. "You should have asked me first."

"You'd have said no, so that wouldn't have been effective." I smile. He does not smile back. "One Friday, Hayes. Just one."

He takes a heavy sip off his drink, sneering even as he does so. "What the hell am I going to do on a Friday?"

I look at him blankly. Yes, I'd anticipated an argument about taking the day off, but I didn't think I'd have to explain the concept of leisure time to him. In the four weeks I've worked for him, he hasn't taken a single day off.

I throw my hands up. "Do whatever people normally do when they get a day off."

His lips press tight. "They normally sit at the DMV for hours getting a license renewed, or grocery shop. I have you for all that."

I prod the inside of my cheek with my tongue, wondering if he has a point. When I have a day off...I work. But if I didn't work, I'd be doing laundry or running errands or jogging while thinking about work. Maybe we need to pull an actual fun person into this conversation, one who enjoys her life.

"Then hike. Or surf. Though I can only picture you doing those things in a suit."

"Well, obviously," he says. "I'm not a savage. But I'm not interested in hiking or surfing. I'm interested in making money."

I exhale wearily. "You live in LA, for Christ's sake. The things you could do are endless. Drive up the coast. Visit a museum."

He gives a slow, exaggerated blink, as if he's been roused from deep sleep. "Sorry, I think I dozed off there. You excel at making leisure time sound dull."

I've got to admit—I bored myself there too. I cycle through memories of times when I was still fun, but only childhood comes to mind: *hide and seek* or *ghost in the graveyard* on a summer night, playing badminton with my sisters while my dad worked the grill, cheering us on. All of my happy memories involve other people, which is, perhaps, why I haven't had a lot of good memories over the past year.

"Go to an amusement park," I offer, more out of desperation than anything else. I picture him standing in a long line, wearing a suit, texting me to demand I explain Dippin' Dots to him. "Roller coasters, funnel cake, arcade games. Hard to get more exciting than that." I try to sound enthusiastic but I think I'm failing.

He sips his drink. "I wonder, when I hear you say these things, how limited your life experience must actually be. But fine. We'll go. You and me. Make the arrangements."

I stare at him in dismay. Sure, I love amusement parks, but I didn't intend to go *with* him. "Why would you take *me*? You've got half the females in this city eating out of your hand."

"Because amusement parks are filthy, and I don't want to be lured into having sex at one." He holds his empty glass up to the waitress. "What's the problem? You seem like the sort of gal who would appreciate funnel cake and Simpsons-themed paraphernalia."

"Wow," I reply. "So, you want me there because I'm tacky and not attractive enough to fuck. You've crafted quite the persuasive argument."

"Are you denying you like funnel cake?" he challenges, folding his arms across his chest.

"You'd have to be born without a soul to dislike funnel cake," I mutter.

"Then it's settled," he says. He's smiling as if he's won something.

৩৩

ON FRIDAY, I ARRIVE AT HAYES'S HOUSE AN HOUR LATER THAN normal. He's already up and dressed, wearing khaki shorts and a T-shirt from some London pub. I freeze, completely struck by the visual before me.

I'm not used to seeing him in regular clothes, and if I'd thought it would normalize him somehow, I was wrong. Now all I see are gloriously fit legs and surprisingly muscular arms, his shirt clinging just enough to his chest and stomach to assure me they're as taut and nicely built as the rest of him.

I, on the other hand, am not much to look at right now. Barefaced, sunglasses, shorts, and a tank top. No jewelry or lash extensions anywhere to be seen, as different from the women he dates as I could possibly be. The closest thing to perfume is the tang of my sunscreen.

I hold my arms out. "You're welcome. I went the extra mile to make sure you wouldn't be *lured* into having sex."

"Is that a *high school* track team shirt?" he asks, alarmed.

"Not fancy enough for you, *milord?* My Gucci amusement-park wear is all at the cleaners."

He blows out a breath. "My problem isn't your lack of style. My problem is you look sixteen. The kind of sixteen that is the definition of jailbait, and the shirt isn't helping. I'm worried I'll get arrested. Those shorts barely cover your ass and that tank isn't exactly *loose*."

I glance down. I guess I'm covering up a lot less than normal. "This is just what I run in."

His eyes sweep over me. "Clearly I should be spending more time in Santa Monica. But that doesn't negate the fact that you're as fresh-faced as a teenage girl and wearing her clothes today too."

I shrug and start for the door. "Try not to act creepy in public."

He follows. "I generally try not to act creepy as a rule."

"I would not have guessed that."

His mouth twitches, and I feel oddly...victorious spying that unwilling smile of his. I suddenly realize how glad I am he's spending this rare day off with me. Along with the more troubling realization that I wouldn't want anyone here in my place.

We leave for Universal—me, eager as a child; Hayes, tolerating me like a weary but amused parent. Once we've parked, I jump from the car and breathe deep. The smell of hot tar and sunscreen reminds me of childhood, back in the days when our family trip to Worlds of Fun was the highlight of the summer.

"I suppose you don't *do* amusement parks in England," I tell him, holding out my phone to an attendant, who scans our admission tickets. "A fun day out is probably a trip to Bath, or a day in the countryside playing with a hoop and stick."

He exhales. "I get the feeling all your knowledge of my homeland comes from reading books about nineteenth century orphans."

"Well, we're about to get a big taste of your homeland in a minute," I say, leading him through the park, my steps quickening. He's so much taller that even when I break into a near-jog his stride remains leisurely.

"Tada!" I cry, arms wide as we walk beneath the faux-stone entry to Harry Potter World. "We're here. Doesn't it remind you of home?"

His teeth sink into his lip as he takes in the rides and shops. "Ah, yes, Ye Olde Butterbeer Kiosk. There was one on every corner growing up."

I roll my eyes. "Fine. Don't show your gratitude. And here I was about to selflessly convince you to buy us both a wand and golden snitch. Which would also remind you of home. I know how you Brits love wands and quidditch."

Something like laughter bubbles in his throat. Possibly a stifled weary sigh. One of many today, I'm certain. "It's like you were raised there, you know us so well."

I make him buy me a butterbeer, which is terrible, and go into the wand shop, though I have just enough pride not to let him buy me a wand when he offers.

With our VIP passes, there is little waiting for rides. I figured a man who hasn't stood in line for anything in years wasn't going to handle a ninety-minute wait for Hagrid's Motorbike Adventure. But as we are ushered past a long, winding queue of whining children and weary parents, I wince. "Are you feeling bad about this at all?" I ask, nodding toward their sad little faces.

His brow furrows. "Bad about making the wisest decision of my life and avoiding parenthood? No, not at the moment."

We watch as a kid old enough to know better gets mad at his father and throws a tray of nachos on the ground. "I feel certain you're missing out on something by not having children," I reply, "though I can't quite think what it is right now."

"You do?" he asks, swallowing as his gaze flickers to me and away. "Want kids, that is."

I shove my hands in my pockets. "I thought I did," I admit. I was eight when Charlotte was born, old enough to treat her like a living doll for several years before she objected. Having kids and being an author—those were my two greatest dreams when I was younger.

He glances at me. "But...?"

"But I doubt I'm ever going to be in a relationship again," I tell him.

"You're twenty-five, and you've only been single a year. How can you possibly claim you'll never meet someone?"

I frown at him as the turnstile unlocks to allow us onto the ride. "Because I knew Matt backward and forward, and there was never a sign he was so...different...from who I thought he was. I can't imagine going through that all over again with someone I don't know as well."

He sighs and runs a hand through his hair. "I understand that better than you can imagine, but not all men are terrible."

I step into the car, holding the lap bar while he slides in beside me. His thigh is glued to mine and his shoulders are taking up more than his fair share of the seat, but I can't say I entirely mind the way we are pressed together. "I just don't trust myself to know the good ones from the bad, and I doubt I ever will. You wouldn't understand. You only want the bad ones."

There's no time for him to respond. The bar locks over our laps and then the roller coaster inches out of the station, climbing up a massive hill at a rickety pace. Fear and anticipation build in my stomach and I let myself lean against his side, just a bit, finding assurance in the solidity of him, though even those muscles of his won't prevent us from certain death if this thing goes off the rails.

"You're nervous?" he asks, grinning down at me.

I narrow my eyes. "Not in the least. I'm just trying to figure out how I can sacrifice you to save myself if this goes badly."

We reach the hill and drop down what appears to be a ninety-degree angle. The lap bar is all that is keeping me in this seat as my intestines seem to lift into my throat and stay there. I'm terrified and thrilled and clinging to the bar while I attempt to press my face into his shoulder, all while we whip around corners at high speed and fly up another impossible hill. I stop screaming just long enough to hear him laughing—not the dry, sardonic chuckle he gives me occasionally, usually at my expense, but a true belly laugh. It makes me smile for half a second, until I start screaming again.

When we reach the ride's end, coming to a shockingly sudden stop, I climb off on weak legs.

I've only been standing for a few seconds when the world turns black. "Whoa." The blood rushes from my head, and I find a strong arm wrapped around my waist, pulling me tight.

"What's the matter?" he asks.

My head falls to his chest as little black dots fill my vision, and even as I struggle to regain my balance, I notice how nice and firm he is, how good he smells—soap and skin and fabric softener, how reassuring his arm around me feels, as if nothing truly bad can happen when I'm standing against him like this.

"Just a dizzy spell," I reply. "I think I need to eat."

Slowly I regain my vision and step away from him. His eyes narrow. "You're sure that's all it is?" he demands. "Does that happen a lot?"

I laugh. "Are you *worried*?" He didn't even look worried when a very famous actress told us she was 'gushing blood' from her incision.

He forces his face into a less concerned shape. "No, never. I just don't want to blow forty bucks on funnel cake for you. But come along."

He leads me down the exit ramp, his hand moving from my shoulder to the small of my back, as if he's suddenly convinced I'm the kind of girl prone to fainting spells.

He orders a funnel cake and two lemonades. "You were wrong before, you know," he says to me.

"I do need to eat," I argue. "My entire caloric intake in the past twenty-four hours has been a sip of butterbeer and a pack of Oreos last night."

"Not that," he replies. "What you said. That I'm only interested in the bad girls."

He carries the funnel cake over to a spot in the shade and pushes me to sit.

"Fine," I amend. "Not *bad* girls. Just temporary ones."

He tears off a piece of funnel cake, examining it as if it's some bizarre curiosity—a winged pig or a tomato with eyes. "Not even all that temporary," he says. "I was engaged once upon a time, after all."

I stop chewing, momentarily...frozen. I can't explain why, but the fact that he was once engaged—that he wanted to spend forever with another person—makes my stomach sink.

"What happened?" I ask. The funnel cake has turned to mush in my mouth.

He lifts his head. His eyes are dark, unreadable. "I went away for a month as part of my fellowship. While I was gone, she fell in love with my dad."

The funnel cake in my hand falls to the ground as I stare at him. I wonder if I've misunderstood somehow. Because it's difficult for me to imagine how anyone with Hayes could choose someone else, but it's *impossible* to imagine that someone chose his actual birth parent. "Your dad?" I ask. "Your *real* dad."

He nods, putting the funnel cake in his mouth at last. "He's a movie producer, extremely wealthy. And still relatively young, since he was only twenty when I was born. It was everything she wanted."

He doesn't sound bothered by any of this. He could be discussing his taxes for all the emotion in his voice.

"But your *dad*," I repeat. "I mean, who does that? And what more did she want?"

He shrugs. "She accused me, when she left, of not loving anyone as much as I love myself."

I hate her, this insane stranger who left the man beside me for his own father and was an asshole about it to boot. I hate her in a way that I never hated the actress Matt cheated with, hate her more than I ever even hated Matt. I don't understand how he can just accept it all. "That's a pretty bitter thing to say to someone you're leaving, especially under those circumstances."

He swallows. "She wasn't wrong. I'd lost a patient and I was floundering, not sure if I wanted to stay in medicine at all, more consumed with my own shit than hers. And I was still finishing my fellowship back then, making nothing, so it's not as if there was any other benefit to sticking around."

I'm still so dumbfounded I can barely respond. I wonder if it's why he's in that ridiculous house—if it's some Great Gatsby-esque attempt to prove his worth to her.

"It sounds like you actually forgave them," I say, shaking my head. "I don't see how."

He wipes his hands on a napkin. Apparently one bite of funnel cake was enough. "I was forced to learn a few hard truths about myself, and I got a little sister out of it, so it's not all bad."

My mouth opens, and he holds up a hand. "Before you suggest that I not write off an entire enterprise based on one bad experience, allow me to remind you, you've done the same thing."

He swipes some powdered sugar off my upper lip with his thumb, small laugh lines forming at the corners of his eyes as he does it. There's so much affection in the look he gives me, so much sweetness, that my heart breaks for him even more. He's taken that bitter parting shot of hers and made it his motto, embraced the idea that he isn't loving or loveable, when nothing could be further from the truth.

If he was mine, I'd have held on with everything I had.

☙❧

WHEN WE'VE HIT EVERY RIDE AND EATEN A YEAR'S WORTH OF junk food (which, for the record, Hayes completely enjoyed even if he wouldn't admit it), we head home. After the heat of the day and all the walking, the passenger seat and air conditioning are all I need to be lulled to sleep. When my eyes open, we're in front of his house.

"It's about time you woke up," he says. "The neighbors are probably calling the cops to report a comatose teenager in my driveway."

I yawn. "They'd have placed that call years ago if they were going to. So how will you spend the rest of your day off?"

"The sky's the limit," he replies. We both climb from the car. I'm strangely reluctant to leave.

He seems reluctant too. He places a hand on the car's roof, in no rush to get inside. "Enjoy your quiet night in, refusing to get a life. I'll think of you while I'm out doing the things you won't."

My nose wrinkles. "I'd prefer you not think of me during *that*, if it's all the same to you."

He gives me the dirtiest smile imaginable. "A man has limited control over where his mind goes at various points."

My body sags a little against the car as I release a quiet breath. I know he's joking, but my stomach is fluttering anyway —like a single baby butterfly trying out its fledgling wings. If I thought he'd ever *actually* imagined me during sex, I'd probably orgasm right where I stand.

I cross the driveway to my car, which looks especially rusted out and ready for the junkyard this afternoon. After a day in Hayes's BMW, it will feel like I'm driving home in a car from *The Flintstones*.

"Hey, Tali," he says, as I reach for the door. "Thanks. It was the best day I've had in a long time." He's being earnest for once, and I can tell it's difficult for him.

Another baby butterfly takes flight. I smile, stifling the impulse to ruin it with a joke. But I can't bring myself to tell him the truth…it was the best day I've had in a long time too.

AT HOME, BEFORE I'VE EVEN KICKED OFF MY SHOES, I GO online to look up Hayes's dad and wife.

His dad is hot for a guy in his fifties and looks a lot like his son, which really just makes the whole thing creepier.

Ella, his wife, is fine-boned and tremulously beautiful in that way only foreign women are: So fragile you'd think a strong wind might blow her over. The kind of woman other women don't even try to imitate because you know, looking at her, that imitation is impossible.

It makes my chest ache. It's not as if I ever thought I would replace her. It just sucks to realize I *couldn't*, even if I wanted to.

❧ 17 ❧

If I thought forcing Hayes to take a day off would teach him the value of leisure, I soon learn I was woefully mistaken. When I suggest he consider a weekend off, he laughs, and when I ask about blocking out another Friday, he only says "maybe", in a tone that sounds a lot like *no*.

But he's coming home nearly every day for lunch, so...baby steps?

On an office day, when he can't come to me, I go to him instead. I need to go anyway, since I've just gotten his oil changed and have to return his keys. The feminist in me winces as I show up at his office, toting a bag from In-N-Out Burger like some 1950s wife bringing her man his midday meal, but... fuck it. He needs to eat.

The receptionist looks at me like I'm taking my life in my hands and suggests I set it outside his door and run. I know he goes out of his way to appear distant and intimidating...I just didn't realize people actually bought the act.

I wander back through the hallway to his office, walking in after I tap on the door.

"I got you a cheeseburger and fries," I say, handing him the bag. "The rest is mine."

He closes a file. I'm clearly interrupting him, but he doesn't seem annoyed. Not that I'd care if he was. "Trying to ruin my social life by fattening me up?" he asks.

"At one cheeseburger a week, it will take me about two hundred years, but I have faith in our longevity."

"You have faith in my longevity?"

I smile. "You might have a point." I nod at the food. "I mean, look how you eat."

I reach out to take the bag back from him, but he points to the chair beside me. "Stay," he says. "I have a few minutes before my next patient."

"I thought you hated people," I reply, slumping in the chair happily and pulling out my fries. "Your receptionist wanted me to set the stuff outside your door."

He spreads the paper wrapper out neatly on his desk and places a napkin in his lap, as if this is a proper meal. "I do hate people. I guess your constant nagging sets you apart somehow."

I laugh despite myself. "Your staff could learn something from me," I reply, shamelessly licking the grease from my fingers. He watches me, a flicker of interest in his eyes. "Maybe I should offer an in-office training."

"Your smart little mouth is plenty," he says. There's a purr to his voice that makes my core clench tight as a drum, something that seems to be happening more and more. I've always had a fair amount of self-control, but one lingering look from him, one low note in his voice, and I feel like I'm another kind of girl entirely.

Remember why it's a bad idea, Tali.

I know his romantic past is certainly littered with examples of bad behavior, but when I scour my brain for them, I come up empty-handed. Even the few reports I've seen about him in the press have been complete bullshit, like the one claiming that girl I saw leaving his house weeks ago is "broken-hearted" over him —though he saw her only once—just because she looked vaguely depressed walking into yoga. Who *doesn't* look depressed walking into yoga?

"Tell me about these *purported* girlfriends of yours," I demand. There's bound to be plenty of douchery there. "I'm still having a hard time seeing it. Start at the beginning."

"The beginning?" He wipes his mouth. "That would be Alice Cook. We were six. I gave her candy hearts for Valentine's Day, and she told me her mum wouldn't let her have sugar and threw them away."

I laugh and ache simultaneously. It's too easy to picture a tiny, crestfallen version of Hayes having his tender heart broken for the first time.

He takes a sip of water, stalling, and I wave my hand to move him along. So far, he's only made my issue worse.

"Then there was Caroline Cutherall, my mate's older sister, who I loved fiercely from ages ten through fourteen," he says. "She was a decade older. I suppose I might have a shot now." He shrugs.

I'm sure he would. I don't know who Hayes was at fourteen, but there's no way it can match up to Hayes, two decades later.

"After that, there was Annie, the reverend's daughter. We dated until midway through my first year at university."

He pops the last of his burger in his mouth. I notice he doesn't mention the *end* with Annie, which undoubtedly means he was at fault. *Jackpot.* "What happened with her?"

He leans back in his seat and holds my gaze. For a moment I'm certain he's not going to answer.

"I came home from university to discover she'd been filling her time in my absence with a footballer from the local club," he says.

Oh.

"She was followed by Ella," he concludes, "who is now, of course, my stepmother."

He gives me a rueful smile and takes another sip of water, as if this is all vaguely amusing and a little boring. To me, it is neither. I struggle with a sudden lump in my throat. Instead of a healthy reminder of Hayes's callousness, I've just watched him die of a thousand small cuts and a few major ones.

I want to tell him he deserved better. I want to tell him Ella was crazy, that they *all* were crazy, but the words are lodged in my throat, too earnest and possibly too invested to be said aloud.

The phone rings, announcing the arrival of his next patient. I quickly clear away our trash, still thinking about what he's said and wishing I could fix it all. He walks me through the waiting room to the elevator, standing with me while I wait for it to arrive. It almost seems as if he wishes I could stay, and...I wouldn't mind. Increasingly, it's hard to remember what my days were like before they included Hayes's smirks and withering commentary about my car and my choices. Without the sweetness in his eyes that assures me he means none of it.

I've barely reached the parking garage when he texts, asking me to return. I *wish* I was annoyed. I wish I didn't feel this quiet excitement at the prospect of seeing him again, even though I just left his side.

I find him in a room with a patient and stop at the threshold, but he beckons me in.

"Tali, meet Linda. She saw you in the waiting room and is telling me she wants to look like you."

I slow, and my last few steps to reach them are faltering.

"I want all of it," Linda says. "The tiny nose and especially the lips. Get mine as close to hers as you can."

Is this normal? To point to another human being as if she's an outfit on display and ask to be recreated? Hayes shows no surprise at all, but he swallows as his gloved thumb presses to the center of my lip. I want to suck it further into my mouth, nip it with my teeth.

"Tali has a lot of volume in her lips, the upper lip in particular," he says. "It would be hard to replicate, but I could use micro doses of filler to turn the border out the way hers does." His index finger runs along the contour of my upper lip. I take tiny, insufficient breaths through my nose, my heart beating harder than it should.

"Yes, let's try that," Linda says. "You've done such amazing work on her."

His finger stills on the center of my mouth and our gazes lock. Being the center of his attention, in this way, is headier than I ever imagined it could be. It's the experience of being exposed, laid bare, but also *seen*. Seen in a way no one ever has before, as if I'm something fragile, something worthy of care. I never want to stop feeling this way.

He drops his hand as if he's been burned.

"Tali's beauty is all her own," he says gruffly, walking away. "I'm going to get the camera."

I stare at his departing back in shock, wondering what the hell just happened. Was it me? Was it both of us? My memory of it is a little too surreal to be trusted.

"I wish my husband would look at me the way he looks at you," Linda whispers. "Like he could be completely content if he never had to look at anything else."

I glance at her—she is lovely in her own right, more than deserving of an appreciative husband—and my heart gives an odd, hard thud at her words. It's the ache of wanting something to be true and knowing full well it is not. "I'm just his assistant," I reply. "He looks at me like that because if I wasn't around, he'd have to get his own coffee and he finds waiting at Starbucks intolerable."

"I just watched the way he looked at you, honey," she says with a knowing smile. "And believe me, that look had nothing to do with coffee."

❧ 18 ❧

Hayes's smoothie is waiting when he joins me in the kitchen the next morning. He's slick and pressed and perfect as ever, but his gaze is just a little more piercing than normal. I wonder if I was weird yesterday. *Of course* I was weird, and I'm still being weird. I can't seem to shake the desire for more of his attention, for the feeling of his hands on my skin and his eyes on my face the way they were in his office.

I picture him cornering me in the kitchen, his hard body pressing my back to the cabinet, invading my space. His thumb on my mouth before his lips seek mine, his hands falling low, to slide over my hips, to tug up my skirt.

The mere thought makes me feel winded. I can't imagine what the reality would do.

"I have a party tonight," he says, shattering the fantasy. "I may need your help."

I hope he can't tell that my head was somewhere else entirely. I close my eyes for a moment and calm my breathing. *Get it together. This is what he does: he makes women feel like they're special and then he moves on.*

"As far as I can tell, you don't need any *help* at parties." It comes out sounding more bitter than I'd intended.

"It's an industry thing," he says with a glib smile, putting his keys in his pocket and grabbing his coffee. "Every actress or female producer I talk to is going to wind up deciding she wants a little touch of something. Besides, you're clearly good advertising. Everyone who sees you assumes I did your work and wants the exact same thing."

I have no desire to stand by his side while he flirts with beautiful women all night. If only I actually had plans so I could refuse. "What should I wear?" I ask, my shoulders sagging.

He glances at me, his eyes falling to my mouth, soft as a snowflake, before they jerk away. "Every eye will be on you," he says, "no matter what you wear."

He sounds as if he regrets it.

❦

I CHOOSE A DRESS I BOUGHT RIGHT AFTER MATT GOT HIS FIRST big part—black and silky, draped low in the front, no back whatsoever.

Matt called it my *Fuck This Party We're Staying Home* dress. I flinch at the memory as I slide it on. He made me feel so desirable back then, and the thing is, I still believe he meant it. He just didn't mean it *enough*, and how do you ever know when someone does?

I pair the dress with sky-high strappy black sandals that will still only bring me to Hayes's collarbone. My hair is down, curling softly over my shoulders, along with a smoky eye and a hint of nude lipstick to play up the lips he seemed to appreciate yesterday. Some distant part of my brain asks why I'm making the effort and shies away from the answer.

The event is held at Black Swan, a massive new bar in the center of Beverly Hills. By the time I arrive, the place is packed. Everywhere I look, I see beautiful women and vaguely familiar faces. It's the kind of event Matt would have sold his soul to attend, back when we first got to LA.

I'd forgotten, until now, how much I hated attending these things with him. The way people would treat him as if he was superhuman and would treat me like the lucky but replaceable straggler along for the ride.

And sometimes I got the feeling he agreed with them. That's what I hated most of all.

I've spent so long telling myself Matt and I were perfectly happy, but as I stand here taking in the crowd, it seems I remember more bad memories than good.

I give my name to the doorman inside and text Hayes to say I'm here. Only moments later, I see him moving toward me. He's in a black shirt, partly unbuttoned, and looking at me in a way I enjoy far too much. Like I'm the only thing in the entire bar, the entire *city*, he can see.

"Jesus," he says, blowing out a breath. "Half the men in this room are old, Tali. And now I'm going to have to defibrillate all of them."

I blush, struggling to remember why I'm here. I'm sure there was something, but all I want is for him to keep saying sweet things and looking at me the way he is.

"So, what is it you need me to do tonight?" I ask, glancing around us.

He hands me a drink. "Relax, first of all. It's a party. I'm not going to ask you to perform open-heart surgery. Just help me with scheduling and save me if I get trapped by someone."

I roll my eyes. "How will I know whether you're trapped or talking her into something she'll definitely regret?"

His gaze flickers over my dress once more. It feels as if we are the only people in the room. "I assure you, she wouldn't regret it. But there won't be any of that tonight."

In truth, it seems like there hasn't been any of that for a while. He still occasionally gets texts from women he's seen in the past, but he ignores them, and there have been no new dates, no naked women in his bed the next day.

As I'm thinking this, though, he turns toward a group of

women who immediately start flirting, gripping his biceps, smiling too widely. Maybe he's just finally learned how to be discreet.

I'm forced to take a step back as the group closes in around him, and those memories of being replaceable seep back in. I lift the glass in my hand and swallow half of it in one go, hoping it will dull my nerves and quiet my thoughts a little.

"You are way too pretty to be standing here alone," says a voice behind me. I look over my shoulder to find a generically attractive guy not much older than me. His smile is confident, then sheepish in turn. "Sorry, that was cheesy. I was gonna offer to buy you a drink but it's an open bar."

"That would weaken the gesture somewhat," I reply, taking another sip of whatever Hayes got me.

He extends a hand. "I'm Chris." His handshake is firm—an adult handshake. "And you look so familiar. What have I seen you in?"

I shake my head. "I'm not an actress."

"Really?" he says, stepping closer. "You just became so much more appealing to me, and you were already appealing."

Is this how flirting works? I really have no idea, and now it feels like I'm too old to learn. But this is the first attractive, single guy I've spoken to in a while. I suppose I should at least *try*, even if it's the last thing I feel like doing.

"So you're an actor?" I ask.

His grin is cocky. "You seriously don't know who I am?"

I'm about to reply when Hayes suddenly appears at my side with his hand on my elbow, making a polite but clipped excuse to my new friend as he drags me away.

"And here I was worried you wouldn't have a good time," he says.

I'm relieved he's rescued me, but I'm not about to let *him* know it. "I'd probably be having a better time if you weren't dragging me away from the first man I've spoken to in months."

"I brought you here to work," he replies. His voice is clipped, devoid of its normal mischief. "It's funny how quickly you forget you're being paid."

I hold up my phone. "And I'm ready to do so. Or was I supposed to—"

My words fall away entirely, my eyes frozen on the man being whisked past the doorman. My heart flops like a fish out of water, in serious danger of collapse.

Matt is here.

With a date by his side.

It's hard to imagine a worse scenario than this one. *He's* even wealthier and more successful than he was a year ago, whereas most of his dire predictions for me have come true. I'm alone, I haven't finished the book, I've taken a lame Hollywood job to make ends meet. If I pack up and move home, he'll be four for four.

I can't stand it.

Sheer panic takes over. I'm trying to think, but I'm a shaky mess, all fluttering hands and weak, skittish pulse. "*Shit.*"

Hayes raises a brow, glancing from me to Matt. "What?" he asks. "Oh, God. Don't tell me you have some deep, undying love for Noah Carpenter? I thought you were more interesting than that."

"No," I say, biting my lip. He's moving through the room. He hasn't seen me yet, but any minute now he will. "No. Can I just —can you just do something for me? *Please?*"

"Fine, I'll have sex with you," he says with a long sigh, "but only the one time, okay? And from behind, so it's not awkward in the morning."

He absolutely doesn't get it. Matt's going to spy me in a matter of seconds, and when that happens, it will be the most humiliating moment of a life positively *strewn* with humiliating moments.

"Hayes, this is important." I clasp my hands together, pleading. "When he gets here, please don't tell him I work for you, okay?"

Hayes is acting like this is the most amusing situation he's ever been in, a lazy smile stretched across his face. "What's in it for me?"

"Jesus Christ, Hayes," I hiss. "You already have my entire life. What more could you possibly want?"

It's then that Matt spies me. He looks stricken, as if he'd forgotten I even fucking existed, and the sudden reminder is a shock. And then his face breaks into that smile—the one I used to love. The one that made me feel like I was the most adorable, special thing in the entire world. Now half the planet loves it just as much, and I finally realize it was never really mine at all.

He skirts around a group of men, ditching the actress he brought without a word, and then he's *here*, pulling me against him.

I freeze in response. My limbs are stiff, unmoving, unable to behave normally. These are the only arms I had around me from ages fourteen to twenty-four, and being in them again is surreal. I've only kissed two other people, and had sex with one other, in my entire life. Standing here is like being reunited with a missing part of myself, one I know is diseased but still *feels* right.

"God, it's so good to see you, Tali," he says, finally pulling away. His hands frame my jaw as he stares at me. It's too much eye contact. It's too intense. I feel sweat beading down the center of my chest. "How have you been?"

I'm about to stammer a reply, when Hayes's arm wraps around my waist, pulling me away from Matt. His lips press to my head in a show of casual possession, and Matt has to look *up* to meet Hayes's eye, a fact I enjoy way more than I should. Matt always did wish he was taller. "Uh...Matt, this is Hayes Flynn. Hayes, this is Matt. Better known as Noah, I guess."

Matt's smile fades as his gaze flickers back to Hayes's arm around my waist, but he extends his hand. "Nice to meet you," he says.

"A pleasure," replies Hayes in that way only a British male can —he sounds polite and dismissive simultaneously.

"I can't believe you're here," Matt says, turning to me, looking...amazed, as if this is some incredible stroke of luck. He seems to have forgotten how ugly it ended. "I texted you so many times and you never replied."

Ah, yes, all those rambling texts, half of them drunk. Always looking for forgiveness. *I will never cheat again, I swear. Can we just talk? You're still my best friend. It's weird not speaking to you at all.*

I really have no response. I'm not sorry I ignored him. He deserved worse.

"How's the book coming?" he asks, as if everything that went wrong between us never happened. As if he isn't the person who tried to squash all my dreams in one fell swoop—not two weeks after my father died. I'm not about to tell him it's still a disaster. I've made some progress, thanks to Sam's suggestions and the addition of Julian, but I still need to spit out about two hundred pages in two months' time.

"It's great," I lie. "They gave me an extension...because of my dad." I'm grateful my voice doesn't sound as shaky as I feel.

His smile flickers out. "I heard about Charlotte," he says. He appears earnest, but who knows? He's an actor, after all. "I'm sorry."

I know I should ask him how he is or mention his movie, but small talk doesn't interest me. What I really want to say to him right now is *how could you? How did I never see it coming? And how much of our relationship was a lie?* A part of me still can't believe it turned out the way it did. This is the boy I attended prom with, graduated college with. I still remember our first apartment, how walking through IKEA with him felt like the start of a grand adventure. I thought I'd gotten so lucky, and I wasn't lucky at all. I was just fooled. But even looking at him now, I can't find it, the sign he'd betray me.

Hayes's arm tightens, pulling me closer. "Sorry, *Max*," he says, sounding anything but sorry. "I need to steal her away for a moment. Excuse us."

He pulls me down the hall, his arm still around me. My body

moves on auto pilot, relieved one of us knows what to do right now. I don't look back at Matt, but I can feel his eyes on me as we walk away.

When we're finally out of sight, I suck in a few desperately needed breaths as Hayes leans me against the wall, his hand on my hip as if I might not be able to support my weight. I focus on Hayes's chest, right before me, trying to get my heart rate back under control. When that doesn't work, I close my eyes, resting my head against the wall behind me.

"I would never have asked you to come if I'd known he'd be here." His voice is soft and apologetic.

My eyes open to find him standing far closer than I realized. I reply to his chest instead of his face. It's easier that way.

"I still don't see it," I whisper. "I thought maybe, in person, I'd see whatever I missed before, how I could have been so blindsided. But he looks exactly the same."

He pulls me against him, and he's so big it feels like I've half-crawled inside him when his arms go around me. "He was an idiot. Anyone who's met the two of you already knows. Jonathan said, and I quote, 'Matt's the stupidest SOB who ever lived. He's never going to do better than Tali.'"

I blink back tears. I wasn't going to cry over Matt, but Jonathan's loyalty is worth more than gold to me. "Jonathan's a good friend."

"It had nothing to do with being a good friend. It was just common sense. I'd never even met *Matt*"— he says the name with a sneer—"and I knew he couldn't do better than you."

It's sweet, but I know he's just saying that to make me feel better.

"Did you see the girl he's with?" I ask. "I'd say most people think she's an upgrade."

His hands cradle my jaw, forcing me to meet his eyes. "You have the purest face I've ever seen in my life," he says quietly. "A face I couldn't possibly replicate, and if I could, she and every other female here would ask me to."

I stare at him. He's so earnest right now I almost think he means it. "She looks like all the women you bring home," I reply.

"Yes, well, one drinks wine from a box when Chateau Lafitte isn't available," he says briskly, releasing me. "As you are clearly in no state to remain—"

"I'm fine," I cut in. I've suffered worse losses than Matt. I'm not letting him run me out of here. "Really."

"You're a terrible liar," he says. "There's not anyone here I want to talk to anyway."

He wraps an arm around me, tucking me close to his side as he starts making his way through the crowd. It makes me feel small and safe and cared for, a sensation I like a little too much.

We are halfway to the door when he stops suddenly, pressing me to one side of the circular bar, his hands cradling my face once more.

"Matt's looking," he says softly. "Just go with it."

And then he kisses me.

He has the warmest, softest, most perfect lips I've ever felt, and he kisses exactly the way I imagined he would...unhurried but as if he's already a step ahead, already planning to pull my dress over my head and take me right where I stand.

I taste the scotch on his tongue, my lungs full of the scent of him.

His hands hold my hips tight, and he presses closer, until our bodies are flush. We have more than proved any point we are trying to make, and I know I should stop him or object, but I can't. There's some wild impulse running through me, destroying every neuron, killing off every reasonable thought. My fingers slide into his lovely, thick hair; his hand tightens around my hip...and then he inhales, sharp and surprised, and pulls back.

His eyes are nearly black under the bar's dim light, his lips swollen. "He's jealous as hell right now."

It takes me a second to even remember Matt was here.

I press my palm flat to the barstool beside me, trying to get a grip. "You're not even looking at him, so how could you possibly know that?"

"Simple," he says, grabbing my hand. He begins fighting the crowd again, pushing toward the exit. "Because I'd be jealous as hell if I were him."

When we finally get outside, he plucks the valet ticket from my hand while I take one lungful after another of the warm air, wishing I could think clearly. Because the kiss is over, but inside me, it's still occurring. It feels like he just let something out of a cage, something too dangerous to be set free. We stand in silence, waiting for our cars, my body so taut I'm certain it would snap like kindling with little effort. It's all I can do not to grab his collar and drag his mouth back to mine.

When my car arrives, he looks at me for one extra moment, and I feel a pulse, low in my abdomen. There's hesitation in that gaze of his, uncertainty. As inexperienced as I am, I suspect if I asked him to get a drink, he'd say yes.

And if I asked him to go home with me, he'd say yes to that too.

"See you Monday," I say instead.

It's the wise thing to do. But it's one of those nights when it feels like wisdom is really overrated.

❧ 19 ❧

The thing about a long-term relationship is that you persuade yourself, when you're in it, that it's good enough. All the little irritations and disappointments are brushed aside. No one's perfect. Why nurture your tiny miseries like a delicate plant you want to see flourish?

Except I brushed aside disappointments with Matt having, essentially, no experience with anyone else. A kiss while playing spin-the-bottle in eighth grade and a sloppy, drunken one-night stand post-Matt are all I had to compare against him...and neither of them held up very well.

I'd believed, for instance, that Matt was an extraordinary kisser. But I could kiss a thousand men, and none of them would match Hayes.

My fingers trace over my lips on the way home, remembering. I try to look at the kiss scientifically: What was so much better? Was it his utter confidence, the way he increased the pressure so suddenly, like water reaching its boiling point? Was it just his feel and his smell, his urgency and his size and that sharp inhale of want and surprise I heard at the kiss's end?

I don't know. But he's not an option, so I really pray that whatever it was, I find it again in someone else.

He appears at the counter Monday morning, all lean, unruffled beauty, that arrogant upper lip of his firmly in its arrogant place, smirking as always.

I slide the smoothie next to his coffee. "Don't freak out on me," I tell him. "I used more kale than normal."

"You know, one of these days you could surprise me and make Eggs Benedict instead."

I bite into a strawberry. "Eggs Benedict, hmmm? I've never pictured you eating breakfast."

"What do you picture, Tali?" he asks, his tone and leering smile so ridiculously filthy I laugh.

"Jonathan coming home so I don't have to get up at six anymore," I reply, leaning my hip against the counter. "That's what I picture."

"You'll miss me," he argues. "My mother says I'm loveable once you get to know me. Well, it might have been the nanny. Someone said it. What's on the schedule today?"

I hand it to him, amazed by how easily things have gone back to normal. They definitely didn't seem like they would all weekend when I flopped around in bed, sheets tangling between my legs, having one dream after another about him: Hayes kissing me, my back pressed to the wall, his hands sliding up my outer thighs as he pushed my skirt to my waist.

You have the purest face I've ever seen in my life.

"Where have you gone, Tali?" he asks. My head jerks up as I blink the memory away. "You're not still mooning over the idiot from the soldier movie, are you?"

I roll my eyes. "Not at all. In fact, I put up a profile on Tinder, you'll be happy to hear."

A muscle flickers along his temple, and his smirk is oddly... muted. "Very good. Let's see it."

I carry the blender to the sink. "I'm not showing you my profile. You're just going to make fun of it."

"Probably," he replies. "You've undoubtedly bungled it. But you must acknowledge I have a lot more experience judging

117

women than you do. And if you don't show it to me, I'll just create a profile for myself and find you."

There's not a doubt in my mind he'll do it too. I reach for my phone and open the app, but when he takes it, he doesn't burst into the peals of mocking laughter I'd anticipated.

Instead, his jaw tightens. "'Not looking for a relationship' is code for 'mostly in this for sex'," he says. "You're not going to find Mr. Right that way."

"Who says I'm looking for that?" I counter.

He runs a hand through his hair and it falls forward messily. "Have you ever even had a one-night stand?" he asks.

"That's an extremely personal question," I begin, but he simply raises a brow, as if to say *and your point is?* "Yes," I admit with a sigh. "Matt had a costar, Brad Perez, who was constantly hitting on me. When we broke up, I..." I trail off with a shrug. It was not my finest moment. I thought I'd feel victorious afterward. Instead, I just felt empty and used.

"A revenge fuck?" he asks with a tight smile. "I didn't know you had it in you. *Literally* had it in you. And you ghosted the poor chap, didn't you?"

I snuck out in the middle of the night like a thief and blocked his calls afterward. Again, not my best moment.

"I was in a bad place at the time. Now I'm fine. I just want to be sure no one gets the wrong idea."

He grabs his bag and his jacket and turns for the front door. "You sound like me now," he says softly. He doesn't seem happy about it.

☙❧

SWIPING ON TINDER IS ADDICTIVE, LIKE A HARMLESS LITTLE game. I do it at stoplights, or as I stand with a contractor while he looks at a plumbing leak in Hayes's powder room. I reject anyone whose first photo is shirtless, or who's posing in a gym—

I'm not looking for Mr. Right, but I would like someone with just a hint of self-respect. I also ditch all the men who say things like *just here to fuck* or *must be D cup or larger*.

There's actually a very long list of things I don't respect, as it turns out. In the end, as pretty as they are, I only say yes to a few guys, and when they write me, I'm mostly revolted.

Hey babe, says the first, which I find demeaning.

The second asks me if I'd rather have hands made of cabbage, or to spit up a full cabbage hourly, which makes me laugh but is also weird. I bet he's got a YouTube channel where he pranks his parents, with whom he still lives. No thank you.

The third says *Dam ur hot*. Even if his text didn't suck, I'd rule him out based on poor spelling.

The fourth says *what r u doing 2night?*

Which is when I give up. Who raised these men? How lazy must you be to refuse to type out one or two extra characters?

"Have you tried Tinder?" I ask Sam later on.

"Everyone under the age of thirty has tried Tinder."

"Why is the spelling so terrible?" I demand, reaching under the bed for my running shoes. "And why do so many people abbreviate words? Like, is it really saving you *that much* time to use the *number* two instead of writing T-O?"

"Then I guess you're dating again," he says. His tone is...careful. Not excited, but not *unexcited* either.

I swallow. "Well, no. I was dipping my toe in the water and now I need to soak my toe in bleach."

"Well, sort of on that topic..." he begins, and my stomach sinks. "I'm coming to LA week after next. Will your ogre of a boss give you a night off?"

My breath holds. It's a crossroads. I either step up and tell him I'm not ready to date, or I decide to let things happen.

"My buddy John will be there too," he adds. I'm not sure if that was always the plan or if my silence freaked him out.

"Sure," I reply. "Just let me know when."

I'm scared, and also, perhaps, a little excited.

Sam is cute and an excellent speller. We'd have plenty to discuss.

But he would not be casual. Of that I'm certain.

🐾 20 🐾

Hayes comes home for lunch, and I sit outside with him. He no longer has to ask me to do it. It's assumed, and that's fine. I guess I kind of like the break in my day.

"How's it going?" he asks.

I tilt my head. "Good as ever. You're booked solid for three weeks straight, aside from Tuesday two weeks from now." I've also left a weekend open in three weeks, but I haven't figured out how to convince him to take a vacation just yet.

I expect him to object but he doesn't even seem to have heard what I said. "Not work. You. Your desperate quest for an orgasm that isn't self-induced."

I flush. I wouldn't call it a *desperate quest*. More of an ambivalent one, at this point. "Poorly. There are a lot of disgusting human beings on Tinder, and even more who don't seem all that bright."

He stabs at his salad—I'm pretty sure he's picking *around* the vegetables—and looks over at me. "Give me an example."

I open up the app and begin scrolling. "Here," I say, handing him the phone.

He swipes through the photos. "This one looks mostly unobjectionable. Not a single nude pic."

"Not his photos. His write-up. *I love to laugh*, he says."

His eyes are light, crinkling at the corners with suppressed amusement. "You might need to find a very specialized dating site if you're looking for someone who doesn't laugh."

"That's exactly it!" I exclaim, throwing out my hands. "Who *doesn't* love to laugh? You've got five hundred words to tell me how you're special and different, and you basically tell me you're a human being with needs all humans have. Why not add that you need oxygen to breathe and take in food for sustenance?"

His mouth twitches. "You're being awfully picky. And Matt didn't look like the sharpest tool in the shed. You can't convince me it was his *intellect* that turned you on."

I frown. "Matt's smart," I argue. "Just not—"

Not smart like you, I very nearly say. Even after all this time, the thought feels disloyal, but I can't deny it's true. It's not as if I felt like something was missing when we were together...but Matt was like a spoon, capable but dull-edged, while Hayes is a blade sharpened to dangerous perfection.

"The things that attract you at fourteen are different than the things that attract you as an adult," I finally reply.

Hayes's nostrils flare in disdain. "I don't understand how you *ever* thought he was worth your time."

"When we met, I was a kid and he was already in high school. And he was so cool. I mean, he played *two* sports and he was dating a *senior*." He grins at my emphasis. "I just felt lucky he chose me."

And then, slowly, I stopped feeling lucky. Maybe it was when I got into Brown, and he convinced me not to go. I agreed in the end, but I remember thinking *I wouldn't have asked this of him. I wouldn't have put myself first*. Or maybe it was in New York when I was working my ass off, but he seemed to be doing more clubbing than auditioning.

I'd still have married him, though, if it hadn't fallen apart, and for the first time I realize how *grateful* I am it did. Matt and I could laugh at the same things, but he was never the one who *made* me laugh. He never inspired that tickling crawl of joy in my rib cage the way Hayes does when he says something ridiculous. And he definitely didn't kiss like Hayes does, which makes me wonder what else I've been missing out on.

"So clearly you're never going on a date again," he says, resting his hands on his stomach. "Shall I stop someplace on the way home this afternoon and buy you twenty cats?"

He's enjoying my singlehood a little too much. His smirk hits like a repeated pinch of a nerve I can't reach.

My chin goes up and I force a smile I don't feel. "I'm going on a date," I reply. I've spent the morning assuring myself the night out with Sam is *not* a date, but Hayes's smugness needs to come down a notch. "His name is Sam."

"I thought Tinder was a wasteland full of horrific men who enjoy laughter."

"I know him from home," I reply. "He's the guy who's been helping me with the book."

Hayes's smug smile fades. I see the quirk of his nostrils before a hand runs through his hair. Something in me wants to push and prod at his discomfort until it's all laid bare.

"What's the matter?" I ask.

"Nothing," he says, setting his bowl down on the side table between us heavily. "It just seems like a bad idea."

21

Later in the week, Hayes's schedule gets so slammed he can't get home for lunch. I have plenty to do, but it's oddly lonely, without his visit to look forward to. When he asks me to meet him for a drink after work to discuss a project, one we could easily discuss via text, I agree without hesitation. I refuse to admit that I might miss him a little.

I've just reached Beverly Hills and found a parking spot when Charlotte's psychologist calls. I blow out a quick, frustrated breath. I don't know why she'd call me instead of my mother, and also...I just want to see Hayes.

"Is this a bad time?" she asks.

"I'm about to meet my boss," I tell her, omitting that I'm meeting him at a *bar*. "But I have a minute."

I climb out and don't bother locking the door. No one's stealing this car. Even criminals feel sorry for me.

"I'll keep it short," she says as I begin walking down the street. "Your mother is not doing well. She was drinking during the last family therapy session and isn't treating Charlotte's issues with the care they deserve. I think some changes are necessary."

I release a small breath, thinking *what now?* At the rate we're going, I will owe the Fairfield Center a million dollars by the time this is done.

"What kind of changes?" I ask.

"Your mother needs to attend AA, and you or your sister will need to assume supervision of Charlotte when she's released."

I step into the intersection, ignoring the blare of a horn as I cross. "But...we both live out of state," I argue.

"Charlotte said you were coming home when she gets out," Dr. Shriner says.

I laugh unhappily. "For a *week*."

I walk faster, bracing myself for what's coming. I'm pretty sure I already know.

"Well, unless something changes, I can't, in good conscience, release your sister to your mother's care."

The argumentative side of me wants to ask what legal grounds she has to hold Charlotte somewhere that costs *me* seven grand a month. But it's sort of beside the point. If my sister needs more than my mother can give her, someone else needs to be there, and I already know who it will be. I'm the one with the flexibility to move home, not Liddie. I'm the one who's single and about to be jobless. What can I even claim is holding me here? I have Jonathan, an unrequited crush on my boss, and little else.

I take a deep breath, silently assuring myself it won't come to that. I'll talk to my mother and convince her to get her shit together.

Because if she doesn't, it means I'm leaving LA, and Hayes, for good. How strange that leaving *Hayes* is what bothers me most.

✦

HE HAS A DRINK WAITING FOR ME WHEN I WALK IN. I TOSS back half of it the second I sit down.

He leans back in his seat. "You're drinking like me tonight," he says. "And while I greatly admire this change, I suppose I should ask if there's something wrong."

I shake my head. The last thing I want to discuss is the bullshit with Dr. Shriner, and for some reason, I *particularly* don't want to discuss it with him. "Just a call from home. What's this project you want me to work on?"

His gaze snags on me over the rim of his glass. "What's wrong at home?"

"My mom's been drinking a lot," I reply, waving a dismissive hand in the air, "and the psychologist treating my sister has some concerns. It'll be fine. Really. So, what's this project? I assume it involves women and liquor, so I'll go ahead and write those two things down."

He hesitates before ceding to my wishes. "I'd like you to host a luncheon. So yes, both women and liquor should remain at the top of your list."

The word *host* throws me off entirely.

"Just a light, catered meal on the terrace," he adds. "I'll set up some aesthetic services inside. It's good for business."

I'm guessing his "just a light, catered meal" actually means *extravaganza for five hundred wealthy women with high expectations*.

"I'm not asking this because I don't want to do that much work, although I totally don't want to do that much work," I say, running my fingertip over the salt on my glass's rim, "but *why*? House calls stress you out, and you don't seem to get any satisfaction from it. You already earn more than you could ever spend, and you only seem to spend on food and alcohol, which I'm guessing you could afford on a surgeon's *paltry* salary."

"Perhaps," he replies. "But it might not pay for you to take care of everything so I can *enjoy* my food and alcohol without the tedium of acquiring it."

I take a sip of my drink and discover I'm down to ice. "Get a wife then. She'll perform all your menial tasks for free."

"I don't know how many marriages you've seen," he says,

looking tired suddenly, "but believe me, there's a price to be paid there too."

It doesn't surprise me that he has a sour attitude toward marriage, so I'm not sure why I feel disappointed. I can't seem to stop wanting him to be someone he's not.

Together, we map out the luncheon and then walk down the street in the fading light, the sky striped in sunset pinks and golds. He's talking about his favorite island in Greece when he comes to a dead stop and points to a mannequin in a shop window, wearing a pale beige dress that fits like a glove. The cap sleeves and just-above-the knee length keep it from being *overtly* sexy...but it's still a very sexy dress.

"You'd look amazing in that," he says.

Just on sight I know it's something I could never afford. "I could buy a year's worth of ramen noodles for what it costs."

"Try it on," he urges, placing a hand at the small of my back.

"What would be the point?" I ask. "I'd have to sell my spleen to buy it."

"No one wants your spleen, so please don't accept any offers. Your liver, possibly. I can even help remove it. Just try."

I'm still carping about what a waste of time this is when I reach the dressing room.

He leans against the door. "Make sure to let Uncle Hayes see," he whispers in an intentionally creepy voice, which makes me laugh and also, weirdly, turns me on. I really do need to get laid if I even find *this* exciting.

I slip out of my clothes and pull on the dress...which is perfection. It skims my curves, the v-neck making my cleavage look ample without revealing all of it. My hair seems to gleam, my skin looks more golden, my lips rosy. After this long year of questioning myself, of wondering if everything I ever believed might have been wrong, I know this one thing for a fact: I look really good in this dress, like the sort of woman you'd expect to see on Hayes's arm.

When I open the dressing room door, I can't help but wonder if he'll think so too.

"Do you like it, Uncle Hayes?" I ask in a baby voice, jutting out my hip. I meant it as a joke, a play on his creepiness, but he looks stricken in response.

"Yes," he says gruffly, turning on his heel and looking at his phone. "You should get it."

I huff in exasperation. "You made me go through all this effort for a dress I can't afford, and you didn't even look."

He sighs heavily, still facing away from me. "The dress and the voice had an unexpected consequence," he says through gritted teeth. "Will you please just get back in the fucking dressing room?"

It takes me a second to understand what he means by *unexpected consequence*. Shock is quickly erased by the mind-bending thought that I made him hard. Standing here in no makeup and bare feet. How is that even possible?

"Talking like a little girl does it for you, huh?" I ask, leaning against the wall with a smug smile. I intend to relish his discomfort as long as possible. "That doesn't surprise me."

"You didn't sound like a little girl," he growls. "That's the problem. You sounded like a very big girl in need of a...Jesus Christ. I'm waiting outside."

He storms off, and I stare in the direction of his retreating wingtips in wonder. I really wish he'd finished the sentence. *In need of a*...shag? A spanking? My cheeks flush as I consider the possibilities. Thank God he doesn't realize how open I'd be to any or all.

I finish dressing and find him when I walk out, standing by the register. I hand the dress to the sales associate and she begins hanging it in a garment bag as if she assumes I'm really *buying* a twelve-hundred-dollar dress. "Oh." I wince. This is why I don't try on shit I can't afford. "I'm sorry. I'm not getting it."

"I just bought it," Hayes says, his voice tight. He still won't look at me. "Let's go."

He takes the garment bag and begins walking while I scramble behind him. "No," I argue. "I don't need you buying me clothes. I'm not poor."

"You're pretty poor," he says. He's walking so fast I have to break into a jog to keep up with him. "And consider it my fine for objectifying you a moment ago. I realize I constantly objectify you, but I keep most of it to myself."

I'm deeply reluctant to accept this, no matter how much I love the dress or love the effect it seems to have on him.

"Hayes, this is *really* nice of you, but I don't even want a dress that costs this much. I'll be too paranoid to wear it."

"You're wearing it to the luncheon," he replies. "Consider it your new uniform. You'll make every woman there want to up her game, because you already sell my work better than any portfolio or brochure could."

"But—" I sputter. "Hayes, I told you I don't want things from you."

"Does Jonathan give you gifts?" he counters.

I sigh. "Yes."

"Then I can too," he says. We've reached my car. He holds the door as I climb in. "Just don't wear it when you're out with *Sam*."

❧

I WISH THERE WAS SOMEONE WITH WHOM I COULD SHARE THE dressing room incident and say, "what do you think it means?" I wish I could tell someone about the way Hayes makes me laugh, and the odd way I sometimes hurt more for him than I think he's ever hurt for himself.

I could tell Drew, who's been texting, but she's in Spain right now and it's the middle of the night. And aside from her, I've kept all of my highs and lows to a very small, closed circle—Liddie, Jonathan, Matt—and now for one reason or another, they're no longer available to me.

That might be for the best, though. Because not one of them would approve of Hayes.

❧ 22 ❧

Even before I began working for Hayes, I'd heard about Ben—Hayes's lawyer and workout buddy, the one person alive other than Jonathan (and now me) who can reach Hayes directly. I've always been curious about this man Hayes allowed into the inner sanctum, so though I'm a little overwhelmed planning the luncheon, I don't object when Hayes asks me to drive across town to pick up paperwork at Ben's office.

The office is large and modern, with gray cement walls, dark floors, and not a single photo anywhere to give me a hint of who Ben is. I wait in the lobby, feeling oddly nervous, as if I'm meeting a boyfriend's intimidating dad for the first time. I tell myself I'm being ridiculous, but also...I'm not. Hayes respects Ben's opinion, so I want him to like me.

For no reason whatsoever I've always pictured Ben a bit like Batman's kindly older butler, a grandfatherly sort, but as a man approaches me with his hand extended, I realize I could not have been more wrong. He's Hayes's age, or perhaps younger, and radiates that same overwhelming self-confidence my boss does. Maybe they bonded simply because they were always the two best-looking, most assured people in any room they entered.

"Tali, right?" he asks, shaking my hand. He smiles as he's pleased by something and tips his head for me to follow him to his office. "I've been hearing about you for weeks."

We turn down the hall together. "Knowing Hayes, I'm sure that means he was bitching about me."

He laughs. "Well, sort of. But it's the same way he bitches about me half the time. I can't believe you got him to take a day off. And smoothies, too. I'm impressed."

"He was eating like a frat boy with a death wish," I reply. "I figured I'd do my best to prevent scurvy until Jonathan gets back."

He holds his office door open, observing me as I walk past and take the seat on one side of his desk. "It's beginning to make sense now," he says, taking the other. I raise a brow and he continues. "Hayes doesn't know this, but I ran a background check on you, before you started. I saw all the photos of you with your ex, and really beautiful women are often not all that interesting. But I get it now. I see why you appeal to him."

I laugh. "Uh, thanks? But I doubt *he'd* say I appeal to him."

He flashes me a smile as he spins his chair toward the filing cabinet. "Of course not. But I've known him long enough to read between the lines. He's gonna miss you when you go."

The idea of leaving Hayes makes something sink in my stomach. And the possibility that he might *miss* me anchors it there.

"I doubt he'd admit that either."

He pulls a file from the drawer and turns. "Probably not. But I suspect you're the first person who's tried to take care of him in a long time, if ever. His mom was dating some cricket player in Australia for half his childhood and stuck him in boarding school and sent him off to his father's every summer. I imagine it was a lot rougher than he'd ever let on."

My heart squeezes tight. I think of those rare moments when Hayes really lets me see his face, the one that rests between the smirks and the innuendo. When he is all bleak eyes and sharp bones, suddenly fragile. I bet that was a face he showed more as a child, until he learned how to hide it. I wish I could travel back in time to fix that for him...and I wish it harder and more fervently than I wish for anything of my own.

"He's been in relationships though," I venture quietly.

He slides the file across the desk to me. "Ella? Well, obviously she's primarily focused on herself. So I don't think that counts."

"You know her?"

He frowns. "I'm not sure anyone truly *knows* Ella, but yes, we've met. She's charming, but given what she did to Hayes, it's hard to tell if any of it's real."

What really happened? I want to ask. Because Hayes seems to blame himself. Did he cheat? Did he shut her out, become cruel and cold? I'm not sure why the answers matter, when they're about a man who's never going to be mine either way.

I take the folder and rise to leave. "I'm sure I'll see you again," he says.

"Jonathan's back soon, so probably not." I'm not sure why that's so hard to say aloud. It's not as if I ever thought I was going to be a permanent fixture of Hayes's life.

"Hey, Tali?" he says, stopping me as I reach the door. "Don't give up on him, okay? He needs you more than he'll ever admit."

I nod, though I don't entirely understand what he means. I'm not giving up on Hayes, but I only have a few weeks left before Jonathan's back. What will happen after that? Will I remain part of his inner circle even then? Could I be more?

I'd really like to stick around long enough to find out.

It's nearly eight by the time I get back to my apartment and call my mother.

"Are you just getting home from work?" she asks. How many times have I called, ignoring the tiny slur to her words? Countless, and I want to ignore it tonight too. She's the adult. It's never felt like it was my place to judge or even wonder about how much wine she might drink at night, but that has to change.

"It's been busy," I reply distractedly, kicking off my shoes. I have no idea how to broach the topic I need to...but I know it won't go well.

Her laughter sounds a trifle mocking. "Busy hanging out with the rich and famous, more likely. I've heard from Liddie about your glamorous little life out there."

My jaw grinds as I fill a measuring cup with water. I can easily imagine the spin Liddie put on things, and it's so like my mother to take her side.

"Since we're judging each other," I reply, slamming the microwave door, "Dr. Shriner is worried about you. She said you appear to have been drinking when you show up for family therapy."

"I'm an adult and we're not paying for Dr. Shriner to take care of *me*," she says. "I'm allowed to have a glass of wine in the evening if I want one."

We aren't paying for Dr. Shriner at all, I think. *I am. And you can't even bother to be sober for it.*

"Mom," I say, taking a slow breath as I lean against the counter, "it doesn't look good when you can't even stay sober for your kid's therapy appointment. She isn't sure Charlotte should be coming home to you under the circumstances. If you could—"

"Oh, for Christ's sake," she says, her voice so shrill I have to pull the phone from my ear. "Shriner's just looking for someone to blame for the fact that Charlotte isn't better."

If she were calmer right now, more rational, more *sober*, I might consider what she's saying. She's the parent. She's supposed to be the one of us who's right about things. But the truth is that she hasn't been right about much in the past year, and she's been perfectly happy to let me figure it out in her stead.

"Mom, she just wants to make sure Charlotte's coming home to someone who's going to be able to take care of her." I pull my hair out of its ponytail and run my fingers through it, wishing I hadn't called. "And right now, she's saying that person will have to be me or Liddie, so I really need you to just...pull it together, okay? Wait to have your glass of wine until after therapy."

"She can't *hold* Charlotte there," my mother argues.

"Jesus, Mom," I snap, pinching the bridge of my nose, "you're missing the point. Charlotte needs to come home to someone capable of staying sober. Can you do it or not?"

"I don't answer to her," my mother replies, "and I don't answer to you either."

I blink in shock when I hear the ring tone and realize she's hung up on me. She fucking hung up on me.

Which means Dr. Shriner probably had a point. And unless something changes fast, I really might have to move home.

❧ 23 ❧

We all have our talents, and mine is avoiding unhappy thoughts. I mostly try to forget the miserable conversation with my mother, and when I remember, I simply assure myself that even if she didn't *sound* receptive, I made my point, and things will turn around.

There's not much time to think about it anyway because I'm so busy getting Hayes's luncheon planned I can barely breathe, much less dwell. It seems almost every attendee wants to bring extra friends, and I swear to God if I hear about one more woman with a "special dietary need", I'm going to lose my shit.

Two days before the event, the gift bags arrive completely botched, which leaves me frantically assembling them myself on Hayes's living room floor. I'm halfway through counting out lip balms when the emergency phone rings, and I'm seriously tempted to let it go to voice mail—it's not as if there's ever been a call to that phone that was *actually* an emergency. They're usually of the *I'm looking especially old today* variety.

Reluctantly, my hand slides beneath a mountain of ribbon and cellophane for the phone, trying to banish the weariness from my voice as I answer.

"I need Hayes," the woman on the other end of the line

croaks. "It's an emergency. My ten-year-old...I think he's got a broken nose. There's blood everywhere."

"Uhhhh..." Hayes does not treat kids, as far as I know, and this sounds a little more pressing than his booked-out-three-weeks schedule will allow. "If he's bleeding heavily, he needs to go to the emergency room."

"No," she insists. "We can't. My son is Trace Westbrook. If we go to the ER, the paparazzi will be all over us asking how it happened."

I know little about him aside from the fact that he has a popular YouTube channel, but I find it deeply suspicious that his mom is more concerned about paparazzi than she is her son's health.

"Hayes understands the situation and has helped us many times before," she says brusquely. "Just call him."

She hangs up, and something sours in my stomach. If Hayes has helped *many times*, that means this kid has gotten injured *many times*. Why would Hayes be going out of his way to help a parent avoid the paparazzi instead of sending him to the emergency room? Surely he realizes how suspicious it all is?

Hayes wouldn't help a family hide abuse. I know he wouldn't.

But you also thought Matt would never cheat, a voice says. *You thought he supported your dreams the way you supported his. You're a terrible judge of character.*

I call him, feeling strangely certain the bottom is going to fall out. That he's going to disappoint me. I pull my legs tight to my chest.

"If this is another party question, you're fired," he answers. "Tell Jonathan his adoption is off. He can get a cat instead of a baby—much easier on everyone."

Please don't disappoint me, Hayes. Please don't prove I was wrong about someone else.

"I just got a call from a woman who says she's Trace Westbrook's mom." My voice is quiet, hesitant. "She said he broke his nose...and she doesn't want to go to the hospital because they'll ask questions."

I hug my knees tighter, waiting for him to clarify this, to explain why he's helping these people instead of letting them hang.

Instead, I hear only a curse and the screech of tires. "I'm turning around. They're in Laurel Canyon, but I don't remember the exact address," he says. "Get it, phone it into my car, and meet me there."

"*Meet you*?" I do not want to be a part of this. And if I meet this kid's parents and it's as bad as it sounds, Hayes might end up dealing with multiple broken noses. Including his own.

"Yes," he says. "I need the black bag in the linen closet in my bathroom. Get it and get there as fast as you can."

He's so cool and collected under normal circumstances that hearing him sound *worried* is deeply unsettling. "Tell me why you're helping these parents cover up a broken nose," I say, my voice hard. I will quit on the spot if I don't like his answer.

"I will," he says, "but first, I need that address. *Now.*"

⚜️

I PULL UP TO A SPRAWLING RAMBLER, FRAMED BY SHORT, stocky palms and gnarled old fig trees. Hayes's car is already there, so I grab the bag and head to the door. A woman answers, looking like death warmed over. "He's upstairs," she says, clutching her robe around her. A small pale face peers over the couch at me, eyes wide and sad, hair matted to her head.

I put my anger on hold and run up the stairs, two at a time.

The kid in the bed looks even younger than I'd have expected, and Hayes is holding his hand, talking to him about skiing with feigned calm. He glances over his shoulder. "Valium," he says. I open the bag and begin fumbling through bottles until I find it. "Get me two and a glass of water." There's no doubt this is an order. There's a degree of *don't fuck with me* in his voice I've never heard before.

I run to the bathroom beside Trace's room and fill a disposable cup with water before I run back, handing it to Hayes along with the pills.

"I need you to swallow these for me," he says to the kid, who begins crying. "It won't hurt, I swear. You aren't going to feel a single thing."

Hayes gives the boy the pills and holds the cup to his lips, still discussing ski slopes, his voice so calm even my breathing slows.

When the boy's eyes droop and then close, Hayes reaches into his bag and withdraws a very, very long needle. Between that and the blood, I feel like I can barely stay upright.

"I need you to hold him down," he says quietly. "Can you do that?"

My jaw falls open to argue, but I see he means it, and maybe it's bad judgment, but I trust him. Implicitly. "How?"

"Grab his shoulders," he says. "Make sure he doesn't jerk while I'm injecting the lidocaine."

Swallowing, I do as I'm told, going to the opposite side of the bed and leaning over him. He looks like he's out cold, but my hands band around his biceps as tight as I can anyway.

Hayes glances at me. "You're looking a little pale," he says. "Are you okay?"

"Yes," I reply, my voice breathless and threadbare.

He holds Trace's jaw with one hand and with the other presses the needle into the upper bridge of his nose, right beside his eye.

"Oh, God," I whisper.

"Hold him, Tali," he growls. "Just look away. I need you. Don't pass out on me now."

I close my eyes, trying to hold it together. I've never thought of myself as someone prone to acting like a girl, but I've also never seen a needle that fucking big aimed at someone's eye.

"What was the name of that ride at Universal?" he asks, in that same calm voice he was using on the kid. "The Harry Potter one."

I breathe through my nose. "I don't...I don't remember. There was the Hagrid one. Oh, or the Hippogriff? Why?"

"You can look now," he says. I open my eyes and his mouth quirks upward. He was distracting me like a child, and it worked.

He starts spraying something up Trace's nose, with a tube. "More lidocaine," he explains quietly. "And now we wait for it to kick in." He begins wiping blood off the boy's face, as gently as he might his own child's.

I've never seen him like this before—acting like he cares. Acting like something matters. I want to look away and I can't.

"Is he going to be okay?" his mother asks behind us, her voice tremulous. I hadn't even realized she was there, and it's hard not to glare at her, not to assume the worst. Would Hayes cover up abuse? I can't imagine he would, yet he does all sorts of things for money I would not. He drives out to houses where women proposition him and let dogs jump on his back. Do I really know where he'd hit bottom? Do you ever know, with anyone?

"It's a basic fracture," says Hayes. "I had them several times myself as a kid. I'm about to push the bones into place, and he'll be good as new."

He gets a tool out of his bag and glances at me. "You probably want to shut your eyes again," he says.

I do, feeling too confused to be angry. I don't understand how he can be so gentle and sympathetic, yet not intervene. These people might be claiming the kid is simply clumsy, frequently hurt...but Hayes wouldn't know if that was the case. That's why they should be forced to go through the hospital, where it will be documented. Where someone who knows the signs of abuse will catch them. And Hayes must realize this too.

I swallow hard. I really thought he was different. I thought he was better than he appeared. Now it seems possible he's worse.

The rest of the work is done quickly. Nasal packs go into his nostrils to support the bones and Hayes splints the bridge. He quietly gives the mother instructions and then pats her shoulder before taking his leave. I follow on wobbly legs and lean against the hood of my car, watching as Hayes throws the bag I brought in his trunk.

"What happened to him? If he's getting hurt a lot..." I feel jittery and out of control. Tears spring to my eyes. "I don't know why you're helping that family the way you are. This should all be getting documented."

He shuts the trunk and turns toward me. "Tali," he says softly, "he's got a heart valve defect. It decreases blood flow to the brain, and he blacks out. Did you really think I'd help someone cover up child abuse?"

I don't know what's wrong with me, but the dam breaks. I press my face to my hands as tears begin to fall. "Can they fix it?"

He comes over and wraps an arm around me, pressing my head to his chest. He smells like soap and starch and home. "I wish they could, but no." His voice is so kind it makes me cry harder. "I think you're in shock. It's okay. It happens."

I shake my head. "I'm sorry. I'm sorry I jumped to conclusions. I just thought..."

"You thought what?"

I struggle to find the right words. I'm glad my face is pressed to his shirt so I don't have to make eye contact. "That I am probably a terrible judge of character," I whisper. "I was with Matt for ten years..."

My voice breaks, and I stop talking. It's ridiculous what I thought. It's ridiculous my experience with one human being out of thousands could make me distrustful of everyone, including myself.

He pulls me closer. "I know," he says quietly. His heart beats faster, just beneath my cheek. "I know exactly how you feel."

I guess he must. He gave up his inheritance for Ella, and she left him for his dad. It would be enough to ruin your faith in people forever, if you let it.

"Is it going to always be like this?" I ask. "Am I always going to feel like I can't trust anyone?"

I feel his slow, weary exhale. "A guy who hasn't been in a relationship for seven years is probably not the person to ask."

I spent so much time looking down on him for the way he lives, but are his threesomes and foursomes any worse than me revenge fucking Matt's closest friend in LA? Are they any different than my long runs at night on the bike path? It's all just a way to drum out the emptiness.

He's me, only with a lot more money and slightly less self-control.

I don't want to still be this version of myself in seven years. I don't want him to be this version either.

❧ 24 ❦

Drew texts the day of the luncheon to see if I want to meet up. She's just back from Spain, where she was visiting Six. I know from her sporadic messages he was both wonderful and terrible. That he alternated between telling her he can see a future with her and then commenting on the size of her thighs. I don't know why she doesn't see through him when she's so clever about everything else.

I tell her I need to take a rain check because the luncheon is consuming every waking minute. And today, when I have to be at my sharpest, I feel like I barely have the energy to push myself into the shower. I've gotten by on Hayes-levels of sleep for days on end, continuing to do my job while setting up the three-ring circus Hayes wants in his backyard: catered lunch, aesthetic services, favors, open bar, valet...the list is endless. There is so much to do today, and I only want to collapse in bed, which means there's no way this thing is going to work out as seamlessly as he'd like.

I arrive at his house with my ridiculously expensive beige dress, my toiletries, and a pair of sky-high heels in one bag, the last of the party favors in another.

Hayes is already downstairs, looking so pressed and perfect and alert that I can't help but resent him for it.

"You look like death warmed over," he says.

I let both bags drop to the floor. I feel like I don't even have the energy to respond this morning.

"What?" he asks. "I'm just wondering how you can look so bad when I know you spent yet another night in, watching Jane Austen movies and dreaming about marriage."

I lean back against the counter, scraping my hair off my face and re-gathering my ponytail. I'm going to be a disaster by eleven AM when the guests arrive. "So that's what you think I do?"

He shrugs. "Mostly, I picture you at home vigorously masturbating."

I pretend to gag, and today I'm not entirely faking it. I wonder if it was the deli sushi I grabbed on the way home last night. I knew I should have stuck with ramen. It might not be the healthiest food, but pre-packaged ramen never gave anyone food poisoning.

It's cool in the house but I'm already sweating and the smell of Hayes's coffee is making my stomach churn. I head outside into the too-bright-morning to discuss table placement with the caterer, and the heat makes my head swim. I have to brace myself against a pillar to keep from swaying as she speaks.

I get through the next two hours, but by the time the linens are down and I've set the place cards out, I'm wondering how I'll survive until the end. The fumes from the chafing dishes alone have me staggering inside to get away.

Hayes is there, looking like a cool dream in a black button down and suit pants while he tinkers with the set-up for aesthetic services. I want to lean my head against his chest, which would be inappropriate and would also destroy his shirt since I can't stop sweating.

"You really are very quiet today," he says. "I don't think

you've nagged me once in the past fifteen minutes, which is certainly a record. What *did* you do last night?"

My eyes fall closed. God, what I would give to lie down right now. "I vigorously masturbated while watching Jane Austen movies."

"Well done," he says. "I've never gotten an erection and had it killed in the space of one sentence before."

I force my eyes open, force my shoulders back. I'm not going to be sick right now because I can't *afford* to be sick right now. "I didn't do anything last night. I stayed up until midnight putting together gift bags, and then I went to bed. I'm just a little tired."

He's silent for once. His mouth is pressed tight, his jaw locked. Which is his worried face but also his angry face, and I'm not sure which I'm seeing now.

"Are you okay?" he asks.

The air conditioning felt so good when I walked in, but now even that's not enough. I've been less sweaty walking out of spin class.

"I'm fine," I reply, pinching the bridge of my nose. "I promise your little luncheon will be spectacular, and you'll have more new patients than you know what to do with."

"I know I'm a demanding asshole," he says, "but is it so insane to imagine I might be worried about you?" He's angry, but even worse...he sounds hurt.

My eyes sting, and I close them before he can see. Jesus, what's wrong with me today? Crying over some tiny indication of Hayes's care has got to be a sign of personal apocalypse. "No," I say. "Sorry. You were making your mad face. I just assumed."

He pulls me toward him. "If you need to go home today, that's fine."

"I don't, but thank you. I'll be fresh as a daisy by the time your thing starts." A daisy plucked several weeks prior and now dead, but still.

I go up to a guest room to change. The pillowcase on the bed looks so crisp and cool that I'd give almost anything to lie down right now and sleep until this was done. I sway at the very idea of it.

I get downstairs just as the first guests arrive, and from then on, it's a blur of people and questions and requests and lost place cards. Lunch is served in the backyard without issue, but I'm almost too out of it to care. Hayes is behind a curtain, doing free filler, thank God. He'd have something to say if he saw me looking like this.

I find the caterer to request a vegan, gluten-free dessert option for a guest who wants something other than fruit. I have to lean against the wall to stay upright as we speak. *Lovely wall. You're my favorite thing in the world right now.*

"Who the hell doesn't like fruit?" the caterer asks me. Her face begins to blur. "I have no idea what I could serve her."

I'm struggling to put my thoughts together. "Water?" I suggest weakly. "A dessert made of water and air."

I hear the caterer giggle as a wave of nausea washes over me. I take a deep breath through my nostrils and close my eyes.

"You might want to slow down with the champagne," she whispers.

I lurch five feet forward, but I've forgotten what I was walking toward, and I'm suddenly so unbelievably hot. I go back to the wall, gripping it tight to remain upright, and seconds later Hayes is looming over me with his hand on my forehead.

"You're burning up," he says. "For fuck's sake, Tali, how long have you been like this?" I'm definitely seeing his angry face.

"Not until the party," I whisper. "I'll be fine. It's food poisoning. I just need to sit for a minute."

"What you need is to go to bed and stay there for three days," he hisses.

And before I can argue, I am airborne, scooped up in his arms like a bride being carried over the threshold or—based on the difference in our respective sizes—a child being carried up to bed by her father.

I know I need to argue, but honestly, it feels so good not to stand up. Hayes's shirt is crisp beneath my cheek. I time my breaths with the hard beat of his heart.

"Put me down," I whisper. "S'embarrassing."

"Yes, I know," he says. "And you're absolutely fine and just need to sit. I'd like to put you over my knee right now."

You'd always like that, I try to say, but the words are slurred.

"You're so sick you can't even speak and you're still trying to one-up me," he says with a soft laugh.

I am too sleepy now to reply, but I think maybe I smile a little. I breathe him in. He smells like the ocean and sunlight. I guess not all smells make me gag. The smell of *him* makes me feel hopeful, as if everything is going to be alright.

❧

AT SOME POINT, I WAKE TO DISCOVER MYSELF IN AN unfamiliar room. It's dark out, and Hayes is there beside me, stripped down to his pants and undershirt.

My stomach lurches. "Bathroom," I beg, rolling out of bed on unsteady legs. I run toward what I pray is a bathroom and not a closet, vaguely realizing I'm only in my bra and panties as I collapse on the tile floor. The contents of my stomach fly out of my mouth, half in the toilet and half out, and Hayes grabs my hair but it's too late by then. I've got it everywhere, and I don't even care. I collapse on the deliciously cool tile floor. I think I'd like to just stay here.

"Come on, Tali," he says softly, trying to pull me up, "let's get you to bed."

I shake my head. "Go away," I beg. "I don't want you to see me like this."

"Worried I'll respect you less?" he asks, but there's a sweetness to his voice that isn't normally there. "And I've already seen you like this. You've been sick *repeatedly*."

"I need to shower," I whisper. "Please."

He pauses. "Fine," he says with a sigh. "I'll wait outside. Please don't take off any more clothes until the door shuts."

Which would indicate *I'm* the one who removed my dress earlier. *God.*

I turn on the water and somehow manage to remove my bra and panties before I crawl into the tub. Even those small actions deplete the little energy I had, however, so I just sit here with my knees tucked to my chest, letting the water hit me. As exhausted as I am, I still have the energy to be humiliated by all of this. *He had to carry me out of the party. He's pretty much seen me naked, and God only knows what I said to him...plus he's now watched me vomit.*

I groan against my knees, wishing I could vanish. I'm not sure how I'll face him when I get out.

I manage to wash my hair from a seated position and pull myself to standing. With the towel wrapped around me, I open the door but have to lean against the frame as I begin to shake.

"Where's my dress?" I whisper.

He frowns and then pulls off his undershirt. "Here," he says, handing it to me. Even in my dazed, sickened state, I am capable of appreciating the absolute work of art he is shirtless. Not an ounce of fat and far more muscular than I'd have guessed.

The shirt falls to mid-thigh and is so loose around the arms that he'd see some side-boob if he wasn't already looking away. I suppose he's seen all the semi-nude Tali he'll ever need to see after the past day. I stagger toward the mattress and collapse in bed on my side, wrestling with the covers but too weak to win the fight. He pulls them from me and lifts them to my chin.

"I'm sorry," I whisper.

I open one eye just enough to see my favorite of his smiles. The sweetest one, that dimple of his blinking into existence. "For what?"

"Ruining your party, forcing you to take care of me, undressing in front of you, vomiting..."

"You ruined nothing, and perhaps you're unaware of this, but

I'm actually a doctor. And a human being who gets sick occasionally as well," he says, resting a hand against my forehead. "You're still running a fever, but your teeth are chattering. I'm going to get some meds and blankets."

"Don't stay here," I say. "You must have patients, and I'm fine now."

"Yes, I know. Just like you were fine earlier. You don't have to do everything alone, you know."

The words leave an ache in my chest as he leaves. I curl into a ball, pulling the blankets tighter, and the neck of his T-shirt rides up to my nose. I get a whiff of sandalwood, ocean, Hayes. My favorite smells in the entire world. As I doze off, I leave his shirt right there so I can keep breathing him in.

WHEN I WAKE, THE ROOM IS SUNLIT AND HAYES IS LEANING over me, taking my temperature. His hair is messy from sleep, eyes a little hooded. This must be what he looks like when he wakes up—soft and delicious. He catches me looking and that signature smirk pulls at the side of his mouth.

"Good morning, sunshine. Your fever's gone. How do you feel?"

"Like I was placed in a crane and repeatedly slammed into a brick wall." And like someone who apparently took off her clothes and vomited in front of her hot boss. I flinch hard at the memory. "Sorry about, um, every single thing I did and said over the past twenty-four hours."

"You're pretty cute when you're sick," he says, perching on the edge of the bed. "And I do have all the photos of you stripped down to your bra and panties, so it's not like I got nothing out of the deal."

I laugh. "You earned them. I'm just glad I don't remember most of it."

He bites down on a smile. "You were your normal prickly self for the most part, although you did at one point suggest I smell like heaven. And then you carped at me for calling the trash can a *bin* and said I need to 'stop speaking British all the time' because I've been here too long for that."

I struggle to sit up. He's got me cocooned in approximately a hundred blankets. "Well, it is sort of ridiculous," I mutter. "You've been here nearly a decade."

I swing my legs off the side of the bed, careful not to flash him in the process and scurry to the bathroom. I wish very much that Hayes wasn't sitting ten feet away while I pee. "Why is it so cold in here?" I shout from behind the closed door.

"Because you complained," he says in a raised voice. "And now you're complaining again, while urinating, like the refined little lady you are, so I'll change the temperature once more." How he manages to make me smile when I'm feeling like crap is a mystery and one I'm not going to think about while I'm half naked in his bathroom.

I wash my hands and brush my teeth with a new toothbrush I find in the medicine cabinet. I still look like garbage, but when I return to the room, he's not looking at my face...he's looking at my breasts—well-displayed thanks to the thin T-shirt and arctic temperature in here. His eyes dart away quickly, but two spots of color remain on his cheekbones.

The completely shameless Hayes Flynn is unsettled by head-lights. Even in my unwell state, it's surprisingly thrilling to see I can affect him at all.

I cross the room to my dress, which is draped over a chair.

"What do you think you're doing?" he demands.

"Going home. I like my neighbors, but not well enough to walk around them in nothing but a T-shirt."

"Get your ass back in bed," he says, making his Very, Very Angry Face and rising to his feet. "You've barely eaten or had anything to drink in over a day, and an hour ago, you were sleeping so heavily even Marta cleaning in here didn't wake you. You're not going anywhere."

I'd like to argue, but the truth is, my legs are starting to wobble, I'm freezing cold, and that bed looks like the blissful, lava-hot cocoon of my dreams. I sink into it.

"I love this bed," I murmur as he takes a seat again. "Would you allow it to marry me? You can take the cost out of my salary."

He gives me a small smile. "Only if you let me watch the honeymoon."

"This is the honeymoon, right here." I pull the covers to my chin. "A perfect one, where I sleep and it cuddles me and doesn't talk."

"Once again confirming your boyfriend's decision to stray was not completely unwarranted."

I laugh. Weirdly, it doesn't even hurt. "Go to work. I'll sleep for a few hours and be on my way."

"I already canceled everything," he says.

I can barely get him to take an hour for lunch, but he cancelled an entire day's appointments for me. Why? He could easily have outsourced this, dragged some poor nurse or resident over here if he was particularly worried. But instead, he watched over me himself.

His unexpected sweetness...is equal parts pleasure and pain for me. Maybe it's just that it's in moments like this I realize how lonely I've been, how badly I want to feel as if someone cares. But it's also that there's this whole side to him that seems to remain hidden. And I wish it wasn't.

"Why did you decide to become a doctor?" I ask as I turn to my side to face him fully, pulling a soft pillow under my cheek. "Was that always what you wanted to do?"

"I did not come out of the womb aspiring to it, no," he says. "I spent a few years wanting to play for Manchester United like everyone else." He rests his hands over his stomach, knees braced apart, thin sleep pants pulling tight over his thighs. Why did I not notice what he was wearing before now?

"But why?" I persist.

He shrugs. "This bird hit the side of our house one day. I put it in a box and decided to care for it. The bird died, but I got it in my head that maybe I could learn how to take care of people instead." Everything about his voice and expression seems bored, as if none of this matters. I've learned with Hayes, that's usually a sign it *does*.

"And why plastic surgery?"

"I saw a documentary about Operation Smile," he says. He leans forward and fixes the top blanket, smoothing it over me. The pressure of his hand, even through three blankets, has me arching into his touch involuntarily. He must notice, because his eyes flick to mine for a brief second. He clears his throat and continues. "They perform cleft palate surgeries on children in third world countries. I was young and idealistic at the time, and it seemed like I could do some good there."

I picture a younger, less damaged version of Hayes. One before Ella left him for his father, before his world started to fall apart. "But then you decided rich actresses were suffering too."

His mouth curves. "Yes, exactly that."

He starts to rise, and I realize I've done it again. I *felt* something when he talked about Operation Smile and had to make a dumb joke to pretend I wasn't feeling a thing.

"Wait," I say, reaching out to grab his wrist. "I actually want to know what changed your mind."

A muscle in his jaw flickers, and his gaze drops to the floor. I hang on the breath of air that passes, hoping he'll tell me.

"I didn't want to live in third world countries my entire life," he says. "And what I do now pays a lot better than performing pediatric surgeries in a hospital setting." His eyes drop to my hand still holding his wrist. "I'm going to get you some food." I let go of him.

I know he hasn't told me the truth, not all of it. I get that there's a big difference in salary, but that doesn't explain why he became someone who cared about that difference so much. He has a lavish house he doesn't use and nice cars he doesn't drive, and he spends little but works like a man who's barely staying afloat.

"Is it the Great Gatsby thing?" I ask as he reaches the door. "Are you still trying to win Daisy's heart?"

I see something melancholy pass over his face, gone as fast as it came, before he grimaces. "If you're trying to imply that I wish to win my *stepmother's* heart, you must be more ill than I thought."

Deflecting a moment of vulnerability with jokes, I think, as my eyes flutter closed. He's as good at my tricks as I am.

ॐ

THE WARMTH OF THE BED AND MY CONTINUING EXHAUSTION must have pulled me back to sleep again, because the next time my eyes open, the light in the room has shifted and there's a note on the nightstand saying he's downstairs and to call once I'm up. My dress, I notice, is now missing.

I ignore his note and walk downstairs, clad only in his oversized T-shirt. My body is sluggish but I'm mostly over the worst of things.

He's in the living room, long legs spread on the couch with a medical journal in hand.

"Get back in bed," he says, his head jerking up.

"I'm fine," I reply, reaching the bottom of the stairs. "I need to be up and about."

His eyes linger for half a second on my chest. "Something about you is definitely up and about." He crosses the room and pushes me into a chair before he drapes a throw blanket over me.

"Thank you for doing all this," I tell him, snuggling into the blanket as he walks into the kitchen.

"It's kind of fun," he says, putting bread in the toaster. "I'm reliving my childhood experience with the broken bird."

"That bird died."

"You should probably speak up if you catch me putting you in a box." He pulls butter out of the fridge and glances over at me—a quick, sheepish glance that darts away almost as fast as it arrived. "I made you custard, if you'd like some. It's what my housekeeper made me."

"I can't believe you knew how to make custard."

He shrugs. "If I managed to get through med school, I figured I could probably master a recipe online." He is acting so casual about this but I can't remember the last time someone took care of *me*.

What a ridiculous thing to bring me to tears.

I blink them away while he hands me two slices of buttered toast and sets the custard on the end table beside me. Suddenly I'm famished.

"I'm really sorry about all this," I tell him, avoiding eye contact until I'm sure I have my emotions under control. "Thank you so much for taking care of me."

"It was the least I could do. I'm sure you caught it from the Westbrooks, which is my fault."

"No, it was the—"

"Food poisoning doesn't make anyone that sick for that long," he says. "It wasn't the sushi. The Westbrooks all had the flu the day we were there. You caught what they had."

My shoulders sag. God, I hope I didn't get all his guests sick. I'm not sure how he's being so forgiving of the whole thing. "Well, I'll finish my toast and get out of your hair."

"Just stay," he says, resuming his place on the couch. "I've canceled my plans already, and you're still too weak to take care of yourself."

I'd be lying if I said I didn't want to take him up on the offer. If I said I didn't want to remain here for hours, days, weeks, with him looking at me the way he is now, as if I'm someone he worries about, someone he wants around.

"Having me here will probably get in the way of your sexy time," I warn. "And you've already gone a few nights without it."

"I appreciate your unwavering consideration of my sexual needs," he says, eyes narrowed, "but I haven't been doing much of that lately anyhow."

Hmmm. I'd noticed there weren't any signs of women here. I just assumed he was doing it somewhere else. I suppose I mostly didn't want to think about it. "What's up with that?"

He runs a thumb over the arch of his eyebrow. "Maybe it's simply that it went hand in hand with the drinking, which a small, shrill voice has been nagging me about."

The words strike me. He corrected course when I nagged him, seemingly without difficulty, though my opinion shouldn't have mattered. But my mother can't do the same, even when my sister's welfare depends on it. Maybe Dr. Shriner had a point.

"So that's it?" I ask. "The bad boy's reign of terror is over?"

"I wouldn't go that far," he mutters, looking away. "It just hasn't appealed lately."

"I know a doctor who can probably give you some pills for that," I reply with a smirk, taking a bite of my toast. Mmm, buttery goodness.

He runs a hand through his hair and closes his eyes. "I'm not having *that* kind of problem. I'm just...going through a phase."

Interesting. "What kind of phase?"

"Not the kind of phase I want to discuss with a twenty-five-year-old who hasn't dated in a year, that's for sure," he replies with a scowl.

It's a strange, unexpected conversation. But the strangest part is he can't seem to meet my eye during any of it.

❧ 25 ❦

I leave Sunday morning and am recovered enough to grab dinner with Drew that evening. She tells me about her trip, and I decide there is no saving Six—he's an awful human being.

I want to talk about Hayes, but find that I just can't. My thoughts about the past few days with him are...jumbled, not ready to be said aloud. Because once upon a time, he was simply a charming degenerate I wanted to take care of and now he's more. There's this small, warm thing unfurling in my chest when I think of him. I feel like a lighter, sunnier version of myself, a *hopeful* version I almost forgot existed. And I'm not sure if that thrills or terrifies me.

I arrive at Hayes's house the next day fully recovered and strangely eager to see him. When he enters the kitchen—his gaze sliding over me, top to bottom—it's as if I'm a little more complete than I was before he walked in. As if *he*, of all people, is my home, my safe place to land.

I hand him his coffee. "I didn't spit in it today. To thank you for taking care of me."

He laughs. "You've made that joke enough times that I'm forced to assume there's some truth to it."

I pull his schedule off the printer. He had to squeeze this weekend's patients into every free hour this week. "No lunch at home today," I say. There's a regrettable hint of sadness in my voice.

His dimple tucks in, just for a moment. He clears his throat. "Do you think you could meet me downtown once I'm done?" he asks. "Just to go over the monthly schedule?"

There is no real reason for us to meet. We could discuss everything by phone in five minutes, plus I've got my non-date with Sam tonight.

Yet I've never agreed to anything more eagerly.

I DRIVE TO THE BAR, SWEARING TO MYSELF I WON'T HAVE A drink. I want my wits about me when I meet up with Sam, for one thing. Plus, I already know how it goes with Hayes. Get a single ounce of liquor in my system and I start looking at him differently. My eyes will linger on the curves of his face, on his perfect mouth, on his broad shoulders and the way he wears his clothes, as if he's constantly restraining himself from removing them. Which is not what eyes are supposed to do when you hang out with a friend, or a boss.

He's already waiting when I arrive. His jacket is off, his shirt slightly unbuttoned, and I find my eyes dipping to the hint of skin beneath his collarbone. My memories from being sick are blurred and dreamlike, but I remember the way he moved as he pulled off his shirt...testosterone-fueled and care-less. I remember his smooth skin, his arms, those surprising abs.

He's got a margarita waiting for me. I decide a drink is called for, after all...I need to cool off.

"How would you feel about coming up to San Francisco with me in a few weeks?" he asks.

I blink. It takes me a moment to remember he's got a conference there, but I still wonder if he's asking me to come as his assistant or something else. I'd probably say yes either way.

"You'd have your own room, of course," he adds, "and it's only for the one night. Fly up Saturday morning, back on Sunday. I just...things go wrong. If the handouts are lost or something needs to be done, it would be good to have you there."

I feel something sink in my stomach. Disappointment, when there should only be relief. Did I really think for a moment he was inviting me on a trip? Apparently, I did.

I take a long sip of my drink, licking the salt from my lips with relish. His eyes seem to snag on my mouth as I do it. "I'm dying to see San Francisco. Just get me up there and I'll find a park to sleep in."

"Excellent," he says with a smirk. "More money for me to spend on cocaine and souvenirs."

I hesitate suddenly. As much as I'd love to go to San Francisco, and go there with him especially...what if he reverts to his old ways? I'm not sure I can stand to watch him carrying on with some brilliant, hot doctor while I pathetically wait nearby, notebook in hand. "I won't be...in your way? I imagine these conferences are like Woodstock for medical geeks."

He laughs. "You've clearly never attended a medical conference."

"Don't act as if you've never done it," I mutter. "You're a walking sexual proposition."

His tongue goes to his cheek, amused. "You're saying, then, that my mere existence makes you long for sex?" He leans forward, a seductive tone to his voice. Smirk in place. "That I walk through a room and make you think of all the itches you'd like to scratch?"

Yes.

"No, although occasionally the sight of you makes me wonder if STDs itch, which I suppose is sort of similar." I glance at my watch. "And on that note, I need to get going."

He looks at me over his drink. "Is there a Jane Austen marathon tonight I'm unaware of?"

"I'm meeting Sam for dinner," I tell him. "The guy from home who's been helping me with the book. It's not a date. We're just meeting at Mezcal for a quick meal and his friend will be there."

A vein throbs in his temple and his grip tightens on his glass. "Right. Your *buddy* Sam is making you feel comfortable by inviting his friend, but after a few minutes his friend will announce that he can't stay." He rolls his eyes, irritated and bored simultaneously. "It's the oldest trick in the book."

"You'd know," I reply, rising. "Fortunately, Sam is nothing like you."

"He's unattractive and dull?" Hayes asks lazily, reclining in his seat. "Seems like you shouldn't be rushing off then."

"He's trustworthy," I reply pointedly.

"And I'm not?" He's as smug and confident as ever, smirking even now, but I sense some tiny wounded thing beneath it.

"Twenty-four hours of celibacy don't make you a candidate for sainthood," I reply. He doesn't argue, and I leave feeling as if I just took a cheap shot. I guess I was hoping he'd tell me I was wrong.

※

THE RESTAURANT SAM'S CHOSEN IS SPACIOUS AND BRIGHT, with open-air walls, polished wide-plank floors, and an exposed beam ceiling. It seems an expensive choice for a guy living off a school stipend.

I find him sitting on the patio and do a double-take. *Holy shit.* Sam has gotten seriously hot since the last time I saw him. His hair is down to his shoulders now, and he's lost that residual bit of childhood softness from his face, revealing a jawline worthy of a superhero. That, plus the nerdy little glasses (which did it for me even *before* he acquired the jawline), make him absolutely edible. The women behind him have not failed to notice his looks either. Construction workers ogle with more subtlety.

"Hey, stranger," I say as I reach the table.

"Tali!" He stands, pulling me into a bear hug. He's added a fair amount of muscle onto his formerly wiry frame. I can't begin to imagine the swooning that will ensue once he's a professor.

When I pull away, he gives me a once-over. "I'm digging the whole naughty secretary look."

I punch his arm. "These are my work clothes, asshole."

He grins. "I bet your dick of a boss enjoys them, is all I'm saying."

A hand is thrust toward me. "I'm John," says his friend. "Not staying long. Just wanted to meet the infamous author, Natalia Bell, who Sam never shuts up about."

Sam gives me a sheepish smile as we sit. Maybe I spoke too soon about Hayes being slightly worse than most men.

"I read the new pages," Sam says, pouring me a margarita from the pitcher on the table. "I hate Ewan a little less, now that he's blameless about turning into a douche."

I give a sigh of relief. "Thank God. My poor agent is emailing me daily about getting the final first half, and I still have most of the second half to write."

He shrugs. "You have plenty of time, and isn't your job almost done? Your friend ought to be back any day now, right?"

My stomach gives a lurch. In two months, Hayes has become such a big part of my life that the future days without him spin ahead like a black hole. Will we be friends when this ends? Even if I manage to stay, California's sunshine, in this imagined future without him, feels like a slap in the face, like the clear blue sky overhead during my father's funeral, a group of teens blasting rap as they drove past.

"Yeah," I say quietly. "They're mostly through the process." Jonathan will take a few weeks to get settled into parenting after he returns on Tuesday, and then it will be over. I'll have no excuse to stay behind, to keep Hayes from working himself to the bone or dying of scurvy.

The women at the table next to ours are suddenly staring at us again. No, not at us—behind us, at someone walking through the restaurant. A shadow looms over our table, and I glance up to find Hayes standing there. I just saw him a few minutes ago, yet my eyes devour him anyway, as if I'd forgotten in that brief period of time exactly how pretty he is.

I straighten, pulling my phone forward to see if I missed a text.

"Hey," I say, glancing from him to my phone. "Did you need something?"

"Not at all," he says with a smile that's a hint too smug. "I was just walking down the street and suddenly was craving tacos."

Bullshit. Hayes has never craved anything but scotch, coffee, and orgasms, as far as I know. I don't understand how I can be happy to see him and deeply annoyed, all at once, but I am. "Sam, John...this is my boss, Hayes Flynn."

"Boss *and* amusement park companion," corrects Hayes, extending a hand to Sam. "Don't be fooled by her current lack of warmth. She adores me. You don't mind if I join, I hope? I'm famished."

Before we can even object, he's taking the empty seat between Sam and myself. My jaw falls open, but Sam is a nice boy, far too polite to send Hayes on his way, though I can tell he'd like to.

"Tali tells me you're driving up the coast," says Hayes.

Sam forces a smile, and with a bewildered glance at me, begins to describe their plans—Big Sur and Monterey, then San Francisco for a few days before going up to the wine country and further north.

Hayes, charming asshole that he is, begins to offer suggestions for all the stops along the way, and I suppose I should be grateful—John is no longer leaving, apparently, and

Hayes has managed to keep Sam and I in neutral waters. But I'm annoyed all the same. How would he like it if I showed up while he was out with *Angela* or *Savannah* or *Nicole* and took over?

"Be careful camping at Yosemite," Hayes is saying. "You need the bear bag, something we discovered too late."

"*You* camped?" I ask incredulously. I can't imagine it, unless the camping involved six-hundred thread count sheets and around-the-clock room service.

"It was quite a while ago," he says quietly. "Nearly a decade by now I guess."

He went with Ella.

Hayes, once upon a time, was someone who took vacations. Who was willing to take road trips and hang bear bags and sleep on the ground. He was someone willing to trust another human being and commit to her.

I stare at him, seeing in his face what he probably sees in mine when I talk about Matt: this low-level shame that he was fooled, that he was so wrong, that he was destroyed by someone who didn't deserve him and fooled himself into believing in her.

As annoyed as I am by the way Hayes has inserted himself into my evening, an ache takes hold in my chest. Discovering I was wrong about Matt was hard. But not as hard as having him beginning a family with my *dad*. How Hayes ever managed to forgive either of them is beyond me.

Our eyes meet, and for one long moment it feels as if it's only the two of us at this table, at this restaurant. We look away at the same time.

"Tell me about teenage Tali," says Hayes, jovial once more. "I understand she had a bit of a Thomas Hardy obsession."

My jaw falls open. "Jonathan has a big fucking mouth, apparently."

Sam looks at me. "How did I not know this?"

"Yes," says Hayes, eyes twinkling at my discomfort, "that's how she and Jonathan bonded as teens, at some writing camp." He turns to me. "You were quite the catch back then it would seem, writing your Thomas Hardy fan fiction. I'm not sure how you kept the boys away."

I'm seriously killing Jonathan. It will be sad for his daughter, I know. I'll find her a better dad. One who can keep secrets.

"It wasn't *fan fiction*," I groan. "It was just an alternate ending to *Jude the Obscure*. Hardy killed off all the children in the end. It was brutal."

Sam leans forward. Victorian-era novelists are his jam. "Thomas Hardy books are never happy. *Tess of the D'Urbervilles*? *Return of the Native*?"

"*Far From the Madding Crowd* was happy," I argue.

"You have a strange notion of happiness. Bathsheba settled." He kicks my foot under the table, grinning. "Though having spent so many years settling yourself, you might not have picked up on that."

I laugh. "I love that you've managed to insult me while discussing the work of an author who's been dead for centuries."

It feels as if we're both kids again, ripping on each other while we sit outside between classes. We've always gotten along well, though. If I'd met him back before I got together with Matt, I'd have thought we were soulmates. And who's to say we wouldn't have been? Who's to say we still aren't? It's the plot of every other second-chance romance: Boy and girl don't get together as teens, only to see as adults what was there all along.

The one person who isn't amused by the conversation is Hayes, whose face is suddenly all angles—sharp cheekbones, hard jaw—as his eyes flicker from me to Sam and back. Perhaps he's seeing what I am now: that there's no reason Sam and I shouldn't be together. We're from the same place. We get along well and could talk about books for hours. If only I was ready for it, which I'm not. Sam is perfect for me, but once we move forward, there'll be no way to walk it back. I somber a little at the thought.

Hayes insists on paying for dinner when the bill arrives, as well he should since he sort of ruined it. John politely excuses himself for the evening, but Hayes is almost defiant in his quest to remain. "Where to next?" he asks, signing the bill with a flourish.

I'm torn between irritation and relief. Hayes has no right to interfere the way he is, but it's also clear Sam wants more, and the prospect terrifies me.

"It's already ten," I say. "And my boss is a dick, so I need to get to bed."

"Where are you parked?" asks Hayes. "I'll walk you."

Sam's jaw shifts. He's frustrated but too nice—unlike Hayes —to argue. I apologize as I hug him goodbye.

"That's okay," he says against my ear. "I'll see you next month. *Without him.*"

The night is a lovely violet-black, the sky dotted with stars, and I'm too annoyed to fully appreciate it. Hayes matches me step for step, and it's only at the end of the block I realize he's scowling.

"You look awfully dissatisfied," I mutter. "Was ruining my night with an old friend not enough for you?"

"Believe me," he sneers, "if I'd known you'd spend the entire meal arguing over Thomas Hardy like the two nerdiest kids in school, I wouldn't have bothered."

I come to a stop, rounding on him. "You barge in on my night out with an old friend, and now you're ridiculing him *and* me for having a common interest? I know you mostly spend time with people who don't read, but there's nothing wrong with the fact *we* do."

People walking past stare at us, and I don't even care. He barely seems to notice them as he pushes a hand through his hair, looking as frustrated as I feel. "Look, I was...I didn't expect him to be..." He blows out a breath. "I like that you have an encyclopedic knowledge of Thomas Hardy. I like that you're well read, far better read than I am. But you and I get along in a way I don't with anyone else, and I guess it bothered me to see that you get along just as well with him."

Under the glare of the streetlight, I see a hint of vulnerability in his eyes. He's known for having superficial relationships, but ours...isn't, and his honesty right now makes that clear. I feel myself softening toward him against my will.

"You're jealous of my friendship with Sam?"

He rolls his eyes. "I'm not *jealous*. And if you think he wants to be your friend, you're delusional. He'd have proposed by the end of the night if I hadn't intervened."

"Why would it matter if he did, Hayes?" I ask. I don't know where the question comes from, but there's a part of me that wants to provoke him. I want to push him toward something, something that would be terrible for us both.

He tugs at his collar. "Because you said you weren't ready for that. And he's not...good enough."

"Not *good enough*?" I demand. "A really nice guy who's about to be a college professor and has never cheated on a woman in his life. How could he possibly not be good enough?"

"You like him, then." His mouth is pressed into a flat line.

"How can I even know when you hovered all night like a third party on our dinner?" My eyes narrow. "And please don't make a joke about threesomes."

His gaze holds mine. "If it were an option," he says, suddenly fierce, "I'd never be willing to share you."

My heart stutters and then speeds up.

If it were an option. There's a part of me—the stupid part that clearly hasn't learned its lesson—that wants to ask why it's not.

I don't look away, and neither does he. We stand in silence, with the words he just said thickening the air between us. They could have meant a hundred different things, and I choose not to let myself consider any of them.

"Good night, Hayes," I whisper, and then, without looking back, I walk the rest of the way to my car alone. He doesn't try to stop me.

If it were an option, I'd never be willing to share you.

I can't seem to move past that phrase as I drive home.

Allowing myself to hope it could mean something is ridiculous and pointless, but the more I think about leaving California, the more it feels like I'm giving up something that matters and matters a *lot*.

By the time I start climbing the stairs to my apartment, I'm reciting a mantra with each step:

I want to stay.

I want to stay.

I want to stay.

I kick off my shoes as I enter and text my mother. We haven't been in contact since that angry phone call before the luncheon, and I just need to know that it made a dent.

Hey Mom, I write. **We haven't spoken in a while and I need to book my flight home.**

Which means: *I need to know if I'm booking a roundtrip ticket. I need to hear you say you've pulled it together.*

And I see that's she read it. But she doesn't say a fucking word in response.

❧ 26 ❧

"**I** have a favor to ask," he announces the next morning.

And here I was hoping he might be a little penitent after last night. How completely unrealistic of me.

"And it's something so big you can't even demand it of me, the way you usually would?" I ask. "I can't give you my liver, you know. I only have one."

He runs a hand through his hair and it flops forward. I wonder if he knows my heart pinches a little at that small sign of uncertainty. Already the answer is yes. *Fine, Hayes, take my liver. Anything you need is yours.*

"It's my sister's birthday this weekend," he says. "I want you to come with me."

Less invasive than losing an organ but nearly as painful. "You need an assistant for a child's birthday party?"

"No," he says, sighing. "I need you to act like you're my girl-friend. I did it for you with your ex, and now I need the same."

My eyes go wide. So wide I probably look like a comic book character, but I can't seem to stop. "*What?*"

"We should run a hearing test on you at some point. I. Need. You. To—"

I wave a dismissive hand. "Yes, I heard that part. I just can't begin to imagine why you need *me* when you have half the women in LA begging for your attention."

"I can't ask just anyone to pretend to be my girlfriend." He toys with the lid of his coffee cup. "I need someone they'd actually believe, someone...impressive."

This I find even more difficult to grasp. "I'm a failed writer who dropped out of grad school, can't pay back an advance and now works for *you*, which is—no offense—sort of hitting rock bottom. How am I impressive?"

"You're attractive and smart, which is a rarer combination than you might think. Though it would help if you wouldn't describe anything involving me as 'rock bottom' when you meet my family."

I hitch a shoulder, uncertain. Not that I won't do it. It's simply that I'm not sure he's thought this through. He should be taking a celebrity or a surgeon, not me. "What am I supposed to tell them I do for a living? They won't be too impressed when they learn I spend my mornings getting rid of the women you bring home."

His eyes narrow. "That hasn't happened once in nearly two months but you're still bringing it up. Just tell them the truth—you've got a book due this fall."

"Oh my God," I groan. "I told you that in confidence. I hope you're not repeating it to anyone."

He shakes his head. "Seriously, Tali—what the hell? How many people write well enough to get a major advance based on fifty pages of a book at age twenty-three? You think that's so shameful? Ask all the women in this city who slept with a bloated old director to get a part. I'm sure they'd gladly trade sources of shame with you."

I mostly got the advance because I was dating Matt, but I suppose he has a point.

"Fine," I say. "What do I wear?"

His tongue glides over his lower lip. He's looking at me, but his mind is far away at the same time. "The beige dress," he says, nostrils flaring a little. "Ella will fucking hate that."

"What's wrong with the beige dress?"

He shoves his hands in his pockets. "Nothing. That's why she'll hate it. When you're in the beige dress, there's nothing wrong in the entire world."

⚜

I PUT FAR MORE EFFORT INTO MY APPEARANCE ON SATURDAY than is called for, cutting short my visit with Jonathan and Gemma—adorably chubby and way more active than I realized she'd be—to see a hairdresser-to-the-stars friend of Ava's.

I walk out with amazing highlights—subtle caramel and gold like I once got from the sun as a child—my hair falling over my shoulders in perfect waves.

I'm trying to live up to this idea Hayes seems to have that I'm somehow capable of impressing Ella and his dad, but perhaps I'm hoping to impress Hayes too.

When you're in the beige dress, there's nothing wrong in the entire world.

No one's ever said anything like that to me before. Did Matt tell me I was beautiful? Sure. But with Hayes, it wasn't simply the words. It was the way he said them, bitten off like they were a curse he'd pay for later.

"Look at you," Drew says over video while I get ready, "putting on *actual* makeup for your date with your boss."

I dab concealer under my eyes. "It's not a date."

"No, it's just your boss who said you were the most impressive, hot woman he's ever met, asking you to pretend you're his girlfriend and meet his whole family." Which is not what Hayes said, but I've already corrected Drew on this twice and she seems determined to believe her own version of the story. "I would kill to have Six say that. I just wish he'd give me some sign what he's thinking, you know?"

It seems to me Six has given her plenty of signs what he's thinking and she doesn't want to see them. Was I any different with Matt? He showed me in a hundred ways that he wasn't the right guy. He talked me out of going to my dream school, he persuaded me to drop out of my master's program. Sometimes the only sign you need is that a guy cares way more about himself than you.

"I think you should find the hottest guy ever and have four amazing months with him," I tell her. "Just go be your best self, and Six will be eating out of your hand when he gets home. Lipliner or no lipliner?"

She leans back in her chair, tapping her fingers over her chest like a vaudeville villain. "Oh, Tali, you're in so deep if you're finally gonna call attention to those yummy lips of yours."

I groan. "I'm not. I just hate this woman, and she kind of fucked him up, you know? I want to do my best to twist the knife."

"Wear the lipliner, then," she says. "I bet you a hundred bucks it winds up on his dick by the end of the party."

❧

HE PULLS INTO THE CIRCULAR DRIVE IN FRONT OF MY building and climbs from the car, eyes flickering over me once and again. He swallows. "The vomit came out of the dress," he says quietly. "That's good."

"You flatterer you."

He comes around to my side and holds the door. "You look amazing," he says, his voice low and gravelly. "I'm...never mind."

The door shuts, and I decide to let it go. This whole situation is awkward enough without us opening up to each other on top of it.

"We should probably get our story straight," I tell him when he climbs in, twisting my hands in my lap. How fortuitous Jonathan talked me into a manicure.

"You're far too worried about this," he says. "It's a child's birthday. No one's hooking you up to a polygraph."

I turn toward him. He's skipped the jacket today and is wearing a deep blue shirt, collar undone, and khaki pants. His hair is a little fucked up, like he's run his hands through it once too often. I've never seen anyone so handsome in my entire life. My gaze drifts to his neck, and I imagine nuzzling his skin there, like a pig after truffles.

"I'm not good at lying," I tell him. "Otherwise, I'd lie to you all the time. I just need the basics."

"Fine," he says, pulling onto the street. "My cock is huge, and you can't get enough of it."

"Yes, that sounds like exactly the kind of classy thing your impressive girlfriend would say." I roll my eyes. "How long have we been together? Where did we meet? Where was our first date?"

A muscle flickers in his cheek. "Just stick with the truth as much as possible. We met six months ago when you were tending bar."

He glances at me and I worry I'm flushing. I sometimes think about how it might have gone if he hadn't rushed out. But we are closer to a relationship now than we ever would have been had he tried something. And if it *were* a relationship, it would certainly seem like a good one. As if we'd really begun to care about each other.

"Where was our first date?" I ask.

"You're not being interviewed for *Cosmo*. No one's going to ask you that."

I don't know how he's so relaxed about this. *He's* the one who'll look like an asshole if we mess this up. "They might. Or they could ask you why you asked me out."

He rolls his eyes. "Anyone who sees you in that dress will know why I asked you out. Though if you're as mouthy as usual, they might wonder why I kept asking."

❧

HAYES'S FATHER AND, UM, *STEPMOTHER* LIVE ON A magnificent estate in Newport, surrounded by fields and trees, completely private. The house itself looks like an English castle, massive and stone-fronted. It even has ivy growing up the sides.

"Oooh," I say delightedly, smiling wide. "I see why she chose him now."

He levels me with a stare. "Yet you call *me* Satan."

We walk inside, and a maid in full uniform takes the gift Hayes has brought—purchased and wrapped by me, of course—and offers us champagne before leading us to a backyard drenched in late afternoon sun, where there's an *elephant* alongside the standard moonbounce/trampoline/swimming pool set up.

He gives me a quick half-smile. He's as beautiful and confident as ever, but I see something uncertain and young in his eyes that breaks my heart. I'm going to be the best fucking fake girlfriend in the world today, just for him. My hand slides into his, soft to rough, small to large. He squeezes gently as his thumb skims across mine, and my body responds to his touch like it's starved for attention. I want to memorize every callous, the pressure of it. Sure, I'm doing this for him...but I think I'm going to enjoy it more than I should.

A little girl, blonde and leggy like Ella, springs at him, throwing her arms around his waist. "What did you bring me?" she demands.

"I made a donation in your name to the NRA," he replies, swinging her into the air. "Happy birthday."

She grins. "Liar! You did not!"

"Hudson," says a chiding voice, "that's enough."

I glance up to see Ella and Hayes's father approaching. His father is nearly identical to who Hayes will be in twenty years, and Ella's beauty is every bit as ethereal and delicate as it appeared in her photos, though there's something a little icy in her blue eyes. Maybe it's simply that I know who she really is.

"Tali, this is my father, Michael, and my stepmother, Ella." I enjoy watching Ella wince at the word *stepmother*.

"Tali, it's so nice to meet you," Michael says, shaking my hand. "I was beginning to think Hayes would never bring a female over."

My eyes widen. I'm not sure if he's making a terrible joke about the *last* time he got introduced to one of Hayes's girl-friends or if he's put it so far out of his head, he's forgotten what he did.

Ella colors prettily. "What a nice surprise. Hayes has never mentioned you."

Acid begins to *drip, drip, drip* in my chest. After everything she did, is she really trying to sabotage the first relationship she's seen him in? Dear *God*, I'd love to put this woman in her place.

"When would I have mentioned her?" Hayes asks calmly. "I haven't seen you since the holidays."

Her smile fades. My hand squeezes his. *Well done.*

"Has it been that long?" Michael asks. "*Madness.* We really need to see more of you. Come get some food." He turns toward the buffet, walking beside us.

"I assume you're an actress," he continues to me. "Hayes might have mentioned I'm doing a remake of *Roman Holiday.*"

Hayes never mentions you, ever. "Oh, I didn't know. But I'm not an actress. Have Hayes tell you about my amazing British accent, though."

Hayes smirks at me. "She sounds like a pirate, and all her knowledge of England appears to have come from *Mary Poppins* and *Harry Potter.*"

"I quote *My Fair Lady* a good bit as well," I agree.

"I wondered where you got it from. *Top o'the morning guv'ner,*" he adds, in a hardcore Cockney accent that makes me cackle in a very non-classy way.

"What *do* you do, Tali, if you're not an actress?" Ella cuts in more forcefully. Her tone has a mocking edge, as if she already knows my answer will be *porn star* or "*I'm between jobs*".

"Oh." I really hate discussing it, but for Hayes's sake, I will. For his sake, I'd claim to be an astrophysicist or world leader if I could get away with it. "I'm actually working on my first novel."

"How lovely," Ella says. "An aspiring artist in our midst." She says it as if I'm a child, waving a stick-figure drawing in the air, and this time, it's Hayes's hand squeezing mine.

"Actually, Tali received a rather large advance for this book when she was still in graduate school," he says, a warning in his tone. "There's nothing *aspiring* about it. If you'll excuse us, I'm going to introduce her to Grandmother."

His arm wraps around my waist, steering me away from them. My hand goes to the small of his back, and it's entirely for Ella's benefit that I then let it slip as low as it can reasonably go.

"Sorry," he says quietly. "I know you didn't want to talk about the advance. I just couldn't stand the way she was trying to belittle you."

"You can tell them anything you want, true or false, if it puts that bitch in her place," I reply, my voice laced with venom. "But honestly? She's a total dick. I'm not sure why you even care about making her jealous."

"This isn't about making her jealous," he says, holding me tighter as we start down the hill. These shoes were not made for walking in grass—or walking, period—and he appears to realize it. "Do you have any idea how miserable it is to attend these things on my own? With every single guest seeing me standing alone and thinking, 'Oh, poor guy. He never really got over her'? Now they're all thinking, 'Well done, mate. You got over her in a big way, didn't you?'"

I feel myself blushing, embarrassingly pleased, as he pulls me toward an older woman, bending low to kiss her on the cheek. "Grandmother," he says, "let me introduce you to my friend Tali."

She peers up at me. "Well, well, well," she says. "This one's much prettier than Ella, isn't she?"

Hayes laughs quietly, holding a chair for me and taking the seat on the other side. "Yes," he whispers, "but you're not supposed to say that aloud."

"I'm old. I can say whatever I'd like," she replies. "And how did you manage to find this fine young specimen?"

I smirk at him. *This isn't a Cosmo interview*, my ass. I'll let him solve this on his own.

"She sat on my doorstep and refused to leave," he says. "Eventually I figured I might as well allow her inside."

She smacks his arm. "You're not as amusing as you think. The truth now, please."

Hayes's eyes flicker over my face. "I saw her photo on Jonathan's desk and started looking for her all the time, because she worked at this bar I'd pass on my way home," he says. Weirdly...it doesn't sound like a lie. "I saw her reading while she was walking in, even though it was raining. And I thought she was the loveliest thing I'd ever seen in my life, so I followed her."

He stops, and my heart thuds loudly in the resulting silence. All this time, I thought he wound up at Topside by accident, but perhaps it was no accident at all. Because it *was* raining the night we met. And I can still remember the book I was reading as I walked in. Maybe he's embellishing this for the sake of our fake relationship...except it doesn't *feel* embellished.

His grandmother clasps her hands together. "And you've been together ever since!'

His gaze meets mine. "Not exactly. My assistant got wind of it and begged me to leave her alone because she'd had a hard year and I wouldn't be good for her." There's a tiny note of bitterness, regret, in his voice. "But it worked out eventually."

I swallow. If this is all true, then Hayes, with his reputation for being careless and selfish, walked out...for me. Is that why he felt so blindsided when I showed up as Jonathan's replacement?

"I'm glad," his grandmother says. "You deserve a nice girl, darling. I always thought you could do better than Ella."

It would never have worked out, of course. Odds are, he'd have hit on me and I'd have shot him down in the rudest way possible. Or he'd have realized I'm generally not a one-night-stand kind of girl. But that *what if* is still ringing in my brain.

Hudson runs to the table and grabs his hand. "Hayes!" she cries. "Come ride the elephant with me!"

He grins at her. "I'm not sure it can support both our weights. You've gotten quite large." She giggles, and he allows himself to be led to the line. I watch as this beautiful man walks off holding his sister's hand, still completely stunned by his admission.

"He's back," his grandmother says, pulling my attention away from Hayes. "I was worried Ella had ruined his faith in women forever, but he clearly adores you. It's such a relief."

I squirm with discomfort. Even if we are pulling this off better than I ever dreamed, it's all a lie. And while I don't mind lying to Ella and his dad until I'm blue in the face, I don't want to lie to this nice old woman.

"You must ignore Ella, whatever she says. The woman's a parasite," his grandmother continues, "the kind that mutates to best attack its host. She met Michael and suddenly became a producer's wife. When she leaves him for someone else, she'll become an equestrian or a go-go dancer or whatever it is her next victim requires."

I shouldn't be prying, but I can't seem to help myself. "Who was she with Hayes?"

"A bit like you—down-to-earth, open. But she didn't pull it off quite as well."

I'm not sure if she's placating me. I only know I *want* it to be true. And I know I want to avoid Ella all afternoon, if possible, but when I help Hayes's grandmother up the hill and stop by the bar on my way back, she suddenly appears by my side. I doubt it's by accident.

"He still drinks this, does he?" Ella asks, lifting the scotch I got for Hayes and giving it a sniff. "You should have seen him at Cambridge, choking it down, trying to impress me."

"That was *so* long ago," I reply, preparing to walk away. "I'm fairly certain he's not drinking it to impress anyone now."

Her head tips to the side as she studies me. "He's not cut out for commitment, you know."

I stiffen. A part of me assumed she must regret her decision —how could you *not* regret leaving Hayes? But I thought she'd at least be subtle about it. Instead, she's openly trying to destroy what he's found in her wake.

"He's charming, and he's obviously smitten with you." She waves a hand as if all this is meaningless. "Just don't start believing it's going to last. One thing goes wrong in his life, and you'll find yourself shut out completely."

I have no idea what the *one thing* was that went wrong, but it also doesn't matter. This bitch was never the right person for him. Never. "Maybe you just weren't someone he felt he could turn to."

Her eyes narrow. "You're delusional if you think he's going to choose you."

I laugh. She is jealous and so painfully *obvious* about it. "What's worse, Ella? Knowing you made a poor choice, or knowing that every person here thinks Hayes dodged a bullet when you left?"

I grab the scotch from her hand and leave her standing there, red-faced and tight-lipped, and return to the table, where Hayes now waits.

He rises, and because I know Ella is still watching, I reach up and make a show of running my fingers through his hair. His eyes go hooded and feral as he observes me, swallowing as his gaze lands on my lips. "You're extremely committed to this role," he says hoarsely. His hands, already on my hips, tighten.

"Ella's watching," I tell him.

He pulls my palm to his mouth, pressing a gentle kiss to it

before he pulls me down to the chair beside his. "I told you I wasn't trying to make her jealous."

"Yeah, I know," I say, "but I am. Because she sucks. I can't imagine why you ever proposed to her."

He prods his cheek with his tongue. "I never actually proposed," he admits reluctantly. "She pulled me into a jewelry store one day and told me it was time. After staying together so long, it seemed like the right thing to do. In retrospect, I think she hoped getting engaged would change me in a way it didn't— the whole thing about making me love her as much as I love myself."

His voice is flat and factual, as if he's accepted her ugly, bitter take on what went wrong. "Hayes, you sound as if you believe her, and you shouldn't."

He shrugs. "A part of me was relieved when she left, which seems to support her point."

Before I can argue, Hudson appears, begging him to go into the trampoline with her. His smile makes my heart ache for him. His own child with Ella might have looked just the same. He must, occasionally, think about it too.

He rises. "Come on," he says, holding out a hand for me.

"You don't seriously expect me to jump in this dress?"

There's a filthy smile on his face. "I'm *commanding* you to jump in that dress."

I should ignore him, but I follow them to the trampoline. I have to hitch my dress up to nearly my crotch in order to climb the ladder after them.

"My plan is working swimmingly so far," he says, his voice low and dirty.

"Enjoy the view while you can, big boy." With a chuckle, he holds out his hand to help me balance as I climb in.

My foot sinks into the floor of the trampoline and I fall forward, into his chest.

He catches me easily. I allow myself a quick inhale—he smells like soap and clean air and *him*, and I want to huff him like glue. I force myself to step away, and we begin to jump in a circle, higher and higher.

In another life, he'd have been a good father, and kids would give him some of that meaning he seems to lack. Maybe he'd have gotten into a different job, or at least not allowed the one he has to take over his life. I wonder if it's still possible for him, somehow.

Hudson falls, and I trip gracelessly in an effort to avoid landing on her. We all end up on our backs laughing and he swings her high in the air overhead. I don't think I've ever seen him look quite so peaceful as he does now: smiling wide, his body loose and relaxed.

When we depart the trampoline, he lifts me so I don't have to descend the ladder—large hands spanning my waist as he lowers me lightly in front of him, sliding me down his body as he does. The contact is not obvious to onlookers, but has us both sucking in a breath. My feet are on the ground but his hands linger, his gaze drifting over my face. It no longer feels as he's playing a part, and I know I'm not. Nothing feels more natural than my hand in his, my head pressing to his shoulder. And I wonder if we are both getting a little lost in playing this role.

I go inside, to a bathroom that's larger than my apartment, wondering how I'll stand to return to a world where his hand isn't on the small of my back or his arm isn't around my waist. I wish I could hoard all these moments and somehow savor them throughout the year.

As I exit, I come face-to-face with his father. I don't think he was waiting for me, but his timing here is odd and there's something eager in his eyes.

"So, you and my son," he says, his voice a little too jovial.

I smile stiffly, unsure where this is heading. Hayes seems to have forgiven his father, but I have not. Because who does that? He's a good-looking man with plenty of money. He could easily have found a woman other than his son's fiancée.

"Yes," I reply.

"I'm glad he's finally found someone," he says, and then he sighs. "He and Ella...I guess he told you."

"He did," I say, my voice flat. If he's looking for a pat on the shoulder, I hope he's not holding his breath.

"You know, they'd never have worked out," he says. "He needs more than her."

My head jerks upward. *What a shitty thing to say about his own wife, even if it's true.*

"I'm not saying Ella is lacking anything," he continues. "She's perfect for me. But Hayes—he needs a firecracker, someone as strong as he is, as smart as he is, an equal. And whether he'd ever admit it or not, she never was."

I raise my chin. "What an *unusual* thing to say about your own wife."

He runs a hand through his hair. It's far cuter when Hayes does it. "I know. And you're possibly the only woman at this party with the balls to call me on it, so you just might work."

If any of this was real, I'd suspect...he might be right. Even based on our limited interaction, I know someone like Ella could never be enough for Hayes, could never challenge him and keep him on his toes the way I would. But me? I could make him happy, and I'd take care of him. For the briefest moment I am staggered by my desire to do exactly that.

Hayes walks in the French doors and stiffens at the sight of us, his eyes going dark.

"I was just telling Tali here what a nice couple you are," his father says, swishing the ice in his empty glass. "She's perfect for you."

Hayes's arm wraps around my waist, pulling me tight to his body. "Glad you approve, Dad." His voice is dry as the Sahara and he stares his father down, as if this moment is about something more. It's only when his father walks away that he turns me toward him. His hand slides to my hip, even though we're the only ones in here. "What was that about?"

"He asked me to have a drink with him later tonight, once

everyone's gone." I wait just long enough for his jaw to drop before I laugh. "Kidding. He told me it was for the best that you and Ella never worked out because she isn't your equal."

"You're shitting me."

I shake my head. In retrospect, it's all pretty appalling. "You won't be surprised to learn I made my disapproval clear."

He laughs, looking younger and freer than he has looked even once, during all the time I've known him. "Of course you did. You about ready to go?"

I nod, though I'm not really ready for all this to end. He takes my hand, and we walk back outside to say goodbye to everyone. Ella hugs us both, barely touching me while she lingers with Hayes, pressed up against him. Everyone watches it happen, and I'm furious all over again with his father. What a horrible situation to put your son in for the rest of his life. I don't care if he did Hayes a favor. He's a garbage human being, and he got the wife he deserves.

❧

I SINK INTO THE SUN-WARMED LEATHER SEAT OF HIS BMW with a relieved sigh, realizing only now how much my feet ache.

"If we happen to pass any bonfires on the way back to my apartment, pull over so I can throw these shoes in."

He glances over at me as we wait for the gates to open. "That you managed to wear them all day was above and beyond the call of duty."

"For real," I agree. "And now that I've done a favor for you, I need you to do something for me."

He smirks. "You're not in much of a bargaining position now that the afternoon is over, but proceed."

I bite my lip. "Take next weekend off. I never filled it in."

We discussed the idea weeks ago. It's possible I simply ignored him when he said he wasn't interested.

His nostrils flare. "Tell me you're joking."

"Come on," I wheedle. "What's two days?"

He sighs heavily. "Do I really have to tell you how much money I can make?"

I throw out my hands. "Think of how much you have, Hayes! For God's sake, what are you working so hard for if you can't even enjoy it?"

He turns up the music as if the conversation is over. "Fill in the days."

"You're just scared," I say, turning the music down again. "You're scared of what happens when there's nothing to do. You fill every free moment with work. That's no way to live."

"I seem to be filling an increasing number of moments with shrill nagging from my assistant," he replies. "I'm not scared of time off. I just don't need it."

"Then prove it," I insist. "Take two whole days off and show me you're not scared. I found a little house you can rent, right on the beach. Swim and nap and read. What could be better?"

"Making ten grand in a day would be better," he replies. "Which would happen if you weren't so averse to doing your job."

That's the last word we exchange on the matter until he pulls in front of my apartment.

"I'll walk you up," he says.

I shake my head. I'd rather he not see how I live—how far apart our worlds actually are. "No, don't. You'll get towed."

Our eyes meet, and butterflies take flight in my stomach. I haven't been in this situation often in my life, but I know what it is: It's when you realize you like someone, and he might like you too. It's the moment when we'd kiss, if things were different.

"Thank you for doing this," he says. "I don't think a single person thought it was fake."

It's an opening. *It didn't feel fake to me either*, I could tell him. Except the very thought of that conversation turns those butterflies into a flock of birds, scattering at the sound of a gunshot, wings flapping, feathers flying loose.

"Surely they realize you're going to pull a George Clooney and not settle down until you're fifty. I'm way too old for you."

"True. Jonathan's daughter is probably a better fit, age-wise," he replies.

I laugh, and then it fades. I don't actually see him pulling a George Clooney. I see him growing a little more alone each year, and I have so little time left to fix it.

"What do I need to do to get you to go away next weekend?" I ask. "I'll work a week for free. Name your price."

He glances at me and swallows. "Fine," he says. "Come with me."

My eyes fly open wide. "*What?*"

"Never fear, I'm not propositioning you." He leans back in his seat. "But it would be fun to have you there, and I want someone to handle the grunt work."

"What grunt work?" I ask. "It's a *vacation*."

"I need someone to do all the shit I don't want to do. Like going to Starbucks in the morning and getting groceries."

I frown. It's not that I'd mind going—I'd sell my liver to go, as short-sighted as that might be, and the book is stalled out again, so I could use a break. But it's not what I had in mind for him.

"Hayes, I think maybe...maybe what you're missing in life is the bad stuff. Maybe what you need is for me not to buffer it all for you."

"This sounds like an elaborate excuse to make me take care of myself, something that doesn't interest me in the least."

My smile is weak. I suppose I *am* asking him to take care of himself, and it's something I have to think through for a moment before I can explain it to him.

"It's not," I finally say. "But here's the thing: I don't like going to Starbucks either. But when I step outside and the sun warms my skin and I take that first sip of my latte, just before I spit in yours, it suddenly feels as if the world is a decent place. You don't get that. Or any of the other moments like it, so you look for your happiness in things that do more harm than good."

His eyes darken. "So much judgment from such a small package."

"I'm not judging you. How could I? I'm in debt up to my eyeballs, I'm about to be unemployed, and my ex is now splashed all over the internet with a girl who's much better looking than me. If I saw an easy fix for any of that, I'd take it, and if your life made you happy, I'd be all for it. It just doesn't seem to."

"She is *not* better looking than you."

I laugh. I can't believe out of everything I said, *that's* the part he heard.

"I still want you to come," he says. "I'll stand in Starbucks with you. Show me what this normal, happy life would be like if you had a weekend off and didn't work for me."

A normal happy life with him if he wasn't my boss. It's the kind of thing I don't even allow myself to *imagine*, and now he wants me to act it out with him.

He raises a brow. "Oh, look how reluctant you are now that *you've* got to go. Not so fun anymore, is it?"

But he's got it all wrong.

I'm not worried about showing him what our life would be like together...I'm worried about showing it to myself.

❧ 27 ❧

We leave on Friday for Laguna Beach, about an hour south of LA. As much as I'd like to take in the view—the city giving way to ocean and sand and distant cliffs—I turn toward him instead, my knees pressed to the console.

We've barely left the city and already I can see how some of that tension from work is easing away. His shoulders are relaxed, his mouth soft.

He has the most glorious profile—a nose that is somehow endlessly masculine and elegant at the same time. What a shame he has no plans to pass those genes on to another generation. He glances at me, and I wonder if my staring unnerves him—but I don't care enough to stop doing it.

"You haven't mentioned your sister in a while," he says. "Is she doing better?"

My stomach tightens. Right now, I want to imagine what his children would look like and pretend I never have to leave him. I do not want to think about my family. "Yes. She gets out in August."

"And your mom? She's not going to be an issue?" he asks.

My mother hasn't replied to the text I sent a week ago, nor

the more demanding ones I've sent since. I know what it means, and I know I should tell him the truth. But my friendship with Hayes is like a flower that's just begun to bloom, and the truth will be a hard freeze, prompting him to cut his losses and back away. And I'm not ready for him to back away yet. "It'll sort itself out," I reply.

I glance out the window, at the sun glinting off the Pacific's endless blue. Yes, it'll sort itself out, but only with my help. Only with my salary paying the mortgage and me there to take care of Charlotte and some concession made on my end to Liddie, who no longer tells me about pregnancy attempts or anything else. And it would be worth it all if only the four of us were going to come out of this okay. I just feel increasingly certain we won't. Me, in particular.

"Have you been to Laguna Beach before?" I ask. A subject change is necessary. Otherwise, Hayes will drag the whole gruesome truth out of me.

He shakes his head. "No. You?"

"Matt and I had this goal to visit all of California's beaches someday. We passed through, but I can't remember if we stopped."

His lip curls at the mention of my ex. "You're telling me, then, that you had sex on most of California's beaches."

A shocked laugh burbles from my throat. "God, no."

"Why not? I'd have tried, were I him."

Of course you would. I squeeze my thighs together and try not to picture sex on the beach with Hayes. Sex on every single beach in the *state* with Hayes. "He'd have never...forget it."

"Oh, no," he says. "You can't start a sentence like that and not finish it. He'd have never *what*?"

"We would never have made sex the focus of a trip. He'd be moody for days after, if we did." A blush crawls up my neck. "He always...finished quickly and it made things, uh, anticlimactic."

I stare out the window again, hoping we're done with this topic. Yes, sex with Matt was anticlimactic more often than it wasn't, but that didn't matter so much. We had other things—friendship and history, a common language. If I suspected I was giving a few things up, they didn't bother me at the time.

"I don't understand why you stayed with him," he says, suddenly irritated. "Is he really *that* attractive?"

"It was more than his looks. He's a really good guy most of the time, and he's kind to everyone, no matter where they are on the totem pole. He did a bad thing, but nobody's perfect."

Hayes's lips press together. "You sound like you've forgiven him."

"I'm getting there, or at least I'm trying to. Holding a grudge takes too much energy."

It's a very mature response. I'm not sure why Hayes looks so unhappy with it.

❧

It's just after six, the sky a symphony of muted rose and gold and dusky blue, when we arrive at the bungalow in Laguna.

I'm so smitten from the minute we walk in that I want to spin in place, like I'm some ecstatic Disney princess singing with woodland creatures.

The cathedral ceiling is walnut hardwood crossed with exposed beams. The back wall is glass, with nothing but water as far as the eye can see. It has a darling shiplap white kitchen and a glorious deck with a hot tub. I couldn't even have dreamed up anything quite so perfect.

His smile is soft. "I've never seen you so in awe of a place."

"Can you imagine living like this? Waking up here every freaking day?" I run a loving hand over the marble countertop. "Forget about your mattress. I'm marrying this house instead."

There are two nearly identical master bedrooms with wall-to-ceiling windows and bleached hardwood. I take the one on the left and stare at the huge bed, covered with a fluffy duvet and pillows. It's hard not to picture a romantic trip here with a bed like that one. But not with Matt, or even Sam. Not with someone soft and safe, but with someone whose nostrils will flare when I'm beneath him, like an animal about to devour prey. Someone who would pin me there for hours, days, weeks...

"You're staring at that bed like it's done something to you," Hayes says, behind me.

I glance back at him. He's leaning against the doorframe with his arms folded, all square-jawed beauty and bulging biceps, radiating dominance.

His nostrils would flare. I bet he'd use his teeth.

My knees wobble with how much I'd like see that for myself. I have to get him out of this room before I do something insane.

"We need to go to the store." My voice is breathy and uncertain.

"That does not sound relaxing at all. You're terrible at this."

"Come on," I say, grabbing my purse and charging past him toward the door. "It'll be fun."

I say this, knowing there is nothing fun about going to the grocery store. And Hayes bitches most of the way there, driving while I navigate. But when we walk in—hit by a rush of cold air and the smell of baked goods—his face lights up like a child's and he makes a beeline for the display of pies in front.

"I think we need some, don't you?" he asks.

"*Pie?*"

He's already got two in hand. "It's a combination of fruit and crust. Quite tasty."

I struggle not to smile. I've seen Hayes's enthusiasm for triple-cask-matured whiskey. I can't believe he's just as excited about shitty store-bought desserts. "I know what pie is, but I'm not sure why you're getting *two*. We won't even be here forty-eight hours."

He hitches a shoulder. "I can eat a lot of pie in forty-eight hours."

Within ten minutes, our cart also holds cinnamon-flavored soda, banana-flavored Oreos, truffle potato chips. It feels as if we are an actual couple, albeit one well on the way to insulin resistance. I want to lean into the experience as much as I want to lean away from it.

"I had no idea these even existed," he says, throwing maple Pop-Tarts in the cart. "Did you?"

"It's been several years since I carefully scrutinized the *Pop-Tart* section of a store."

"And look at these," he says, holding up something claiming to be a healthy breakfast food that looks a lot like a Snickers bar. "Perhaps normal life isn't so bad."

"Normal people probably don't leave a store with seventeen boxes of Pop-Tarts," I reply, pushing our cart toward the register.

The checkout girl eyes Hayes, then gives me a look that says *don't let this one go, my friend*. It fills me with completely undeserved pride, and I have to check myself.

Remembering it's not real is vital.

◈

WE MAKE DINNER TOGETHER WHEN WE GET BACK. I'VE NEVER pictured him as the dad who works the grill and helps with the dishes. It was safer to see him as the kind of guy who's not going to offer the life I want—and he won't—but it's getting harder to remember. Domestic bliss comes naturally to him...and it seems to make him happy.

We eat on the deck in a double chaise lounge, our plates resting in our laps. To my right, a bottle of shiraz sits on a small round table with two glasses. A light breeze blows as the surf pounds the shore and the sky turns from hazy violet to ink blue. Long after dinner is over, the two of us remain right where we are. *This* is what he should be doing every night. What would his life have been like if Ella hadn't left? Would he be tucking a child into bed right now? Would it all have gone wrong anyway, or did it really just hinge on that single event, the one that had him questioning his career and pulling away from her?

I bite my lip. "Can I ask you something?" I wait for his wary nod before I proceed. "Ella said something the other day...about how one thing would go wrong and you'd shut me out. What happened? Between you two, I mean?"

He stares off at the ocean, looking so tired and sad I wish I hadn't asked.

"I had a patient, Dylan. He was thirteen. He had a congenital abnormality that made his lower jaw severely asymmetrical," he begins.

He reaches for the wine and refills my glass and then his. "He'd spent his entire life being bullied and ridiculed, and this oral surgeon and I thought we were going to sweep in and fix everything." He flashes me his trademark smirk, only this time, I just see pain in it, and self-hatred.

"I guess...it didn't work out?" I pick up my glass and take a sip, simply to give him the space to answer. My heart is in my throat as I wait.

He swallows. "No," he says. "He died. Not on the table, but later that night after I was gone. His airway collapsed."

My chest tightens as a lump starts to form in my throat. I look away for a moment, blinking back tears. "Was the airway even your part of the surgery?" I ask, my voice muted, slightly hoarse.

"It doesn't matter. He was my patient, and I told him he'd be fine. I was so fucking sure of myself." He flinches, as if it's just happened, the hand closest to me curling into a fist.

Even if he'd never ask for it, he needs something right now. He needs to be reminded he isn't alone, that not everyone loathes him the way he seems to loathe himself. I scoot closer, until my arm presses to his, and rest my head on his shoulder. His closed fist relaxes. "And you left?"

"I stuck it out a few more months, completed a training at the Cleveland Clinic as planned. Then Ella left and I just...called it. It's all for the best. I make ten times what I would in pediatrics."

I hate Ella more than ever now. How could she have done that to him? Did she really not understand how guilty he must have felt? All she had to do was be patient, and she couldn't even give him that.

It makes sense to me that he'd choose a more painless path. What I don't understand is why he went so very far in the other direction.

"If you don't want Ella back, does the money really matter that much?" I ask softly.

He glances at me and away. "I suppose not. But I had a certain future ahead of me, and suddenly it was gone...I needed a new goal."

Except he chose a goal that will never make him happy. I wonder if he realizes it. I wonder if it's ever occurred to him that he could have a life like this one with someone: waves crashing in the darkness a few yards away, a woman with whom he can share things, one who wants to give him everything.

Our bare calves brush against each other—smooth to less smooth. I picture sliding my legs over his, glancing up at him to gauge his reaction. Would his hand land on my hip to pull me into his lap? Would he roll me beneath him, his weight pressing me hard to the seat?

Would we ruin everything?

I set my wine on the table and climb to my feet. "I should get to bed. Big day tomorrow."

His eyes travel over me for one long moment, climbing from hips to breasts and settling, finally, on my mouth. "Ah, yes, the line at Starbucks. I can see where you'd want to rest up for that."

I scurry back to my room, certain I've narrowly avoided making the worst mistake of my life. But then I lie awake, twisting in the sheets, wishing that, just once, I could stop being so fucking responsible.

❧ 28 ❧

Light is filtering through the windows when I wake. I push the hair out of my face and roll to look at the clock on the nightstand.

8:32.

It's a punch to the stomach, remembering. A year ago, nearly to the minute, my father was in the car with Charlotte on the way to get donuts. It was his idea, of course—he'd use any excuse to get his hands on junk food—but he said it was to get Charlotte more practice behind the wheel.

I picture his heart attack from her vantage point, again and again: panicked and inexperienced, with no idea how to help him and unable to find a place to pull over. She hasn't been behind the wheel since.

I assume there will come a time when I can think of my father without imagining his last moments. When I can remember him and feel happy instead of lost. But it's probably a long way off.

I release a single slow breath, waiting for the grief to lessen, and then I throw off the covers and force myself to move on with my day. I rinse off quickly before donning a T-shirt and shorts and brushing my teeth. My hair remains unruly and I refuse to do a thing about it...I'm on vacation after all. Plus, I secretly suspect Hayes is the sort who likes things a little untamed.

"Rise and shine, pumpkin!" I call as I venture into the living room. "It's time for Starbucks!"

He wanders out in shorts and a T-shirt, hair rumpled and deeply in need of a shave, sweetly sleepy-eyed. He yawns, stretching his arms over his head, and I picture waking up to him just the way he looks now, though in my imagination both the shorts and shirt are entirely absent.

Great. It's not even nine AM and I already need another shower. As cold as possible, this time.

"I was sort of hoping you'd surprise me by getting the coffee before I woke," he says, taking a seat at the counter. "I really hope Starbucks isn't the extent of today's plans."

I roll my eyes. "You know this is *supposed* to be my weekend off. Maybe I figured you'd entertain yourself."

"I did that last night in the shower. Now I want *you* to entertain me."

I laugh, unwillingly, but not before I picture it in all its hard, wet, soapy detail.

Whoa. Down, brain.

Hayes jerking off in the shower is not where I need my thoughts focused today. "Fine. We're going surfing. I know you'll claim you're not interested, but Matt and I went a few times and I think you'll like it."

"I suppose *Matt* was extremely good at surfing," he says, his lip curling.

"He was kind of good at everything," I reply as I head to the door. Except it no longer feels true. I'm mostly saying it to annoy Hayes...which it does.

"I can think of one or two things he wasn't so good at," Hayes mutters from behind me.

At Starbucks, the line takes longer than it should, thanks to the woman taking ninety minutes to choose a cake pop.

We get our drinks, and he stirs in his very own sugar like a big boy. "So," he says, glancing at the door, "we're about to experience the magic of walking outside. Will it feel like absolute inner peace or more like an orgasm that lasts and lasts?"

My shoulders sag. I'd hoped to make Hayes see the value in time off, but how can I when he's hell-bent on proving me wrong? "I knew you'd be an asshole about it."

I walk out without him and turn my face to the sun. The air smells like scrub oak and primrose, the weather is perfect and I have a day at the beach ahead of me. It will have to be enough, whether Hayes is grousing the entire time or not.

He comes up beside me, and his arm brushes mine.

"I'm having fun, Tali," he says softly. "For some reason complaining to you about things I don't actually mind is just my favorite thing to do."

It's not an apology, but it's close enough and something inside me warms a little.

"Better than banging three girls at once?" I nudge him with my shoulder.

He looks around. "Is that an option at the moment? Is *that* what you meant when you said we're surfing? Because if so, I'm one hundred percent in."

"Sadly, no," I reply.

"Alas," he says. "But yes, this will be fun too."

***

I ARRANGED FOR THE SURF INSTRUCTOR TO MEET US OUT IN front of the property at ten. I slip on my bikini, grab sunscreen, and wander to the deck where Hayes is already waiting.

His eyes roam over me—face to chest to legs, back to the chest where they remain. My body reacts to his obvious approval —skin tingling, nipples hardening under my bikini top. I try not to squirm, to let him see how his attention affects me. He turns away and I see him adjust his shorts. I like that I affect him too.

"I kind of figured you for the sporty-swim-shorts-and-tank-top kind of gal," he says.

"The surf instructor is bringing us wet suits. Otherwise, you'd be correct."

He turns and his eyes flicker over me again, and linger. "Probably for the best. That top looks like a light breeze could send it flying."

We walk down a flight of the stairs to the beach, where Gus, our young, shaggy-haired instructor, waits. We struggle into wetsuits and then he makes us practice popping up on the board until he's deemed us ready to paddle out.

He nods toward the surf and leads the way, but Hayes hesitates, looking from me to the water. "You're sure you're going to be okay? Those don't look like pygmy-size waves."

I fight an affectionate smile as I nod. In every important relationship I've ever had—with Matt and with my family—I've been the rock, the one who worries, not the one who is worried about. It's a role I think Hayes would refuse to let me play, and there's a part of me that is so, so tired of playing it, that wishes badly I could lean on someone the way my family leans on me.

I catch a few waves while Gus helps Hayes. After several false starts, Hayes manages to stay upright for a solid ten seconds. Within an hour, he's better at it than I am.

We're straddling our boards and staring at the horizon, waiting for the next set, when Gus points ahead of us.

"Whales," he says, and they emerge not thirty feet from where we sit. Out of nowhere, grief hits. It was a dream of my father's, to go on a whale-watching tour and for a moment I allow myself to think of him here with me. The sun on his shoulders, the water lapping at his legs, a huge smile on his face as he enjoys the wonder of it all. I pinch my lips together and swallow hard as a sharp pain pierces my heart.

Hayes says nothing, but he reaches out and pulls my surfboard so we are side by side, knees bumping, as they pass.

"Are you happy?" I ask quietly.

His hand rests on my knee, making small circles with his thumb. "Very," he says. "We should do this again."

I glance up at him and his mouth lifts, one dimple blinking to life. It's a perfect moment at the end of a very imperfect year. I'm not sure my father would approve of Hayes, but if he's watching, he's probably smiling despite himself.

❧

"YOU'RE GOING TO RUIN YOUR APPETITE," HAYES SAYS WITH A sigh, eyeing the large slice of apple pie I've cut myself. He's stretched out on the chaise—already irritatingly tan while I've been applying SPF 50 every hour this afternoon to keep from burning—and being awfully judgmental for a guy who just bought his weight in baked goods last night.

"Ruin my appetite for *what*?" I counter. "I assume we're eating Pop-Tarts for dinner. At least this has fruit in it."

He snatches the fork from my hand and pops its contents in his mouth. "We've got dinner in an hour down the street. And the place is nice" —his eyes trail over my bare stomach, lingering on the side tie of my bikini bottoms for a moment —"so you might want to be slightly less naked than you are."

He made us a reservation. I stick the pie in his lap and jump to my feet. I have no idea why, as I rush inside to shower, I'm smiling as wide as I am.

I take my time getting ready before donning a strapless white sundress. I dab my lips with a rose-tinted balm and get a good look at myself in the mirror. The girl who smiles back at me— the one with glowing eyes and sun-warmed cheeks—looks like she's on the cusp on something big, something exciting. I try to remind her she's not, but it's hard not to feel like this is a date when I walk out to find Hayes waiting in the living room, his eyes consuming me as I approach.

His teeth sink into his lip and I feel a stab of desire so sharp I almost stumble from it.

It's not a date, but if it were, I'd press up close and whisper in his ear, suggesting we cancel dinner entirely. Then I'd press my lips to his jaw just to feel that five o'clock shadow of his against my skin. I'd finish unbuttoning the shirt he's got on, running my hands down his chest, letting my fingers trace all the hard hills and valleys of his stomach before they trail lower...to his belt, which I'd rip loose so fast my speed would shock us both.

But, of course, this is absolutely not a date.

"Let's go," I say. "Since someone ate all the pie."

His mouth slips into a smile. "I believe that someone is you."

"I'm just pointing out that pie is no longer an option," I say, lips twitching. "I'm sorry you feel the need to assign blame."

We walk two blocks down to the restaurant, which is ocean-front and insanely expensive. He orders a bottle of wine that is worth more than my car—not that that's saying much—and tastes like happiness in liquid form.

Dinner is served while we watch the sun dim and then set in an explosion of reds and fiery orange. He eats off my plate and I eat off his. *Not a date*, I remind myself. *Definitely not a date.*

"What an amazing day," I say, twirling pasta around my fork. "I can't remember the last time I felt this relaxed."

I wish we were staying longer. Or never planning to leave at all.

He leans back in his seat, holding his glass of wine to his chest. "Was a day with me better than a day with Matt?"

It's so weird how competitive he is with someone he's not actually competing against. "Anything with you is better than it was with Matt." My reply is instant, as I reach across the table to take another bite of his risotto. "Don't get too flattered. I've finally realized he wasn't all that great."

"I could have told you that within thirty seconds of meeting him. Men like him want to be the center of someone's universe and look elsewhere the minute they're not."

I lean toward him. "You date all these girls who act like you're a superhero. Is that so different?"

"I date women who don't expect anything, and the rest of it... just comes with the territory. You don't actually think that's what I want."

It's not a question, but a statement. And he's right. I don't think he enjoys the way women treat him. He simply chooses women who understand what he's willing to offer and who, I suspect, won't make him want more either.

It will never make him happy.

But I could, a voice whispers.

What a ridiculous, dangerous thought to entertain.

A waiter clears our plates, but we nurse the last of the wine, neither of us in a rush to leave. It feels, here, as if he's mine—the pleasure of his words and his smile and his gaze. I try to ignore the part of me that, increasingly, wants more. Wants to feel the rough press of his skin, his weight above me, hear the sounds he makes when he's losing control.

The adorable elderly couple at the table opposite us is served a large bottle of champagne on ice and they then rise and bring it to our table. "We're celebrating our anniversary, but we can't drink this alone," the man says. "Do you mind if we join you? My wife keeps talking about how much you remind her of us when we were younger."

Hayes and I share a glance—he looks as reluctant as I do to give up even a minute of our time alone, but it would be almost uncivil not to agree. "Of course," Hayes replies, his smile forced.

They introduce themselves, and then Jacob, the husband, calls the waitress over for glasses while Hayes asks Barb, the wife, how long they've been married.

"Fifty years," Jacob answers for her. He looks at our hands. "How about you two? I don't see any rings."

"Oh," I say, startled. "We're not—"

"Tali's my assistant," Hayes says smoothly. Why do we sound like we're lying? Probably because you don't have a romantic, oceanfront dinner on a Saturday night with your assistant.

"I know what it looks like, but neither of us are married or anything," I add hastily. "I thought he needed a break from work, so I arranged this, and he doesn't know how to get his own groceries or coffee, so he made me come with him." My words come out rushed, nervous.

It still sounds like we're lying.

"Would you rather swallow ten large spiders or sleep in a bed of rats?" Jacob asks suddenly, filling our glasses.

We look from him to each other. "Spiders," we both answer simultaneously.

"Okay, you can only bring one person with you to an uninhabited island and you have no way of leaving. Who do you bring?" he asks.

My eyes flicker to Hayes, who's already looking at me.

"I'd have to bring Tali, obviously," he says. "I can't make my morning smoothie on my own."

I laugh. Only on Hayes's uninhabited island would there be electricity and a Vitamix.

"Tali?" Barb asks.

I grin at my boss. "That's a very hard question. I'd have to give it some thought."

"You know you'd pick me," Hayes argues. "Who could possibly be more fun?"

I shrug. "My niece is pretty fun."

"You'd knowingly choose to make a young child suffer on an uninhabited island solely for your amusement?" he scolds. "With no access to health care? An uncertain food supply? And you call me a narcissist." His eyes sparkle with amusement.

"Only behind your back. And I was under the impression this island somehow had a bounty of organic vegetables and Vitamixes, but you've made a good point. I'm more willing to make you suffer."

We both laugh, and it's only then I see Barb and Jacob staring at us again, wondering what our deal is.

"Well, if you're both single, why on earth aren't you together?" asks Barb. "You'd make the cutest couple."

I feel as awkward as a twelve-year-old sitting beside her crush. I couldn't look at Hayes right now if my life depended on it.

"Tali doesn't trust men," says Hayes. "And I am wholly untrustworthy. That pretty much sums it up."

There's something in his voice that draws my gaze to him, and for a single moment I see hunger on his face, stark and desperate. As if it's only the presence of others that keeps him from pushing up my skirt and taking me right here on this table.

I would let him.

Jacob starts talking about how poor they were when they got married: all the canned tuna and potatoes they ate, the car door tied shut with a rope. I am barely listening, watching Hayes instead. If he were mine, I would have no recollection at all of tuna, potatoes, or how we kept a car door shut. I'd only remember wanting him closer and closer, until I couldn't tell where he began and I ended. I'd suffocate to death trying to get more and more of his gloriously smooth skin.

I'm still fantasizing when Barb coughs politely and tells her husband it's time for them to go. I wonder how obvious my thoughts were.

We stand, and Barb hugs me. "Even if you don't trust men," she whispers, "this one's a keeper."

She obviously doesn't know much about Hayes's careless approach to women. But then again, as he stands there watching me with that look in his eye, he doesn't appear all that careless to me either.

※

WE GET BACK TO OUR RENTAL AND WALK OUT TO SIT IN THE double chaise, where it's silent but for the crashing waves and the incessant call of crickets. Our night here is ending, and we leave in the morning. I want to dig in my heels and refuse to go.

"In a perfect world, I'd stay in this house and never leave," I tell him.

I see a flash of his dimple. "Would I be here with you? Before you answer, let me remind you I'm good at buying pie."

"Hmmm, true," I agree. "And Pop-Tarts. I suppose you'd have to stay."

There's silence. I lean my head back and shut my eyes. As much as I love this house, it's Hayes that's actually made me happy here. If I were to create a Tinder profile now, I'd seek... him. Mischievous eyes, a willingness to always say the rudest possible thing, a mouth that twitches when he's trying not to smile. Someone who holds my door without thinking, but is happy to slam it in my face if it will make me laugh.

We only have two weeks left before Jonathan is back full-time. I wonder if it bothers him at all. I wonder if the thought of it makes his heart clench the way it does mine, if it sometimes hurts to breathe when he considers it. Doubtful, when he doesn't even know I'm leaving for good. He's never asked where I'll go when Jonathan returns, and I never volunteered it. I guess there was this small part of me that just wanted to see every possibility played out. That wanted to see how things might be with us if I were able to stay.

"And in your ideal world," he says, "would Matt be here too?"

I stretch and roll on my side to face him. "I swear you talk more about my ex than I do. Do you want me to set you two up? Is that what this is about?"

"I'm just wondering to what extent you're over him," he says. His voice is quieter than it was, less certain. "And don't reflexively tell me you are. I saw the way you looked at him that night, Tali."

Has he been thinking, all this time, that I still want Matt back? "I was just shocked. It was the first time I'd seen or talked to him since the breakup, and I felt like such a failure by contrast. It wasn't about missing him."

"You must miss him a little," he argues. "He's basically the only person you've ever been with."

I think about this. "The things I miss are pretty stupid. I miss having someone to eat with, someone to talk to while I brush my teeth at night. I miss having someone who will listen to the stupid stuff that happens each day, the stories that don't really have a point."

"I feel like much of what you say is pointless, if that helps?" he asks, and I kick him. "At least he was so deeply unsatisfying in bed you don't have to miss *that*."

"I never said it was deeply unsatisfying," I argue. "But I guess it's nice not to have the pressure." This grabs his attention. He turns his head to look at me, and his body follows, adjusting his position so he is on his side.

"What pressure?" he asks.

I flip onto my back. "I'd need a lot more alcohol to discuss that comfortably."

He grabs the bottle of wine and refills my glass.

I take a heavy sip, wishing I'd had more to drink before this discussion began. Or that I hadn't said anything to lead to it in the first place.

"It bothered him," I begin haltingly. "It bothered him if I didn't...finish...which I often didn't for the reason I mentioned earlier. He took it personally, so I was always kind of worried."

"Lots of women don't come through intercourse. Why didn't he just go down on you?"

The ease with which he suggests it, as if it's the most obvious thing in the world, plucks a string in my core. I picture it. I picture Hayes like that...how open and shameless he'd be.

God.

"What?" he asks. "You can't come that way?"

"I have no idea," I groan, as I cover my face with my hand, humiliated. "And I can't believe we're discussing this. I've only slept with two people, and neither of them tried. It doesn't matter. It probably wouldn't work anyway."

"It would work," he says. His voice is low and raspy. I shiver at the sound of it. "I could make you come in two minutes flat."

My gut clenches. I picture him sliding down between my legs, pushing my thighs apart. The rasp of his scruff against my skin, that first flick of his tongue... *Stop thinking this way. There will be other men in the future. It just can't be him. It'll ruin everything.*

Hayes is perfectly still beside me, silent. I'm about to brave looking at him, but I'm scared of what I might see.

And then his hand circles my wrist. "Tali," he says quietly, pulling my hand away from my face. "Let me." The look on his face is almost pleading, but there's desire too.

His smell is everywhere—ocean and soap and fresh air, making it impossible to think.

I stare at him, my tongue darting out to tap my lip as I hesitate. I know what he's asking, and I know it's a terrible idea. "I don't want to mess up—"

"It won't," he says. "It won't, I swear. You don't have to touch me. Just let me do this. Let me be the first."

I've never heard him like this before. I've never seen him act like he really wants something, and wants it badly. I'm shocked by how compelling it is.

I don't think I'm capable of turning him down when he asks like that.

"Only this," I whisper. "Nothing more. And it all goes back to normal in the morning. We're friends again. No weirdness. Promise?"

His fingers push into my hair, and he turns my face toward his.

"I promise." He grabs the wine glass out of my hand, putting it down on the little table to his right, and then comes back to me. His hand rests on my waist, face inches from mine and I suck in a breath at his closeness. He glances at my mouth and for one endless second, I think he will kiss me. He swallows and then his lips move lower—to my jawline, then my neck. They linger there and he breathes deep, as if I'm wine he's just decanted. Already I'm arching toward him, like a flower toward the sun.

I feel the flutter of his pulse beneath my palm, faster than normal. His hand moves up my body, skimming my breast. He runs his fingers along the top of my sundress, dipping for a moment into the cleft between my breasts.

"This," he says quietly, his eyes never leaving me, like I'm a meal he's waited a lifetime for. "This made me crazy all night."

Grasping the fabric, he slowly lowers my dress down to my waist, freeing my breasts to him completely. His quiet groan grazes my skin, pebbling my nipples, and he traces one with an index finger before his mouth lowers to grace it with a gentle kiss.

I arch upward as something bursts open inside me. My blood is racing, my body taut and reckless.

"Oh," I gasp. "That..."

I can't really form the rest of the sentence, and I don't need to. He knows. He knows I need more, that suddenly I need *everything*. He does it again, using his teeth this time. A pulse beats in my core, insistent and demanding. My knee bends as my foot slides up the back of his leg, in a silent plea for action.

I want to tell him to forget about his plans. I want to reach for his belt and pull him inside me. But already he's noticed the way my skirt has fallen to my waist, exposing me. His hands trail along my inner thighs and then he pushes my legs apart, his eyes following their progress as if the Holy Grail is at the end of their path.

And then his fingertips press against my panties.

Oh. Even that tiny brush of his fingers is waking something up in me, something I'd almost forgotten existed. My eyelids flutter closed, but not before I see him watching my reaction, avid and satisfied.

His index finger hooks under the elastic and drags along my core. My head falls backward, arching my neck. "Oh, God," I whisper. *But what if it doesn't work?* the voice in my head echoes. I don't want him to look at me like Matt used to afterward, silently resentful.

"Stop thinking, Tali," he whispers, pressing his lips to the soft skin of my inner thigh. "This is just you and me, no one else." He strokes me again. "Do you feel my fingers against you?"

I swallow as he refocuses my attention. The calloused pad of his index finger brushes against my clit before it slides lower. That tiny brush lights me on fire. I'm not sure it's even possible to worry when he's doing what he is right now.

"Yes." The word is breathy, desperate.

His mouth moves up my thigh, his shoulder forcing my legs further apart, allowing him more access. He presses his lips to my clit, outside my panties, before pushing the panties to the side entirely and swiping his tongue over me, top to bottom.

"Jesus, you're so wet right now." He glides his fingers up and down, and then pushes one inside me, to emphasize his point. I let my knees drop open even more, encouraging him. His fingers circle my opening and I groan out loud before he slides two fingers inside me, his tongue continuing to flicker over my clit in the most torturous way.

It's unlike anything else. I rock my hips against his fingers as he starts to move them in and out of me. I'm not even going to last a minute and I *want* it to last. I want him to keep doing exactly this until we have to check out in the morning. Preferably, until I have to move home.

His thumb replaces his mouth on my clit as he applies more pressure and my head starts to spin. My breath comes out in small gasps, in rhythm with the thrust of my hips. I hear him moan and the clank of his belt as it falls open, followed by his zipper, and then...the sound of his free hand, moving over his own length.

My eyes open to watch him. His mouth is slightly ajar, his gaze dark and drugged, his grip on his cock so tight it looks painful.

That's all it takes.

Every muscle in my abdomen pulls tight. "Oh, God," I whisper. "I'm gonna come."

He buries his face between my legs and licks hard as I arch against him with my hands in his hair. Fireworks explode behind my eyes as I finally let go, crying out as the entire world falls away. He doesn't let up for a moment until I reach down to wrap my hand around the one currently gripping his cock.

"Come here," I gasp, and he knows exactly what I mean, rising quickly, climbing over me to press his cock to my lips like he'll die if he doesn't get it there soon enough.

"I'm close," he hisses, as my tongue slides over him. "Oh, fuck, I'm so close."

I take him as far as I can, my fist sliding over his base, and when I pull hard with my mouth, he inhales sharply. "Coming. *God.*"

He starts to pull out but explodes before he can, and I wrap my hands around his hips, holding him where he is, taking everything he gives me.

He finishes with a low, delicious groan of relief, the most gorgeous sound I've ever heard him make.

He's breathing heavily as he collapses, his head on my chest.

"Holy shit," he gasps. "I think I understand why your ex came so fast."

Before I can laugh, he's pulled my mouth to his and he's kissing me hard, urgently, the same way he did between my legs. It's not what we agreed to, and I just don't care.

Once. It could mean one time, or it could mean one *night*. We can't really make things worse, and...I want more. His mouth lowers, pulling at one nipple and the other. He's already hard. I can feel him there, swollen against my inner thigh.

"Condom," I gasp. He reaches toward his shorts, still hanging off his thighs and grabs his wallet. He tears the packet with his teeth and raises above me to roll it over his—predictably huge —length.

"Are you sure?" he asks, positioning himself between my legs.

The way he's looking at me right now—as if this is all he wants in the world, hits me deep in my gut. I feel empty for him, and my hips arch, pressing him into me before I've ever answered.

"Jesus, Tali," he whispers. "I've wanted this for so fucking long."

He thrusts inside me, and I'm suddenly full, so unbelievably full. My gasp is small, almost inaudible, but he hears it.

"You're okay?" he asks. His voice is tight. He's not moving, trying to let me adjust to his size.

"Yes." I'm breathless as a sprinter. "God, yes. The, um, rumors were true."

He gives a quiet, pained laugh, and then he begins to move. *Push in, slow drag out. Repeat.* I want to do this for the rest of my life. This and nothing else.

"It's so fucking good with you," he hisses, moving faster, his tight control starting to lapse. I love seeing him like this. I love that I'm capable of producing it in him, this lack of restraint. His fingers move to my clit, light but fast. He changes the angle of his hips and thrusts hard, hitting deep and in just the right spot.

"Aahh."

Something opens up inside me, and no sooner has he begun than heat rushes up my body, my muscles stiffen, everything wound so tight I feel like I might snap in half.

"I'm gonna—" I gasp, and then I clench around him and my head digs backward. My back arches, pushing my breasts into his chest, intensifying my orgasm as I spasm around him, my core gripping him tight.

"Fuck," he hisses, his thrusts jerky and hard and uneven and perfect. "*Fuck, fuck, fuck.*"

Finally, he's still above me, breathing hard. When his eyes open, he looks as stunned as I feel. I'm not sure why. Surely this wasn't as radically different for him as it was for me.

My God. To think I almost went through life without this. Without even knowing it could be this way.

His lips find mine once more before he flops to my side and pulls my head to his chest.

"I'll show myself out," I mumble against his shirt.

His chest rises with a quiet laugh. His arm tightens. "I knew you were going to say that."

And then there's silence.

I still want more. But he just came twice in a row, and he's gone quiet...undoubtedly because he assumes I'm now planning our spring wedding and choosing our children's names. Any minute now, he'll say something to place distance between us, to remind me what this was.

The mere thought of it makes my stomach drop. I need to extricate myself before it happens. I don't want this to be awkward for either of us.

I sit up and fix my dress. "I'd say 'let's do this again sometime' but I know that's not your M.O."

"Rushing off?" he asks. "Am I the new Brad Perez?" It's phrased like humor, but there's a bite to it. As if it bothers him, when we both know I'm simply saving him the trouble.

"Who will kick me out in the morning if I'm not available to do it?" I ask, climbing to my feet. There's this desperate thing inside me that wants him to say *this is different, I wouldn't kick you out, I want you to stay*.

"I guess I deserved that," he replies. It makes me feel guilty, like I aimed too low, but it's not as if he's stopping me. It's not as if he can argue I'm wrong.

My tread is heavy as I enter the house, like I'm fighting my way through mud. I wish I hadn't rushed off. All I want in the world right now is to be curled up against him, and I just walked away from my only chance to do it.

As Matt said at the end, maybe I'm not as smart as I think.

I OPEN MY EYES TO THE SKY ALIGHT WITH THE COLORS OF THE sunrise. The soft bed sheets wrap around my legs from a restless night's sleep. I can still remember the feel of him above me and in me, the sound he made when he came. The way he looked— mouth open, eyes squeezed tight, head thrown back. One day, the memory of him like that will dull, and it's probably for the best because right now, it's almost too sharp to bear.

My skin smells like him. My lips, and other areas, are sore from him. I feel him everywhere, and the only way to recover from this is to wash it all away and start fresh.

I shower, lathering my sensitive skin in soap to disguise his scent. Once I'm dry, I pull on shorts and a tee, throw all my shit in a bag. As much as I love this house, I just want to leave now. I need to move forward, as soon as possible, and I don't think I can do it here.

He's already in the living room, already showered. I don't think he's ever woken before me in his life, which means he's probably as desperate as I am to get through the awkwardness of our trip home.

"Aren't you the early bird?" I ask. My good cheer sounds as forced as it feels. "Sex with me transformed you into a new man. I assumed it would."

His jaw tightens. "I didn't figure you for the type to be so...uncomplicated the morning after."

I go to the kitchen and start unloading the dishwasher, clanging flatware and pans as if I don't have a care. "Best just to put it out there. Otherwise, it turns into The Thing That Shall Not Be Named."

He comes to the other side of the counter. "I *did* figure you for the type to work a Harry Potter reference into any given conversation, so that lines up."

I can tell he's watching me. I continue to focus on the dishes, as if the task requires all my attention. If our eyes meet, he'll see every single thing I'm feeling. He'll see I'm the stupid girl who wants more when she should know better.

"Now I just have to decide what I should say on the flowers I send myself."

"And you'll want breakfast, too, I imagine. Will Starbucks suffice?" he asks, tying off the trash bag. "Probably not. I'll get you a gift card. Applebees? That seems like a place a person from Kansas would enjoy."

I started this, but I'm a little stung that he's replying in kind. The dumb teenage girl inside me wanted him to hold my face lovingly and explain how much it all meant to him. And maybe if I stopped being so offhanded about it, he *would*. But I feel too raw for that. I just can't. I need to protect my heart.

"I'm deeply impressed by your thoughtfulness," I reply. "I'll frame it as a permanent reminder. Although testing positive for syphilis in a few weeks will probably be permanent enough."

He sets the trash by the front door and returns. "As far as I can recall, we were careful. And I'm clean."

"That you just referenced a sexual encounter with '*as far as I can recall*'," I reply tartly, "indicates my concern is valid."

The kitchen is spotless. I'm forced to meet his gaze at last. His eyes are dark, and his face is drawn. I wonder if he ever went to sleep at all.

"I remember, Tali," he says, his voice quieter, more earnest, than normal.

I swallow. "Yeah, me too," I whisper, reaching for my bag.

This is precisely what I *didn't* want—the awkwardness of *I know you want things from me I can't give*. It's not how I pictured our trip ending.

ॐ

THE DRIVE HOME IS FINE. HE DOESN'T SEEM TO MIND MY running commentary on every car and building and view we pass, which I find absolutely necessary. If I'm silent, I start looking at his profile and remembering the scrape of that jaw against my thighs, the way he'd push in hard and drag out slow, eyes shut as if I was expensive scotch, meant to be savored. The sounds he made as he came. Oh, God, I hope I always remember the sounds he made.

We finally reach my building. As uncomfortable as the morning has been, I don't want to leave his car. I'd take discomfort over being apart from him, hands down.

I force myself to open the door, and he climbs out too. The air no longer smells like him. Santa Monica suddenly seems like it's nothing but pavement and reflective surfaces, and I'm not sure I've ever felt more alone.

"Thanks for bringing me," I say, swinging my bag over my shoulder. "It was fun."

"I'm glad you came," he replies. Our eyes meet. "That wasn't meant to be a double entendre."

I laugh. He beat me to the joke.

By the time I reach the stairs, he's driven away, probably eager to put this behind him. I get to my apartment, collapse face-down on the bed, and cry like a child.

How is it possible I got over ten years with Matt more easily than I did ten minutes with Hayes?

L atte? *Check.*
   Smoothie? *Check.*
   Stomach in knots? *Also check.*
He looks like garbage when he gets downstairs—either tired or hungover—albeit garbage I would eat with a spoon and lick thoroughly afterward.

His eyes flicker to me and rest there for half a beat before he forces a smile. I know it's forced because his mouth curves upward on both sides, the way a normal person's might, but his lips are tight. No dimple. No teeth.

"Advil?" I ask.

He gives a small shake of his head. "I don't drink before surgery days. You know that." There's a sharpness to his tone that takes me aback. He hears it too. "Sorry. I couldn't fall asleep last night."

I slide him the schedule just as he reaches for his vitamins and our hands brush. I snatch mine back as if I've been burned.

He sighs and runs a hand through his hair before he grabs the smoothie. "I'll drink this on the way," he says.

Well done, Tali, I think. *You've driven the man out of his own home.* As if I needed further proof it should never have happened.

People only recover from what Hayes and I did in movies. Otherwise, they're exactly as we are now...slowly backing away from each other until a safe distance has been established, until they're far enough apart to pretend it never was.

Our trip to San Francisco next weekend is promising to be the most awkward two days of my life.

❧

HE DOESN'T TEXT ME ALL DAY, AND I DON'T TEXT HIM. I watch for it, of course, like a lovesick teen, wanting even the smallest hint that we haven't ruined everything. When he finally calls that afternoon, just as I've finished up his errands and am nearly back to his house, I want to weep with relief as I answer.

"What are you doing?" he asks.

"Busy serving your every whim as always," I reply. Awkward silence falls in the space where he'd normally growl *you're not serving all of them* or *if every whim is on the table I have a new list.*

And my heart stutters in its absence. "This is why we shouldn't have slept together," I tell him as I reach his street. "You're holding in all your dirty jokes. You probably don't even know what to say instead."

"Sorry. It's hard to revert to *mild* sexual harassment now. I'd kind of need to go straight to major, lawsuit-worthy harassment at this point." I turn into Hayes's driveway and slow when I see a bright yellow Ferrari sitting there.

I stop entirely when Matt climbs out.

"What the fuck?" I gasp.

"What?" he asks. "What's wrong?"

"Matt's in your driveway," I croak.

"Your *ex*?" he demands. "Stay in the car, Tali. He has no right to show up at your place of employment. I'm calling the police."

"Don't do that," I reply, easing off the brake and pulling up to the front of the house. "It's not like he's dangerous. Let me get rid of him."

I end the call and climb out, more irritated than nervous. It was bizarre, unexpected, to run into Matt at that party, but that he's here on purpose is...a little creepy.

His mouth slips up into that lopsided grin I used to love. I don't smile back. The part of me that once hoped he'd at least apologize is long gone. Now I just want to get rid of him. "What are you doing here?"

He leans back against the Ferrari, untroubled by the lack of welcome. "How else was I supposed to reach you? You've been blocking my calls. I was worried."

"Worried?" I repeat, slamming the door shut behind me. "Your concern is coming a year too late. But I've never been better, so I guess you can be on your way."

He shoves his hands in his pockets, pretty brow furrowed. It's almost comical how childish he now seems, in contrast to Hayes. "Look, I thought you were just working for this guy but fuck...you went *away* with him for the weekend? What the hell are you even thinking?"

I freeze. I didn't tell a soul about this weekend. Not my family, not even Jonathan. "How do you know about that?"

"I've been having him followed," he says without a trace of guilt. "I didn't trust his intentions."

I release the air I was holding in a single, dumbfounded laugh. "Holy shit, Matt. Are you serious right now? *You* cheated on me while I was burying my father."

"I cheated *once*, Tali, because I had too much to drink. I let the fame go to my head. I can admit that. But this guy...it's what he's *known* for. And maybe I didn't catch him at anything, but have you seen how many women's homes he enters over the course of a day? You really think he's not fucking someone in one of them?"

I'd probably have said the same, last winter. Now I know better. "I've never seen him be anything but unfailingly honest and level with every single person he encounters, myself included," I reply. My arms fold across my chest. "And what you don't seem to get is that I didn't end things with you because you cheated. I ended them because you never fucking believed in me. You told me I wouldn't have gotten the book deal without you, remember? And the minute I started to struggle, you told me to give up. I would never have done that to you."

He hangs his head, ashamed of himself. Or perhaps merely pretending to be. He's an actor, after all—I imagine he's relatively good at faking emotion by now. "You're right, okay? I shouldn't have said it. But you know what? If you'd ever told me to give up, I wouldn't have *dumped* you over it. I'd have argued. The real problem is you don't believe in yourself, and you were scared I was right."

My stomach sinks as the words hit home. I've spent a full year thinking I need to prove him wrong about me without ever asking why I cared what he thought in the first place. Maybe it was never *his* mind I was trying to change.

"I didn't come here to fight," he says softly. "I miss you."

"I don't miss you," I reply. I'm not even saying it to hurt him. It's simply the truth. I missed the idea of Matt and the security of having someone, but I'm not sure I ever actually missed *him*. And I'm certainly not missing him now. This conversation is just making me ashamed I stayed with him as long as I did.

He laughs, incredulous. The arrogance that seemed to take hold in New York has clearly flourished here. "I don't believe you. What could this guy have that I don't?" he demands.

"Brains," I reply. "And morals." Height and a big dick, too, but I manage to keep those to myself.

His response is cut off by the man himself, who flies into the driveway, stopping beside us with a screech of brakes and a haze of dust.

He jumps from his car and moves toward Matt at a pace that would scare almost anyone.

"This doesn't concern you, asshole," says Matt.

I hear more than a little false bravado there. On screen, Matt looks every inch the superhero. In real life he's five ten, a hundred and sixty pounds, and Hayes looks like he could break him in half, one-handed.

"You come onto my property to ambush her and want to tell me it doesn't fucking concern me?" asks Hayes. "Think again."

Matt's mouth twists. "Oh, so you're the big hero now? I know exactly what you are, and on your best day, you're still not good enough for her."

"I'm well aware I'm not good enough for her," Hayes growls, pushing Matt against the Ferrari, "but *this* stops now. If I ever hear of you approaching her like this, in public or in private, I will fucking ruin your life, and don't think for a minute I can't."

Matt feigns boredom, even though he's very clearly outmanned. "Tali, call off your watch dog."

Someone once told me hatred isn't the opposite of love...apathy is. I get that now. Because I don't want revenge or anything else. I just want him to leave.

"Please go," I reply. "I'm not interested in anything you have to say."

"Are you serious?" Matt asks. "You think this guy is a better option? He'll have dumped you in a week."

Before I can reply, Hayes's fist flies into Matt's face.

I'm as stunned by it as Matt clearly is, wide-eyed, blood pouring from his nose. I'd have thought Hayes more the type to wound with a few cutting words, or a well-timed lawsuit.

Matt pulls his T-shirt up, trying to staunch the flow of blood. "If my nose is broken, the studio will take you for everything you're worth."

Hayes releases him with a shove. "You're on my property, asshole. Good luck explaining how you're the victim."

"Tali—" Matt says, still certain I will intervene on his behalf, as if all my love for him still rests inside me, and will now come blazing forth in his defense.

I shake my head. "You'd better go before he hits you again. Or I do."

"You're making a mistake," he says, climbing into his car.

It's a relief to realize as he drives away that I just don't care.

Hayes turns and takes a step toward me before coming to an awkward halt.

"How did you possibly get here so fast?" I ask.

"Some traffic laws were broken," he says. "But I was worried about what he'd do. Plus, you hung up on me which was, by the way, a fire-able offense, but I'll let it go this once."

I smile. "Just this once?"

"Yes, we seem to do a lot of things just once, so why not add this to the list?" He places a hand at the small of my back. "Come on. Let's have a drink on the terrace. A shrill little person I know has been insisting I need more sunlight."

I'm ushered through the house and out back, where he pours me a glass of red, watching me carefully, still concerned. Because he puts me first, even when he's pretending he isn't.

Matt breezes through life on his sweet smile, and people take him at face value, no matter how petty and selfish he is. Hayes goes through life wearing this mask of indifference, of smug certainty and hauteur. People take that at face value, too, never noticing the ways he is gentle. Never quite seeing he's also the same man who pushes an adoption through for an assistant, who jumps on a trampoline with his half-sister, and rushes out of his office to defend an employee.

"Matt's been having you followed," I tell him. "I'm sorry. I had no idea."

"*Me?*" He freezes, the bottle of wine held in midair. "Why?"

"I think he was looking for evidence you were 'cheating' on me. I guess we're lucky he didn't catch Miss *It's So Big* here."

"Still calling her that, are we?" he asks, sinking into the seat next to mine. "I rather thought you'd stop, having said something similar."

I release a shaky laugh. "It sounded cooler when I said it."

Our eyes meet and the air between us seems to heat. It feels as if we are back there—the weight of his body pressing me into the lounge chair, him thick inside me, struggling not to come. I look away as I try to scrape the image from my head. It feels like I can't get a full breath.

"About this coming weekend," he says. His voice is gravelly, less certain than normal. "If you're uncomfortable..."

"I'm not," I reply, too quickly. "I want to come. *Go*, I mean. I want to go."

Awkward.

Our eyes meet again, and I wonder if we will ever get back to normal.

And I wonder if I want us to.

❧ 30 ❧

Five days later, I'm flying business class for the first time in my life. Any awkwardness between us is briefly overcome by the sheer pleasure of it.

"It's a *bed*, Hayes," I whisper. He's been working steadily since we got on board, while I've done nothing but mess with the seat, play with all the buttons to see what each one does, and unwrap all the complimentary goodies they gave us—once again making it amply apparent why one of us is wealthy and one of us is...me. "My God. Why don't I have this at home?"

He raises a brow. "You don't have a *bed*?"

"Of course I do. But I don't have a seat that *transforms* into one." I push the button until I can lie flat. "No wonder so many people try to join the mile-high club. These seats are made for it."

His eyes flicker over me. I wait for him to make a lewd offer and instead he returns to his laptop. I hate that there's no sly grin, no innuendo. All signs indicate he got it out of his system last weekend, while for me it's like a virus that's replicating in every cell.

I wish I hadn't run off last weekend. I wish I'd kept him up all night long.

I wish I was brave enough to tell him I want more.

⚜

THE CONFERENCE PLANNER HAS PLACED US IN A TWO-BEDROOM suite. It's a romantic room, with a shared balcony overlooking the Bay of Alcatraz. Hayes appears as surprised as I am by the configuration, so I guess that means he didn't suggest it.

My phone flashes, a reminder of the voice mail my mother left while we were in the air, which I'm ignoring until Hayes leaves. I confirm that all the handouts made it safely, change clothes, and then the two of us walk back into the elevator—him, pressed and perfect in a designer suit; me, in shorts and an oversized college sweatshirt, looking like someone's kid.

"Are you sure you don't need me to do anything today?" I ask.

He shakes his head. "As long as the handouts are here, I'm fine. What do you have planned?" He's speaking to me like a polite stranger, one who isn't really interested in the question he's asked. I catch his eyes flickering down to my sneakers and back in the mirrored door.

I hand him my map, highlighted in advance with everything I want to see.

"I'll be back in time for dinner," I tell him, and then silently curse myself. Maybe he doesn't want to have dinner with me. Maybe he's eating with colleagues and now will feel compelled to bring his lame, underdressed assistant along. "I mean, unless you have other plans."

His tongue darts out to tap his lip. "I don't have plans. But don't rush back on my account."

We are being too tentative with each other now, and I miss the old Hayes, the one who would bombastically demand my free time as if it were his due. We should never have slept together, and you'd think with as many times as I've had this thought over the past week, I wouldn't still be letting myself fantasize about him at every turn.

We exit the elevator, and he's stopped by someone he knows just as my mother calls again.

I turn away from Hayes, walking toward the tall palms that divide the lobby from the downstairs bar. When a parent calls twice in a row, you probably ought to answer...even if it's *my* mother in question.

"It's about time," she says by way of greeting. "I met with Dr. Shriner this morning, and she told us you're moving home for good. I can't believe you're going along with this nonsense. Shriner has no right to keep Charlotte there. None at all. She's bluffing."

I close my eyes, trying to rein in all the other words I want to say: *Dad never would have abandoned his duty the way you have. He'd never have put me in this position.* "Mom, it's not about whether or not she *can*. It's about the fact that she doesn't think you're up to the job."

"Because I won't go to AA!" she yells. "Which I don't need!"

I no longer know what to believe. It's hard for me to truly imagine my mother is an alcoholic, the way you see them in movies and cop shows. But it's getting increasingly easy to believe she's not the best person to care for a fragile child.

A bell rings signaling the start of the keynote session, and suddenly a herd of people is moving behind me toward the ball-room doors. I need to end this call.

"Look, I don't care if you need it or not," I snap. "But the fact that you won't listen to Shriner at all means she's definitely right about one thing: I have to move home because you are not willing to do what's best for Charlotte."

I hang up and turn to look for Hayes...only to find him standing right behind me looking stunned. And *stung*.

"What the hell is going on?" he asks.

This is not the way I want to be telling him. And not now, when he's about to go into a conference for an entire day and we can't really talk.

"I...I'm, uh, going home next month. To Kansas. My sister's doctor is requiring it."

He stiffens. "For how long?"

I glance away. "I don't know. I guess until she graduates. I don't see my mom stepping up and there's no other option." My teeth grind as I say it, making the words sound more defiant than forced.

He pushes a hand through his hair, his jaw clenched tight. "And you never managed to tell me this?" he asks, his voice rough. "I see you every day, and you never managed to tell me you're *moving*?"

I want to claim it never came up, but it did. He's brought it up repeatedly, and I thought I could simply ignore the problem until it solved itself. "It's not like we were going to be hanging out together in a month anyway." I sound like a child, trying to defend the indefensible.

His nostrils flare and his eyes are darker than they've ever been, all pupil. I've never seen him so angry before.

"That," he says, turning to walk away, "is absolute bullshit."

As I walk the streets of San Francisco, a sick feeling settles in my belly.

Would Fisherman's Wharf—loud and crowded and slightly tackier than I expected—excite me if the conversation with Hayes didn't just happen? Perhaps not, but it wouldn't feel like *this*, as if I can't see anything clearly, as if my stomach is folding in on itself and I can't quite take a full breath. I should have told him. He knows almost everything else about me, and I concealed this from him intentionally, for reasons even I can't fully acknowledge.

What upsets me most about all this is simply that he knows. Because it means I can't keep pretending—to him or myself— that I'm able to stay.

My feet are throbbing and my shins ache once I get back to the hotel. I shower and collapse into the soft chair on the balcony in my robe to wait for Hayes. There's a naïve part of me that hopes he'll simply be over the whole thing so we don't have to discuss it.

When I hear him enter the living room, I call out. He comes to the sliding door, eyes flickering over my robe and wet hair.

I don't know where we stand. My lips open, on the cusp of offering a reluctant apology, when he speaks instead.

"How was it?" he asks.

Relief rushes through me. Maybe we can keep pretending. Maybe we can go to dinner and things will feel normal again. "Good, but I've still got a lot more to see. I hope you weren't planning to make me do any actual work tomorrow morning."

"I generally try to assume you won't be doing any work whatsoever," he replies coolly. "That way, my expectations are met."

He pulls off his jacket and slumps into the chair beside mine. I pour him a glass of wine, which he accepts but doesn't drink. Instead, he stares off at the water, his expression pensive. Perhaps we aren't as good as I thought.

"How was your conference?" I ask. "Are you ready for your big talk?"

He rubs his temples. "I just wish it was over."

Hayes is so smugly overconfident most of the time. It never occurred to me he wasn't every bit as blasé about this talk as he is everything else. "You're *nervous*?"

"I'm just tense. It's fine."

"What helps?" I ask.

His eyes flicker over my face, remain a half second longer on my lips. My nipples tighten under his perusal. "Exhausting myself."

I can think of so many ways we could accomplish that. But there's never been a greater distance between us than there is in this moment.

I climb to my feet and stand behind him. Back in New York,

I used to give Matt a massage before auditions. I even took a massage class for him, which seemed loving at the time and now seems kind of pathetic.

"Here," I say, placing my hands on his shoulders, which are...so fucking nice. Broad and rounded muscle, perfect for anatomy drawings and *Men's Health* covers. I begin to rub.

"Tali," he says, a warning in his voice. And then he groans. "My God. How are you so good at this? I'd have had you do this every day if I'd known."

"It's not a standard thing I offer employers, oddly enough. But I guess that argument no longer applies given that I don't usually blow my employers either."

He lurches forward, out of my grasp, elbows on his knees and his head in his hands. "Jesus Christ," he says. "You need a warning bell on your mouth sometimes."

I stand frozen, my hands hanging in midair.

He runs a palm over his face and climbs to his feet. "I'm going to call the concierge about dinner. What would you like?"

Focus, Tali. Be normal. Save this. "I—" My mind is absolutely blank. "I've, uh, heard there's good Italian in North Beach."

His eyes narrow. "Who told you that? *Sam?*"

I blink. Yes, of course it was Sam.

He takes one look at my face and sets his drink down on the table so hard the glass splinters. "Fuck," he hisses. He pushes both hands through his hair and then glares at me. "You know what I'd like to know?" he asks. "How long you've been keeping all this to yourself. How *fucking long* have you known you were leaving and failed to mention it? Did you know when Sam was here? Has that been the plan all along—move home, settle down with your dull old mate?"

I want to be mad at him but feel some inexplicable urge to cry instead. I swallow hard. He has no right to make me feel bad about anything. "How could it possibly matter?"

"Don't give me that shit," he says. He takes one long step

toward me. I step back to the wall, and he closes the distance. "You know it matters."

My heart is thumping so loud it's audible, echoing in my ears. "I—"

His mouth lands on mine, rough and unrestrained, as if he's been pushed slightly too far. And all the tension I've held for the past week—tension I didn't even know was there—snaps loose and unfurls like a sail in a storm. I've dreamed about those minutes on the deck, have woken each day feverish and desperate for more. And I've spent a week hating myself for the way I ran, like a coward.

I lean in to him, giving in to all his frustration and my desperation. My fingers grip his hair, pulling him closer, deepening the kiss even more. His jaw scrapes my skin and his lips move over my neck. He slides one hand inside my robe, the heat from his palm gliding along my torso, to the underside of my breast. My nipples tighten so hard they ache.

He started this, but I take over, pulling him through the balcony door, my eyes never leaving his face. He looks as hungry, as desperate for this, as I feel, and I don't stop until I have him in my room, where I shove the suitcase off the bed with a clatter. I half expect him to laugh at my haste, but instead, he lays me down on the duvet and looks me over like a feast he's about to devour.

He unbuttons his shirt and wrenches his belt free. There's no hesitation, no uncertainty. The pants fall, and then he's standing before me in nothing but boxers, the thick swell of his cock jutting against them.

I'd be a little intimidated now if I didn't already know how perfectly he'll fit.

He climbs over me and traces a path—clavicle, sternum, down to the sash which he flicks open with a single finger.

And then his lips find mine. I wrap a leg around his waist, pushing my hands into his hair. When he starts to slide lower, I stop him. "No," I whisper. "I want you inside me."

He winces. "I'm not going to last. Let me—"

"Make it last the second time." My voice is husky, made confident by sheer desire.

I arch upward again, and he inhales sharply. "Fuck," he groans, squeezing his eyes shut. "Wait." It sounds like he's speaking to himself, not me. He climbs from the bed and is back seconds later, throwing his travel kit on the nightstand, pulling a condom on.

He lines himself up with my entrance and slides the tip over me once before his hips push forward. He seats himself inside me, all the way in, thick and hard and perfect. His eyes are feverish, at half mast. "I'm going to need more than a second time," he warns.

Good.

Slowly he pulls out, dragging over nerve endings that have never been as sensitive as they are at this moment. I'm tight as a clenched fist around him.

There's that ever-present part of me that wants to know what this all means, or how it will end. But then his hips snap forward and I gasp as if I've been impaled. It's too good for me to worry, it's too good for me to think.

His head lowers, pulling my nipple into his mouth with his tongue, catching it with his teeth, and he pulls out again and again, snapping back hard. I can feel the coming explosion already. A small twinkling star at the base of my stomach, spinning and unfurling. "Faster," I hiss, and with a groan he complies, moving ruthlessly in and out.

I come so hard that the world goes silent and dark, that it takes me a second to even realize he's above me, his thrusts jerky and violent. "Fuck," he hisses. "Fuck. It's so good with you. I can't—" he gasps, and then he goes still above me.

He falls down to the mattress and pulls me against him. "*Bloody hell*, Tali."

His chest rises and falls, breathing heavy as we both take a moment to recover.

"Should I joke about ordering my own flowers, or do you already expect that?"

His mouth nuzzles my neck, nipping at the skin. "After last weekend, post-coital awkwardness on your part is kind of a given."

"On *my* part?" I pull up, elbow in the bed, to look at him. "You've been the one with a stick up your ass all week. Today especially."

"Because I was *trying* to fucking behave," he growls. "And then you drove me off the edge, talking about blow jobs whilst rubbing my shoulders." He pulls the sheets away from my body, rolling me to my back, and begins to slide downward. His lips press to my hipbone. "I never imagined we'd wind up in bed thanks to a fight over *Sam*."

"No?" I ask. "What did you imagine?"

"You have three holes. The permutations are infinite."

I laugh. "Not really, unless you're imagining Angela and Savannah with us too."

He looms over me, pinning me to the mattress as his mouth moves to my neck. "As I've told you before, I'd never be willing to share you." He doesn't look away as he says it, sincerity written all over his face. And some of the barriers I've built around my heart crumble, though I wish they hadn't.

⊱✿⊰

IT'S THE MIDDLE OF THE NIGHT AND I'M ABSOLUTELY exhausted but too exhilarated to sleep. He's been silent long enough that I suspect he's dozed off when he speaks, suddenly.

"When would you have to leave?" he asks. "To get your sister."

I'm glad the room is pitch black. It feels safer, somehow, discussing this in the dark. I suspect he's still mad about the way I handled things...or failed to handle them. I'd be mad too.

I roll toward him and rest my head on his chest. "She's

supposed to come home the third week of August, right before school starts."

"Surely there's some other way to handle it," he says. "Unless you *want* to go. She can't just come to LA?"

Beneath my head, his heartbeat is strong and steady. He's a rock, and I wish with all my might that I could keep leaning on him the way I am now. "It's her senior year of high school. I can't uproot her, and she needs someone there who actually cares about her and will listen. If I can't trust my mother to do it, I'm definitely not trusting a stranger."

He's quiet, and I brace myself, wondering if he'll tell me this can't go anywhere. And hoping at the same time he'll tell me it can.

"I felt blindsided today," he says instead, his voice low and reluctant. "It was like Ella all over again, waiting in the apartment when I got home from Ohio, saying she didn't want to tell me over the phone."

I hear the pain there, the wound I reopened with my stupidity. "I'm sorry. That's not what I intended. I just kept putting it off, I guess. I thought if you knew, it might change things."

He pulls me beneath him, and his mouth grazes my neck. "It appears to have changed things," he says, with a quiet laugh.

Yes, I think, *but for how long?*

WHEN I WAKE, IT'S LIGHT OUT, AND HE'S SHAKING MY shoulder.

"Tali," he says, "our flight leaves in just over an hour. Our car will be here in fifteen minutes. Can you be ready?"

I'm so tired it feels like I'm swimming through water as I try to form words. It was after dawn when we finally fell asleep, and he's making no sense. "Our flight's not until two," I slur.

"It's twelve forty-five."

"Oh my God. Your speech!" I bolt upright. Surgeons came

from all over the country to hear his talk, and if he slept through
it...

"All behind me." I suddenly realize he's wearing a suit and
appears very relaxed. "But I got stuck down there afterward, and
now we're cutting it close. Can you be ready, or should I change
the flight?"

I fling myself out of bed, freaked out enough not to worry
that I'm running across the room butt naked. "How did it go?" I
shout as I climb into the shower, shuddering at the blast of cold
water. "Were you nervous?"

"I was too exhausted to be nervous," he replies, coming to
the bathroom door. "Congratulations on finally making me feel
my age."

"You stay up all night frequently," I reply, frantically soaping
myself. The water still isn't warm. "Don't blame that on me."

He laughs under his breath. "We had sex *sixteen times*, Tali,
and as you love to point out, I'm ancient. I probably won't be
capable of having sex again for a month."

His words sink in my stomach with an audible *plop*. A piece
of me waited all last night for something to indicate this wasn't a
one-off. Mostly I was too busy enjoying him to think it over, but
now that I am, now that I search all the words he *did* say, I find
nothing. *Wet, tight, hot,* and *hard* are great in the moment, but
they're not really the stuff of wedding vows.

He was stressed about his talk, and he wanted to exhaust
himself. Mission accomplished for one of us. But there were
things I wanted, too, things I was stupid to have even hoped for.
And I will need to let them go.

I'm ready to leave quickly. Hayes takes both our bags as we
go downstairs to checkout. "We hope you'll join us again," the
clerk says.

"I'll be back in October, actually," Hayes replies. He doesn't
say *we'll* be back. *He'll* be back. My chest aches.

"I'm going to find the car," I tell him quietly. I reach for
my bag.

"I can get that for you," he says.

"I have it," I reply.

I spent last night hoping for a happy ending, and now it's time to pay the price for that. Although I want more, I have to be realistic with my expectations. I'm not some cosseted princess who lays about in a plush bed ordering room service and being pleasured. I'm a desperately poor twenty-five-year-old with a book she can't finish, a family she can't fix, and a commitment-phobic boss she might be in love with. And it's best if I allow reality to intrude right now, because it always intrudes eventually. Hayes might not be capable of giving me more. And maybe, at the moment, I'm not capable of it either.

☙ 31 ❧

Monday morning, I'm full of adrenaline and dread.

The trip home to LA yesterday was silent, and awful. He asked if I wanted to come to his place when we arrived, the question so forced it was painful to listen to. I told him I had to do laundry, and we haven't spoken since.

When I arrive at Hayes's house, I find him downstairs already, looking less pulled together than normal. He's wearing scrubs instead of a suit, and his hair looks like he's run his hands through it once too often. I want to ask him what he's thinking, but I'm not brave enough, and he's in a rush anyway.

He grabs his coffee as he rises. "How was your night?" he asks abruptly.

I swallow. "Good. Yours?"

"Fine." His mouth closes, then opens, then closes again. "Can we talk later?"

My heart starts to hammer in my chest. *Can we talk* is never good. It's like "no offense, but…" or "with all due respect…": a warning you won't like what you hear next. I give him the smallest nod imaginable in response, my stomach in knots, but I pull myself together quickly. I knew this could be Hayes's reaction to our situation and for both our sakes, I have to accept his choice.

I'm not the same girl who was devastated when Matt cheated, nor am I the one who snuck out of Brad Perez's house and ghosted him for a full month after. I can survive whatever Hayes has to say ...but I'm glad I've got the rest of the day to psych myself up, because at present, the specter of it is making me a little sick.

I dump out my coffee and get on with my day. I've been at work for two hours when the doorbell rings, and I find Jonathan standing there with Gemma on one hip. In spite of my foul mood, I smile at the sight of them together. "You look like an old pro."

"*Old* is the keyword, because I feel extremely old," he says, putting Gemma down. She promptly runs in a wobbly toddler style for the stairs, and he lunges to catch up with her. "I'm aging about a decade per week. Keeping her alive is a full-time job."

"Huh. Not water once in morning, prune weekly like you thought?"

"Ha ha," he says without humor. "She has a death wish. She can't go two seconds without pulling a chair on top of herself or trying to scale a bookcase."

I scoop her up and bounce her on my hip while Jonathan sinks into the couch. "You don't know how good it is just to sit," he sighs. He closes his eyes. "I love her to death, but it's exhausting caring about someone all the time."

How exhausting is it? I wonder. Is it so exhausting that he wants to return to his job early? This was always his life, not mine, and I was lucky he let me be a part of it, but I really need time to set things right with Hayes.

"If you want to come back early," I say quietly, unable to meet his eye, "I understand."

He leans forward, pressing his elbows onto his knees. "It's kind of the opposite. Now that I'm home with her, I can't imagine working those hours anymore. In an ideal world, I'd come back part-time. I know you're going home, but I wondered if you'd want to stay on part-time until you left."

Would anything change between me and Hayes if I stayed on? Probably not. I'm still leaving at the end of August, and that's not enough time to build something lasting. But already, I feel myself growing weak, longing for a shot at something I want, no matter how unlikely. My breath releases in a long, resigned sigh as I contemplate it.

"What's going on, Tali?" he asks.

I meet Jonathan's eye. He's known me nearly as long as Matt has, and probably knows me far better. I'll wind up telling him the truth eventually, if he doesn't guess it outright. "I like him. I like him in the very way you warned me not to."

Jonathan's smile is soft. "I never warned you not to *like* him. I warned you not to bang him and sneak out like you did to Brad Perez."

"Why would you care?" I ask. "You couldn't have been worried that *I* would hurt *Hayes*?"

He hesitates. "Because I saw the potential in you both for more. And nothing could ruin that faster than another of your grisly one-night stands, or his. I wanted you to get to know each other first before one of you could hit the self-destruct button."

"You almost make it sound like you did this intentionally," I say. "Like that's why you hired me."

And in response, he is silent.

My gaze jerks from Gemma, toddling in front of me along the glass coffee table, to her father. "Oh my God," I whisper, staring at him. I couldn't understand why Jonathan had been so devious in hiring me, and now, at last, I do. "You hired me on the *off chance* that we'd fall in love? Did you even adopt Gemma, or is she just a prop baby you're borrowing for this?"

He laughs. "I didn't leave the country for two months solely to set you up with my boss. I'm not *that* much of a romantic. But, yeah, I thought there was a chance."

I pinch the bridge of my nose. "Why? I was a marginally

employed bartender with a bad attitude about men, and Hayes is...well, he's *Hayes*. The two of us together make no sense."

He shrugs. "He was so smitten with you that night in the bar, and when I told him to back off because you'd had a hard year, he *did*. He actually cared about you, even then, more than he cared about himself."

"So that really happened." I whisper the words in disbelief. Sure, I heard Hayes say as much at the party...I suppose I didn't want to let myself believe it was true. "But he doesn't want a relationship."

"From the sound of it, Hayes is already *in* a relationship." Jonathan's mouth tips into a smirk. "*Laguna Beach*, Tali? And before you claim you were just assisting him on vacation, let me tell you how many *vacations* I've taken with Hayes in the two years I've worked for him."

I want, so badly, to believe him. But it will only lead to me being more crushed when I discover he was wrong. I need to protect myself. I've come a long way since Matt broke my heart, but with Hayes it would be so much worse.

"That doesn't mean he wants a relationship. That doesn't mean he wouldn't freak out if he thought this *was* one. And I can't just wait around for him to be ready, because that might never happen."

He nods. "So, I should look into hiring someone else?"

I can't stand that either. I can't stand to imagine some knock-out who looks like Ella here in my place every day. I bury my face in my hands. "I can stay on part-time until mid-August," I say. "And after that, can you only interview men?"

"Oh, Tali," he croons, as if I'm a child who's skinned her knee. "Maybe by then it'll all have worked itself out, and it won't even matter who I hire."

I allow the tiniest part of me to hope he's right, to trust in some future point, weeks and weeks away, where Hayes magically fixes everything or I find some way to fix it myself.

And then that hope dies when one of the nurses at Hayes's

office texts me, saying he's sewing up right now and wants me to meet him in an hour. *It's best to never end things on the property, in case they refuse to leave*, he once said.

Apparently, it's my turn. The only surprise is that I didn't see it coming sooner.

❦

HE GLANCES UP AS I WALK INTO HIS OFFICE AN HOUR LATER. I see fatigue and reluctance in the gesture, which pisses me off. I did everything right. I never asked *anything* of him, and yet, here I am, being treated like some desperate girl with a crush.

"Hey," he says. "Can you shut the door?"

My jaw grinds, but I do as he's asked. He comes to my side of the desk and takes one of the two seats there, turning it to face mine.

His tongue darts out to tap his lip, searching for words. I'm half inclined to tell him not to bother.

"I was performing what is possibly the most complex surgery I do," he begins haltingly, staring at his hands, "and I spent the whole time thinking about this. The thing with us. It's stressing me out."

My eyes close. "I never expected anything from you," I say between my teeth. My throat swells, and I swallow hard. I refuse to cry in front of him, because really, it's entirely my own fault. I gave him so much grief about the way he treated women, the way they might expect things from him, but they were all fine. *I'm* the only idiot he's had to give this speech to. "I thought I made that pretty clear yesterday when I went back to my own place."

"Exactly!" he says, pushing his hands into his hair. "You're acting like I'm some creep you can't get away from fast enough."

I blink. I was expecting complaints about the way I'm wearing my heart on my sleeve and how uncomfortable it is for him...but not this.

"You didn't say a word on the way to the airport," he continues. "You wouldn't even let me touch your *bag*. I ask you to come back to my place, and you say you've got to do laundry. I have no idea what you actually want. Based on the way you're acting, I assume you want nothing at all."

"Does it matter what I want?" I whisper. "*You* don't want anything."

"What have I ever said to lead you to that conclusion?" he asks. "I've spent every free moment I've had with you for *months*, Tali. I've gone out of my way to find excuses to spend time with you any chance I get. I've taken four days off this calendar year, and I spent *all* of them with you."

I place my hands in front of my face. "I'm the person you hired to get rid of girls like me," I whisper. "I was just trying to make sure you didn't have to ask me to go. I knew what this was going into it. I didn't want to put unrealistic expectations on you."

He pulls me onto his lap, and I go willingly—straddling him, finding his mouth. And I don't know how I can miss something I'd barely had until two days ago, but I know it deep in my gut: I've missed this. I've missed him, as if he's a critical organ I was failing in the absence of.

"I can't believe you'd still lump yourself in with them after this weekend," he says, leaning back to grasp my face in his hands. I don't answer, but simply pull his mouth back to mine. His lips slide, then, from my mouth to my neck, with soft, adoring kisses that wind me up in ways he can't even imagine. We've barely begun and already I'm craving more—the scrape of his unshaved jaw against my thighs, him inside me.

I want him so tight against me that not a whisper of space can exist between us, and he is throbbing under his scrubs, which suggests I'm not the only one. I reach for his waistband.

"You were stressed about your talk. I had no idea if it had anything to do with me at all."

"I don't get nervous before speeches," he says, sliding my

skirt up my thighs to my waist, his fingers slipping inside my panties. "You said it, and I let you think it when really, I'd been tied up in knots over *you* all day." His thumb moves in circles over exactly the right spot. "Shit. I don't have a condom."

"I do," I say on a gasp, reaching for my purse without leaving his lap. He raises a brow—wondering why the girl who sleeps with no one has a condom. "Don't judge me. I like to be prepared."

He tears the wrapper with his teeth and rolls it on. "For now, I'll just be grateful."

Pulling my underwear aside, he lifts me enough that he can free himself from the scrubs and his boxers. I reach between us and grasp him. He's heavy in my hand, hard as nails. My thumb brushes over that vein pulsing down his length, and his eyes squeeze shut. "I'm not going to last," he says. "*Again.*"

I'm not quite recovered from the weekend. The fit is so tight it hurts as I slide down him, but it's the best possible kind of pain, the kind that has you thrusting your hips forward for more.

His eyelids lower as if drugged, but beneath them, his eyes are fever-bright. His mouth falls open. "I've thought about nothing but this for twenty-four hours," he says between his teeth.

Obsession like this is a fleeting thing, but I'm not going to worry about how long his interest will last. I'm just going to relish every minute of it while it does.

❧ 32 ❧

Rats die after nine days without sleep. Even allowing for the longer lifespan of humans, I figure Hayes and I have only a few more days before we change or perish. At least I'll die happy.

For five days now, we've been like this. Barely eating, definitely not sleeping, abandoning work the first minute possible. We don't really discuss the fact that I'm leaving. One day he asks if I *want* to go, as if what I want is even relevant. When your family needs you, you step up. He lets it drop after that. He never mentions what happens to us after I leave, but why would he? A guy who hasn't been monogamous in a decade isn't going to suddenly try it *long-distance*. Which is fine, I remind myself. We are having fun, living in the moment. I'm simply enjoying it while it lasts.

I am in nothing but a T-shirt, making him a smoothie, when he gets downstairs. His eyes run over me from head-to-toe, no longer subtle the way they used to be. Under normal circumstances, me wandering his kitchen half-dressed leads to sex on the counter or couch or even inside the pantry, during one especially interesting round. Except today he's already running late.

"You're trying to torture me," he groans.

I laugh. "Is it working?" I turn on his fancy coffee maker—the upside of fucking the boss is that he doesn't want me getting up early to make his Starbucks run anymore—with some excessive leaning over so my ass is on display.

His eyes go dark. "Fuck," he groans. "I'm going to be out of a job if this keeps up."

"You should be out of a job." I stir the sugar into his latte—weirdly, I now like doing this for him—and cross the kitchen with it. "Yours makes you miserable."

"Despite what you may think," he says, "I'm not independently wealthy. I do need to work."

"But you hate house calls, and you seem to dread half the surgeries you do," I argue. "If pediatrics is what inspired you in the first place, maybe that's where you're meant to be."

His jaw shifts. "I don't think so."

He takes a sip of his coffee and I wait. I've found with Hayes that sometimes silence, rather than badgering, is the best way to get information from him.

"All I remember from that period of time when Dylan died and Ella left, other than the guilt, is feeling terrified of going through it again," he finally says. "I don't need that kind of pressure."

I lean forward, drawn by the possibility of finally getting to the heart of this. "Pressure?"

"The pressure of caring so much."

I'm not sure if he's talking about the pressure of caring about his patients, or the risk of loving another person. I suspect it's both.

"Hayes," I say, my voice quietly pleading, "I'm not sure feeling nothing at all is really a better option."

I want him to agree with me. To tell me what we have is different. A smarter girl would probably make note of the fact that he doesn't.

ON MY LAST FULL-TIME DAY, JONATHAN COMES BY TO GET THE phones. For the next few weeks, he'll handle the calls and schedule from his house while I deal with everything else.

If it were up to Hayes, I'd do no work at all, and he's said as much, but getting paid by a man to wander around his house naked feels like a turn in the wrong direction, and I still have enough free time after I run his errands to get some writing done. There is no more time spent staring blankly at my laptop —the words are flying now, because I've finally realized this book is not Aisling and Ewan's love story. Theirs was the love of children, not adults. It's Julian and Aisling who pop off the page, whose every clash comes through with a flash of color, a burst of sound. It's their story now, even if it wasn't when the book began.

I've just finished writing the sex scene—it's mild enough for a young adult novel but still has me worked up—when Hayes texts from his car, saying he's done early.

Show me what I'm coming home to, he demands.

I kick off my shoes and go to his room, stripping naked and climbing into bed. It's been a long time since I've attempted to take a nude photo. I'd forgotten how hard it is to get an angle without double chins or boobs flopping weirdly, though I feel oddly certain he'd be happy with anything as long as I'm naked.

I send the only decent shot I managed to take, and he texts me immediately, telling me to stay right where I am.

Within minutes, I hear him come through the door, taking the stairs two at a time, then he's standing at the threshold.

"Remove that sheet," he growls, looking me over in a way that gives me the best kind of chills.

I comply, and his gaze devours me as he moves to the foot of the bed. He wrenches his shirt off, all clenched muscles and urgency. The pants follow. My legs spread as he climbs over me, bracing on his forearms, his mouth pressed to mine.

I will never tire of this, I think, as I look up at him. Hayes, open to me, eyes heavy lidded as he pushes inside me.

You won't get the chance to tire of it, some cynical voice in my head counters, and I will it away. Our time is fleeting and I refuse to let the truth ruin everything.

An hour later, I've come more times than I can count and am curled up against him. These moments are my favorite: the smell of his skin against my nose, his hand smoothing over my bare back, the way he seems so completely content. I'm nearly lulled to sleep by exhaustion and the rise and fall of his chest when he speaks.

"When do I get to read your book?" he asks.

The question wakes me. I'd never even considered the possibility, nor do I want to. Reading a story that parallels our time together would tell him so much more about how I feel than I'm ready for him to know.

"Never," I reply.

"Why?" he asks with a hint of a smile. "Because I'm Julian and Matt is Ewan? And if Ewan is actually *Sam* I'm going to be *really* put out."

His arrogance, so infuriating once upon a time, just makes me laugh now. Besides...he's right. "What makes you think Julian's *you?*"

"Tall, dashing, irresistible. Obviously, it's me. Although I can't believe you named me *Julian*. Couldn't it have been something manlier—Steve, perhaps, or Chuck?"

"Yes, both Steve and Chuck totally sound like popular names for fae royalty in the 1800s." My hand glides over his chest. I bet he can go one more round before dinner.

"At least tell me how it ends, if nothing else."

My palm goes flat and still. "I don't know how it's going to end yet," I reply, quieter now.

Aisling does not end up with Ewan, but I still don't see how she can end up with Julian either. And the mere fact that I'm struggling to come up with a believable happy ending, when I have infinite fae magic at my disposal, reminds me a happy ending in real life, with Hayes, is even less likely.

❧ 33 ❧

I know better, I do.

I know I can't ask a guy who remains uncertain about commitment where we stand when I'm moving, and I wouldn't have the guts to do it anyway. But that doesn't stop me from hoping he'll bring it up.

I mention Kansas every once in a while, as if the reminder I'm leaving will jolt him into action. And it never does, not once. Yet I keep trying.

"Thai food back home tastes nothing like this," I tell him one night as we share red curry chicken and drunken noodles on his back deck. "It's closer to paprika sprinkled over a chicken pot pie."

This isn't entirely true. I mostly say it in order to mention *home*, the place I'm returning to very, very soon. As if he's going to say *speaking of home, let's talk about how we can continue this when we're far apart.*

"I'm surprised you even have Thai food in Kansas," he says instead.

"You act like I live in Siberia. I'm ten minutes from a college town." And a small airport. "Of course we do."

"You're there a lot, then," he says. There's something hard

242

and certain in his voice that makes it feel as if he's saying another thing entirely, but I have no idea what it is. He pushes his plate aside, the food barely touched, and pours himself a glass of wine.

"Is something wrong?" I ask.

His eyes have gone almost black in the dim light. "It's still unclear to me why all of this is falling on you. You've paid for everything. Why can't your sister step up?"

"Liddie has a kid and a husband in another state. I'm the only one of us who's unencumbered."

He stiffens but doesn't argue. We've only been together a few weeks, with not a word about commitment spoken, so I'm certainly not *encumbered* by him.

"They seem very happy to let every ounce of the weight fall on your shoulders, Tali," he says quietly. "I guess what I'm wondering is why you never object to it."

I feel a pinch of frustration. It's as if he's blaming me for being mature about a situation I can't really control in the first place. "What good would it do to object?" I argue. "Charlotte and my mom are both pretty fucked up by my dad's death and need help. End of story."

"And you weren't?" he asks. "I see the way your face falls whenever I bring up your father."

"I wish you weren't ruining our nice night by bringing it up *now*. Why do I feel like you want a fight?"

His jaw tenses. "I don't. It seems like you're leaving something out."

He doesn't understand because he doesn't really have a family. Neither of his parents have shown him much in the way of loyalty or obligation. And when I leave here, he'll be alone again. That, of all this, is hardest for me. He will probably fill my seat with a thousand Angelas and Savannahs and Nicoles, but I know they won't care about him the way I do. I know they won't fill him the way I do, but I'm not sure he really sees the difference.

We are silent for a minute, him sipping his wine, me pushing around my food while I worry about him.

"Let's go away this weekend," he says suddenly. "I'll do the planning."

My mouth falls open. I can think of nothing I'd like more. And then I smile like an absolute lovesick loon. "What are we going to do?"

"It's a surprise," he says. And for the first time since this conversation began, the light returns to his eyes.

⚜

"WHERE DO YOU THINK YOU'RE GOING?" DREW ASKS ME breathlessly over breakfast in her cottage at the Chateau Marmont—which is far more *1950s traditional* than *celebrity luxe*, but at least the food is good.

"I have no idea," I sigh, digging into my omelet. I've begged, cajoled, attempted to barter. I've walked in on whispered phone calls to Jonathan and Ben, seen papers couriered to the house. It's a whole new side of him—a playful, doting side—and I adore it, even if the mystery is driving me crazy.

"It's sweet, though," Drew says. "That he wants to surprise you. I just want Six to *invite* me somewhere. He doesn't even have to surprise me."

"I thought we agreed you were going to go out and meet someone else and have an amazing time?"

"I can't!" she cries. "Who's going to go out with me, looking like this?" She's convinced she's gained weight, which is why we're hiding out in her cottage—otherwise there will be the inevitable photos, accompanied by a story implying she's broken-hearted. Worse this time, she says, because it's true.

"Anyone in the sane world would go out with you," I reply. "You're gorgeous."

She grabs a croissant and tears off a piece. "Not according to my manager. He wanted me to lose five pounds before my tour, and now I've gained five instead."

I set my fork down. Drew seems to surround herself with people who are awful to her, who say the worst things to her with absolute impunity, things that aren't even true, and she believes every one of them. "You don't need to lose weight. You *do* need to fire that manager, however."

She shrugs. "He wouldn't say it if it wasn't true. It's fine. I'll go on an all-cocaine diet for the next week and the weight will come right off." Her eyes light up, suddenly. "Maybe he's going to tell you he *loves* you this weekend!"

"I don't think you need a lawyer for that." I still have no idea why Ben's involved.

Her eyes grow wide. "Maybe he's going to *propose*. It's a prenup!"

I force a smile. "We're only a few weeks past 'oh good, you got the vomit out of the dress'. I seriously doubt it's anything like you're thinking."

And it would need to be, wouldn't it, to have this all work out?

34

On the morning of our trip, my phone rings early. Too early.

It's barely light out and Hayes, beside me, doesn't even twitch at the sound. I grab his T-shirt off the floor and head toward the stairs.

"Tali?" my mother asks, her voice tremulous and strained, as if she's been crying.

"What happened?" I can barely get the words out. "Is it Charlotte?"

"It's me. I was in a car accident last night and broke my leg. They say I won't be able to drive for months. I know you weren't due home for a few weeks, but I can't even get to the store."

I blow out a breath. If I were a better daughter, I'd go rushing out there. But surely, she can wait until the weekend is over, at least?

"Okay," I tell her. "I'm going away, but next week I'll—"

"I need you here today," she says. "The situation is...complicated."

"Complicated *how*?"

"I'd had a little to drink," she says. "So, I got a DUI and the officer is claiming I hit him and...well, the upshot is that I'm now in police custody and the moment I'm released from the hospital they're taking me to jail. I need you there to post bail."

"God, Mom," I whisper. There's so much to say that I don't even know where to begin. She's the parent. It's not my job to scold her. But how could she have been so irresponsible? I take small, shallow breaths. Blaming her and blaming myself. I'd been secretly hoping she'd pull herself together before Charlotte returned. It was impossibly stupid of me. And selfish. I just wanted that extra time with Hayes so, so badly.

"I'll come home. I'll fix it," I tell her, but something hardens inside me. I always felt like my loyalty to my family was infinite. For the first time ever, I'm seeing an end point. I'll do whatever is necessary for Charlotte, but I'm not sure I'll ever forgive my mother for making me give up what I'm about to.

I hang up and take a long, shuddering breath.

"What happened?" Hayes asks.

I look at his face and want to weep. These weeks have been amazing, but there've been no promises made. I had no reason to be in LA anymore anyhow, and I couldn't ask him to wait for me.

"I have to go home," I whisper. "My mom's broken her leg."

He kneels beside me, still in nothing but boxers. "For how long?" he asks.

He's probably doing the same math I am: wondering how long this would have lasted anyway, wondering if it's worth suggesting we continue.

I swallow. "A long time," I reply. "At least until Charlotte's in college next year."

I bury my face in my hands, and he pulls me against his chest. My tears aren't really about my mom or my sister, because nothing there has changed. I'm crying because this is the end of what I had here with Hayes, and it just feels so fucking unfair.

Eventually, he helps me off the floor and books me on a noon flight home. "Do you need to go to your apartment and pack? I'll drive you there."

I shake my head. "You've got patients. You'll be late."

"I don't, actually," he says. "We were going to leave this morning for our trip."

My heart *hurts*. He's changed so much over the past few months. He's happy, and he's taking time off, and he did this for me and now...what will happen? "What was the surprise?"

He swallows. "I'll tell you another time." I simply nod, too sad to even push him on it.

I let him drive me to my apartment. We climb the stairs, saying nothing. And with every step, I'm realizing all the experiences with him I'll never have again.

He'll never wait at the counter for another smoothie, his gaze on my ass the entire time. I'll never see his face light up as I walk into his office, catch that relieved smile when he sees me waiting for him at the end of the day. Never again will he undress me, growling some complaint about how I'm wearing too many clothes as he moves me toward the bed.

It's all in the past, already, when it feels like it barely began.

When we reach my apartment, I walk in, but he remains at the threshold, rigid. That we are ill-matched has never been clearer than it is now. I'm used to the way I live, but to him, it must look like I'm practically homeless, squatting in a place that's roughly the size of his closet. In his home, I never felt like my debt made me less of a person, but now I'm seeing it through his eyes, and how could it not?

"Now you see why I never wanted you to come over here."

"Why were you living like this?" he asks. "You've been making good money."

"I was saving to pay back the advance if necessary, and pay for the rest of Charlotte's stay. I wasn't joking about all the ramen noodles."

He takes a seat on the bed, shoulders hunched, jaw grim. "Why the fuck didn't you tell me? I would have helped you."

"Because I don't want help," I reply. I wanted it to feel like we were equals, which seems laughable now that he's here. We were never equals.

I pull my suitcases out of the closet and start to pack. He opens a drawer and then stops. "What are you taking?"

"Everything." I don't know why it's so hard to say it out loud. "My lease is up soon anyway. I'll take what I can and see if Jonathan can get rid of the bed."

I want, with my whole heart, for him to suggest an alternative, but the flicker of a muscle in his cheek is his only response. And what could he possibly have said? By the time I get free of my family, there will be nothing here to come back to. No job, no apartment. Hayes will have moved on. And I'll be so grossly in debt I won't even be able to afford a dump like this.

We're nearly done when I get to the beige dress. I'll never even have a place to wear it again. Maybe Charlotte's graduation from high school, or the baptism of Liddie's next child. The only big events I see ahead of me now belong to my sisters, not myself. I'm going to stay in Kansas, living with my mom, and people will reference the one book deal I got like it was my only accomplishment. And all that pales next to the fact that Hayes won't be beside me for any of it.

I find myself pulled against his chest—I didn't even realize I was crying. And it only makes me cry harder, because how many more minutes of this will I have in my life? How many more times will I lean against him and breathe him in, and how the hell am I going to survive without it?

His mouth finds mine, and though I'm embarrassed by my tears, he doesn't seem to mind. There's a desperation to our kiss, but his hands are gentle as he removes my T-shirt and shorts, revealing me as if I'm something to be treasured. He's above me, inside me, when he suddenly stops and holds my hair back from my face, looking at me as if I'm the only thing in the world that matters to him.

And I realize something: I never felt this way with Matt. I never felt content and heartbroken and complete with him. I never felt *seen*. He was never so deep in my blood that I felt his sadness and his joy as if it was my own, as if it mattered *more* than my own.

There wasn't a sign from Matt because he was never right for me in the first place.

And Hayes is, but I've discovered it too late.

❧

WE'RE QUIET ON THE WAY TO THE AIRPORT, HIS HAND TIGHT around mine. He pulls up to the curb and flags down a porter to help with my bags.

It's time to say goodbye, and I'm not ready for it.

My mouth opens but Hayes pulls me toward him instead, his hands framing my face. He kisses me hard, as if he can squeeze in a lifetime's worth of kisses into a single moment. "Tell me what you want," he says.

My throat swells. I want him. I want a life with him here. But even if he agrees to it now, over the course of the next year he'd wind up breaking my heart.

"Nothing. There's no point. It isn't going to happen."

He stiffens, and the color seems to leech from his skin. A part of me wants to take it back, but we're best off being honest about this. I can't ask him to wait a year for me. It wouldn't be fair, and eventually it would feel like one more failure to him, one more way he convinces himself Ella was right when it was never reasonable in the first place.

I go on my tiptoes and kiss his cheek one last time, memorizing the delicate scrape of his unshaved jaw, the smell of his soap, the feel of his skin. "Goodbye. And thank you. I've loved every minute of this."

And then I turn and leave California, and the thing I loved here most, behind.

35

When Matt and I lived in New York City, I used to dream of home, awake and asleep. I dreamed of heat lightning on summer nights, and the way the sky would turn still and yellow before tornadoes rolled in. I dreamed of huge snowfalls in winter, balmy air rolling in through my windows in late spring. Even those fucking box elder beetles that came through every crevice of the house in the summer...I missed them too.

Now I'm back, and it's no longer home. Everything has remained the same—same time-worn carpets and scratched oak table, same beaten-up couch in the family room—but there's no meaning attached to any of it.

There isn't a ton to do, other than taking my mother to see an attorney and getting the house ready for Charlotte's return, yet I feel overwhelmed. So, I ignore Jonathan's texts, and Drew's. I avoid the calls—from old friends who've heard I'm home, from Fairfield, claiming there's a billing issue, from my agent, wanting those last few chapters of a book I can't seem to finish. Most of all, I don't read the gossip blogs. Not a single one of them.

Hayes has texted a few times, asking how it's going. Nothing personal. Nothing indicating we are anything other than distant friends. From the sound of it, his life has gone on as it was. I guess that's for the best, even if I can't claim the same.

Everyone—from neighbors to cashiers to the librarian—asks me if it's good to be back. I have to lie, because I can't tell anyone that home, for me, is no longer a place. It's the sound of Hayes's laugh, and the sight of him brushing his hair out of his eyes, or reluctantly drinking a smoothie he hates solely because I made it for him. It's the way he struggles not to smile when I imitate his accent, his singular willingness to always say the worst possible thing.

Home is Hayes, and I am going to miss him every minute of the day for a long, long time.

⚜

I LIE IN BED ON THE MORNING OF MY MOTHER'S FIRST AA meeting—her lawyer's suggestion, though it's me she seems to resent for it—wishing I could just remain here. Eventually, I force myself to get up, to shower and take out the trash and collect the paper and feed the cat. I even make my mother a smoothie, the way I once did for Hayes.

"What's this?" she asks, pushing it away before I've even answered.

"It's good for you," I reply. "Six kinds of vegetables. It'll help your leg heal."

Her eyes narrow. "Don't patronize me."

I roll my eyes and walk away. It's only when I'm out of sight that I feel tears come. Hayes had every reason to refuse the smoothies, and the vitamins, and the vacation. Instead, he took every single thing I was willing to give. Who's going to make sure he's okay if I'm not there? Who's going to force him to take a day off? Who's going to love him with her entire heart, the way he deserves to be loved?

I grab my phone. It would be pointless, and embarrassing, to ask him these questions. To show all my pathetic cards when nothing can come of it.

So, I ask him in my own *Tali* way—caustically and with little emotion.

Me: **The olives in your martini don't count as vegetables. Just wanted to mention before you revert to your old ways.**

I wait breathlessly for his response, watching those three dots swirl as he types.

And then it comes. A single line that fills me and destroys me at once.

I miss you.

Tears drip down my face as I stare at those words. And they continue to fall as I sit, helpless, wanting to say a thousand things in response. I want to tell him I love him, that I wish I'd never left, that I'd give anything to be back there.

I want to ask if there's any chance he'd be willing to wait for me, but I'm not brave enough.

Instead, I just write **I miss you too.**

I see the three dots again. They disappear and come back. They disappear entirely, and I sit with my head to my knees on the bedroom floor and weep like a kid.

I really wanted him to say something, *anything*, more. But he can't be here, and I can't be there, so what else was there to say?

At least I know how the story ends.

❧ 36 ❧

I'm not surprised when my agent calls to express her displeasure with the book. While it was certainly realistic to have Aisling leave Julian behind at the wall, with everything they felt unspoken, people aren't paying good money for *realism*. Realism and sad endings are something most of us get for free.

"It's not going to fly, Tali," she says. "I'm not saying it's bad. But you sold them a romance, and a story that doesn't have a happy ending isn't a romance."

"*The Hunger Games* and *Divergent* don't have especially happy endings. They seemed to do okay."

"They *had* romances but they weren't *solely* romances. Unless you want to have Aisling actually *overthrow* the kingdom, this book is."

I don't really know what to do without rewriting everything. Aisling and Julian can't end up together: she needs to be home with her brother—it was the whole point of the book—and it would be unrealistic to have Julian come through the wall to her. He's fae royalty. What would he do among humans—*farm?*

I tell her I'll think about it some more.

But the only conclusions I can think of at this particular moment are bittersweet at best.

◈

SAM RETURNS FROM HIS TRIP TO CALIFORNIA AND COMES OUT to see me the night before Charlotte is released. We sit together on the front porch, talking about his trip and potential endings for the book my agent won't hate.

"Maybe there can be someone back home for Aisling," Sam says. "Someone less flashy than Ewan or Julian, and it took the adventure in Edinad for her to see it." His hand covers mine, leaving no doubt what he's really talking about. It's sweet, and if I were going to move on with anyone, it would be him, but I'm not ready for there to be an *us* yet.

"I started dating Hayes," I say. "A few weeks ago. I just want to be honest with you. It's not going to work out with him but I'm...not in a good place right now. It's made coming home a lot harder than I expected." I know the day will come when we will sit on this porch and I'll feel something other than sadness, because humans are made to bounce back. If I can recover from my father's death, I can recover from Hayes too. But it's going to be a while.

Sam gives a short, unhappy laugh. "I can't say I'm surprised. He was jealous any time you even looked at someone other than him. But you must realize that guy isn't waiting around for you out there. He's not the type."

I rub at my chest, at the ache his words create. I'm not sure why they hit me so hard, given it's what I've been telling myself all along too. But even after Sam leaves, I can't seem to get them out of my head. *You must realize that guy isn't waiting around for you.* It's the reason I haven't been returning Jonathan's calls, why I've shut down in so many ways: because I was scared the truth would break me. But dreading the truth is hurting nearly as bad.

"You've been avoiding me," Jonathan says when he answers.

"I just knew how busy you must be." I fiddle with the hem of my T-shirt. "And I felt bad leaving the way I did, when you had no one to replace me."

"I hired someone the day you left," he says smoothly. "Things are fine. Delia, your replacement, is amazing."

My stomach falls.

"Delia?" I ask weakly. I'm not ready to hear Hayes is dating if I can't even stand the thought of a female *assistant*.

"Super competent. MBA."

"That fucking figures," I mumble.

I sink to the floor as I picture her—blonde and beautiful like Ella, good at everything. She comes up with an innovative way to organize his inventory, has better lingerie than I do. Her MBA is, undoubtedly, from Harvard.

"Are you not even going to ask how he is?" Jonathan asks. There's an edge to his voice I haven't ever heard directed at me.

"Are you *mad*?" I ask. "I'm sorry I left the way I did, but you know I had no choice."

"Yes, I'm mad, and it has nothing to do with the fucking job," he says. "How could you leave him like that? Without ever telling him how you feel?"

My throat seems to swell, and it's hard to swallow around the lump there. "Because there was no point. We barely dated. It wouldn't have been reasonable to ask him to wait, and hearing him say so would break my heart."

Jonathan snorts. "You have this set up in your head like you're Little Red Riding Hood and he's the Big Bad Wolf. Has it ever occurred to you he might be even more terrified to trust someone than you are? I know what Matt did sucked, but can you please look at how different that is from having your fiancée leave you for your father?"

"I didn't know it was a competition."

"You're intentionally missing the point, which is that you're acting like you're the only person here who's broken, or vulnerable, and you're not."

The desire to argue with him springs up, reflexively, but my stomach is bottoming out at the same time, because I know he's right. I didn't suffer having the rug pulled out from under me the way Hayes did. I was naïve with Matt, but even if I never admitted it at the time, I knew we were having problems.

"You say all this as if Hayes begged me to marry him and I said no," I whisper. "He didn't say a thing."

"That's not what he told me," Jonathan counters. "He says he asked point blank what you wanted, and you said you didn't want anything at all. While moving twenty minutes away from the friend you planned to date."

My eyes close. It sounds bad, when he puts it like that. Far worse than it sounded in my head at the time. "I was just letting him off the hook," I argue. "I wasn't about to ask a guy I'd barely begun sleeping with to wait a year for me."

"You took the decision out of his hands," Jonathan replies softly, "and maybe you should consider how much that must have hurt. Because no matter how awful you feel right now, *you're* not the one who just got dumped."

I think back to that moment in the airport, and suddenly realize how wrong I was, how sickeningly wrong, because I'm seeing Hayes's face clearly for the first time...and I know he was crushed.

Hayes, who trusts no one, trusted me. He opened up to me and took the first risk he'd taken in a long time. And what he heard in response was that I didn't care enough, that I didn't trust him enough.

I feel like I've been punched in the lung.

"Ask me what the surprise was, Tali," Jonathan says softly.

My eyes close. "What was it?"

"He bought the house you stayed at in Laguna," he says. "He bought it for the two of you. His somewhat inept way of telling you what you meant to him, and what he was hoping for."

I cry for a long time after we end the call, fully realizing how badly I messed up.

Every step of the way with him, I've wanted to avoid pain. I've been the one to jump and run, to make the poorly timed joke before any exchange felt intimate. But I hurt him in the process of protecting myself, and that's so much worse.

The point was never whether or not I could trust again, because love isn't an exchange. It's not something you hand out only if it can be returned in equal measure. Love is handing your fragile heart to someone else because you want him to have it, no matter what he'll do in response. You do it because you love him more than you love yourself.

I couldn't even bring myself to let Aisling, who's *fictional*, take that risk. Maybe it's time both she and I become a little braver than we've been.

I pick up my phone. No matter how Hayes feels about me, what matters is that he knows—if it were at all possible—I'd have chosen *him*.

Hey there, I begin typing, but the tone is too breezy, too conversational.

*So I was talking to Jonathan...*That doesn't work either. I can't soft-shoe my way into this. I need to lay it all on the table.

I told you I didn't want anything, I type.

Really, it was that I couldn't stand to hear you tell me no to the things I do want. I don't expect you to wait for me, so I'm not writing this now asking anything of you. I just want you to know I love you more than I've ever loved anyone.

And then, before I can change my mind, I hit *send*.

The message is delivered. He doesn't have to respond, but if he wants what I do, he simply has to say *let's try*. I see those three dots. He's typing.

Typing more than a simple answer, which isn't necessarily bad, but isn't necessarily good.

They disappear again. Return again. And then they disappear entirely. Failing to answer...is still an answer. And it hurts. My stomach is in free fall. My chest aches, exactly as I knew it would. It's too late.

But I'm still glad he knows.

The next morning, I sit next to my mom on the couch for an online meeting with Dr. Shriner to discuss Charlotte's transition home.

I know I need to focus for my sister's sake, but it's hard to hear anything when my head and heart hurt like this. When, every few seconds, I find myself thinking *I can't believe he didn't write back*. Even if it was simply to politely decline, to tell me he didn't see it working...I really thought he'd leave me with *something*.

Dr. Shriner is reviewing ways to help Charlotte when she's struggling. I feel overwhelmed, listening to it—mostly because I suspect it's all on me. Liddie nods along from Minnesota, and my mom seems focused primarily on throwing out objections as if Dr. Shriner is asking too much of us when nothing matters *except* what Dr. Shriner's asking.

"She's supposed to be applying for college," my mom says now. "She's not going to have a lot of time for therapy over the next few months."

Dr. Shriner, who has remained almost entirely expressionless during the time I've known her, stops just short of rolling her eyes. "Therapy needs to be a priority right now," she says to my mom.

"But college—" my mother begins.

"I'm not even sure Charlotte will be ready to go away for college in a year," Dr. Shriner says.

My mother sits up straight at this, ready to do battle. "She will definitely be going to college." I love how she thinks she can pull off the *concerned parent* routine at this late date. "It's not like she has to be off in a dorm alone. Tali could get an apartment and live with her there off campus."

My head jerks toward her, and for a moment, I wonder if I heard what I did. I paid for Charlotte's time at Fairfield, I'm paying my mom's mortgage, I gave up my life in LA to take care of her and Charlotte this year and now...she wants *more*?

She didn't even ask. She just assumed it would happen, as if I'm some chess piece to move around their board, protecting or attacking when called for.

I wait for someone—Liddie or Dr. Shriner—to object. To say *enough is enough*. But Dr. Shriner simply looks at me with that placid face of hers and Liddie *nods*, looking toward me on the computer screen, as if my agreement is a given.

I laugh, and the sound is distinctly unhinged. "Are you *fucking kidding* me?" I demand.

"What?" my mom asks, turning toward me. "You'll be fine. You can work anywhere." Her tone is so dismissive. As if I'm needlessly whining.

"Let Tali take care of it. Let Tali pay," I reply, my hands pressing tight to my scalp. Hayes was right. I've been shouldering all the weight...and I'm officially done. I lost Hayes, and I'm not giving up anything else. "Your only plan for this family going forward appears to be *me*. Has it ever occurred to you maybe I deserve a life of my own? That I've been living in an eight-by-eight room and eating ramen for a year to pay for everything you all need? What have any of *you* given up?"

My mother and sister are both open-mouthed, undoubtedly

preparing their arguments. And I already know what they'll be: *It's easier for you. You don't have a child, you can work anywhere, you'll figure it out*. And all that may be true, but it doesn't mean it's easy. It doesn't mean I should have to do *everything*.

"Have you expressed these feelings to everyone before?" asks Dr. Shriner.

"I didn't think I had to!" I cry. "I thought maybe they already knew I'm a human being with wants and needs of my own, but apparently that has to be pointed out. And I also thought things would eventually sort themselves out. But they don't seem to be."

There is absolute silence. Even Dr. Shriner looks a little shocked by my outburst, and there's a part of me that feels as if I should back down and apologize, but...no. Hell no. I'm here, and I've lost Hayes, and I'm so sick over it I no longer care about adding my hurt to theirs. I just don't care.

"Families—" begins Dr. Shriner.

"Things always work out for you, though," argues Liddie. "You get scholarships. You date and dump celebrities. You move from coast to coast and get book deals. You just...always land on your feet."

"How is this landing on my feet?" I ask. "I'm alone and living in my childhood home taking care of our mother, a woman who doesn't want to work and doesn't want to stop drinking and is perfectly willing to throw me under the bus. You behave as if everything is so easy for me when the biggest problem you have is that you aren't getting pregnant fast enough."

Liddie's jaw falls. I probably went too far with the pregnancy comment, but at present I'm too irritated to care. She can't selectively name the high points in my life while ignoring the lows.

"Families tend to assign each child a role—" begins Dr. Shriner, but she is cut off my mother.

"Is that really how you see this?" she asks, her voice tight. She is staring at her lap, her hands tightly clasped.

"How could I not, Mom?" I ask. "You take and take, but don't seem to have any plan for yourself. You won't stop drinking even when you know it means I have to move home. How could it possibly be seen any other way?"

She covers her face with her hands, and I feel a tiny pinch of guilt. A voice says *she lost her husband, Tali, cut her some slack.* But what about everything *I've* lost?

"You always seem so strong," she says quietly. "And I'm not. I've never held a job in my life. Who's even going to hire me? And with the drinking...I wasn't trying to force you to come home. But I thought Dr. Shriner was wrong, and it felt like you were taking her side. Why didn't you say anything?"

I try to come up with an answer, but my mind is blank. "I have no idea," I reply. "It just seemed best to keep it to myself."

This is the point where I'd normally apologize. I'd tell Liddie my comment was insensitive. I'd assure my mother that it's fine that I'm here, that I'm happy to help as long as she needs me. For once in my life, though, I stay silent.

"Tali, it sounds like your role in the family is 'the competent one'," says Dr. Shriner, finally able to get a word in edgewise. "The question is whether you want to keep playing it."

I think of Hayes again at the airport and that lost, crushed look on his face I refused to acknowledge. For the past year, I've shoved down everything I felt, like I was a soldier in the trenches just trying to survive. And I took Hayes down with me. "No," I reply, rising, my voice rasping. "I don't."

I walk out of the house and down the street, trying not to cry as I picture Hayes's face at the airport, or the way he looked at me that last time we were together. My hatred for Ella could fuel the state's power grid, yet I was hardly any better to him, in the end. I go up and down the street until Mrs. Deal next door calls out to me from her garden to ask if it's good to be home.

I feel myself gearing up to fake a smile and give her the answer she wants, but quell it.

"At the moment," I reply, "not especially."

I return to the house, fully expecting recrimination from my mother, now that Dr. Shriner is no longer online to witness it. But her shoulders slump when she sees me.

"I'm sorry," she says. "I had no idea you wanted to stay in LA that much. And I did try...I tried to get a job. I sent out resumés, but when I studied marketing, there was no Twitter or Facebook or Google. My degree is useless, and I'm not sure there's anything I can do about that. But I'll try to pull myself together. I promise."

I nod, but my eyes pinch with tears. It no longer matters. Without Hayes to go back to, LA is just a city with better weather and shopping, and I may as well stay here.

❧

IN THE AFTERNOON, I LEAVE FOR TOPEKA TO PICK UP Charlotte, trying to get my head in a better place. For her sake, I need to find a way to fake good cheer.

There is paperwork to be filled out when I arrive, and they tell me—like the vultures they are—I'll need to talk to finance about the billing issue. I'm not in the mood. I wish I hadn't been avoiding their calls.

I'm ushered to a desk where someone named Lisa looks up the chart. "We've called you a few times. There's a credit on the account," she says.

"A credit?" I repeat. It must be a mistake. There's a desperate part of me that is already considering letting them make it—my family needs the money more than they do.

"Right. We were wondering if you wanted it to apply toward the rest of your sister's stay, but I suppose if she's leaving, we'll cut you a check."

I sigh. As desperate as I am, having them actually *give* me money would be taking it too far. "I...think there must be a mistake. I haven't even paid for Charlotte's last month here yet."

She taps something on her keyboard and peers at the

monitor for a moment. "No, her entire stay was paid in full two weeks ago. We were told to credit back to you what you'd already paid."

I blink at her. It takes me longer than it should to realize who paid it. Even after I left Hayes at the airport, saying I wanted nothing to do with him, he still spent almost fifty grand helping me get out of debt.

I'm swallowing hard as she submits a request for the reimbursement check. In an ideal world, this wouldn't be the end of our story. But at least I know he cared.

It will need to be enough.

⚬❧⚬

CHARLOTTE EMERGES FROM THE INPATIENT AREA WITH A WIDE smile, pretty as ever. She seems more like her old self, instead of the pale, destroyed girl who arrived here. A guy is on the other side of the door, watching her with lovesick eyes.

"Who's that?" I ask, nodding toward him.

She waves goodbye to him. "Just a guy who was here," she says. I suspect she has no idea of the effect she has. Of the three Bell sisters, she definitely got the looks.

We stop for Slurpees on the way home. It's what my father used to do with us on the first and last days of school. "Do you think he did it because he wanted to celebrate?" I ask. "Or was it an excuse to have junk food without Mom yelling at him?"

Charlotte laughs. "It was totally about the junk food. Mom said they found like fifteen bags of Skittles in his desk at work. He was *dead*, but she was still so mad."

We start exchanging stories, recalling the time when he couldn't figure out Uber and ended up walking home ten miles because he didn't want to admit it. The way he would demolish half a tub of ice cream and then later claim he'd barely eaten all day. The time he couldn't get the hood of his car open and took a saw to it, destroying it in ways even the autobody shop couldn't fix later.

It's good being able to talk about him like this. Not in hushed, sad tones, and not as if he was infallible. But as the funny, loving, flawed man who raised us. It feels a little bit like getting him back, in an odd way.

Too soon, we arrive at home...to find a tiny orange Ford in the driveway.

"Who's that?" asks Charlotte.

For a single, heartbreaking moment, I wonder if it's Hayes. If he flew out here like the hero of some Nicholas Sparks movie to declare his love for me. And then I laugh at myself. There's no way Hayes would rent an American car. Certainly not an *orange* one.

The door opens, and my niece Kaitlin comes running outside to us, throwing her arms around Charlotte and then me.

"We're here for a whole week, Aunt Tali!" she shouts, squeezing my legs as I lean down to pick her up. I laugh. My chest still aches, but it's hard to be entirely sad when you have a three-year-old wrapping herself around you like you're her favorite teddy bear.

Liddie, who followed Kaitlin out, hugs Charlotte and then gives me a tentative smile. "It was last minute. I hope that's...okay?"

I wince. I took things too far this morning if Liddie feels like she has to ask permission to be in her own home. "I'm sorry about what I said. I know the pregnancy thing matters to you."

She shoves her hands in her back pockets. "Dr. Shriner asked me about it, after you stormed out. She says sometimes people create a problem or throw themselves into a project in order to avoid their own grief. It's possible that's what I've been doing."

"But you're allowed to create projects or problems," I tell her. "Especially if it's what you need to move forward."

She shrugs and wraps an arm around me. "I can probably do it without acting like I'm the only one suffering, though. I'll do what I can to get down here. We're going to figure this out, but all of us, not just you, okay?"

I'm too choked up to do anything but nod.

It's not a perfect resolution, but it's...a better one, and sometimes better is all you can hope for.

My mother starts making cookies with Kaitlin, and I order pizza for dinner. There is noise and light in the house for the first time in ages, and it feels as if we might have all turned a corner, even my mom.

"Should I open a bottle of wine?" she asks.

Liddie and I both turn to her, jaws open.

"Oh, lighten up, girls," she says with a wave of her hand. "It was a joke."

I'm grabbing cash for the pizza when I hear my phone *ping*, and though I know it's probably not Hayes, hope is a defiant little thing. It goes on about its business, no matter how vigorously you insist it shouldn't.

I see Sam's name and my stomach drops a little. A few more moments like this and the hope will start to fade and so will the ache. Eventually, I'll be able to smile at the memories of Hayes the way Charlotte and I did today about my dad. Maybe it will even feel as if it's for the best.

How's Charlotte doing? Sam writes. **Did the trip go okay?**

He really is a keeper. Thoughtful in ways Matt wasn't, and with far more common interests.

It went well, I tell him. **And Liddie is here all week, which should be fun**.

Maybe they can spare you for a night, he replies. **Let's go out for dinner. I know you're not ready for more, but I'm still your friend. And I hate how sad you looked last night.**

I stare at the phone. I'm not ready for more. At the moment it feels like I never will be. But it's one of those times where you see how your story will turn out. Like Aisling, I've learned about love—what it is and what it is not—and I will carry that lesson forward into the next chapter of my life. Someone like Sam is probably the right choice for me. Maybe the day will come when I can look back to this moment and see it was for the best, how things fell apart with Hayes. Right now, though, it just makes me want to weep all over again.

The doorbell rings, and I grab the cash and jog to the front door, where both Charlotte and Liddie already stand.

"Wow." Liddie's got her hands on her hips. "I don't know about this."

"That's fascinating," comes the drawled response. "But it's actually her opinion that matters." The voice is deep, arrogant. *British*.

Hayes.

I push my sisters to the side and the sight of him—thinner and more tired than he ever was before—cracks me wide open. He's suffered every bit as much as I have, and it was all my doing.

I burst into tears, and throw myself against his chest. His arms come around me and I'm lifted off my feet. "I'd hoped you'd be a little happier to see me," he says with a small laugh, burying his head in my hair.

I cling to him as if I'm drowning. "Why didn't you reply?" I ask. "I tell you I love you and then there was *nothing*. I thought...I thought..."

He takes my jaw in his palms and kisses me. He kisses me as if he's starved for me, and that makes sense. I'm starved for him too. It feels as if I'll never get full.

Behind us, though, my family is offering a steady stream of commentary. "Maybe we shouldn't be watching this," says Charlotte, still standing right there in the doorway.

"I *knew* she was sleeping with him," says Liddie. "Little liar."

"Isn't that her *boss*?" asks my mother. "And why's he wearing a suit?"

Hayes flashes them his most charming smile. "I look forward

to explaining everything. But a little privacy, for now?" He raises a brow, and Charlotte finally shuts the door.

He pulls me close. "I'm sorry I didn't reply right away. I had to think."

"How...romantic?"

He laughs. "It wasn't a question of what I *wanted*. I just had to figure out what could be done, how it would work. Because I'm not waiting a year for you to come back to LA."

My mouth trembles. "Things are improving, but I really do have to stay here. Even if my mom sticks with AA and is able to keep her license, I still can't leave Charlotte with her alone."

"I know," he says. He wipes a tear off my face with his thumb, his mouth curving into a soft smile. "I spoke to the other doctors in my practice this morning. I'll need to be in LA half the month, but the rest of the time I'll be here with you."

I'm speechless, half waiting for a punchline or amendment that doesn't seem to be coming. "But your job is everything to you," I finally say.

"Tali, I'm so in love with you it terrifies me," he says. "And you're the only thing that's mattered for quite a while now. Do you really think I'd take off work to go to an *amusement park* otherwise?"

No, I guess not. I saw he was changing, but it's only now I realize he was changing for me. I go on my toes to kiss him.

"Hayes Flynn living in Lowden, Kansas, population three hundred," I say, with a laugh. "It sounds like the premise of a bad sitcom. One in which you're constantly expressing dismay about the quality of the sushi and wearing Tom Ford suits to Chili's."

His hands palm my ass, pulling me against him. "I'm not eating at Chili's. One of us may need to learn to cook, probably you. But that can wait. Right now, I would like, very much, to go somewhere without your family listening." He nods at the door behind us, where my sisters have their faces pressed to the glass. "It's going to be loud tonight, I assure you."

My body goes taut at the very idea of an entire night having

Hayes to myself. But a Prius with a pizza logo is pulling up in front of the house, and I suppose if we're really doing this, we better start now. "Yes," I tell him. "But first, you should probably meet everyone. And get used to our version of fine dining."

"Hey there, Tali," says the kid coming up the porch steps. "Heard you were back. Good to be home?"

I look up at Hayes, blinking back tears. "Yes," I tell him. "It really is."

EPILOGUE

Four Months Later

Electric stars hang from every lamppost, framed by the black velvet sky.

Snow begins to fall as we climb the church steps, a luminaria on each of them to light our way. It's perfect. *Almost* perfect.

God, I wish Hayes was here to see it.

The church is warm and already crowded, the entry full of jostling children dressed like shepherds and angels, anxious about their performance, eager for tomorrow. It's a night when everyone is happy, and I should be too, given how much better off we are now. Charlotte has bad days but is doing better, Liddie is pregnant again, and my mom is taking marketing classes and figuring out her next steps. They are nearly ready to be left to their own devices, and just in time: My first novel comes out next summer, and the publisher wants a sequel. In the end, Aisling got the same fairytale ending I did—Julian found a way to come through the wall to her. In book two, they'll return to the other side together.

It would be perfect, if Hayes wasn't stuck at the airport, waiting out a storm over the Rockies that shows no sign of letting up. It kills me that after so many holidays spent alone, he's going to spend this one alone too.

I'm not the only one who's disappointed. Though it took some time to adjust to having a man around the house again—especially one whose jaw falls open in dismay when served staples of my mother's cooking (including, but not limited to, Hamburger Helper and Crockpot Cheeseburger Pie)—everyone's grown to love him. Even Sam, who comes out whenever Hayes is here to watch soccer with him and get a home-cooked meal…while ignoring the longing glances from my lovesick younger sister, who could very well end up as one of his students next year.

Hayes has also come to enjoy Kansas—leisurely mornings with coffee and the paper, twilight walks, or a few hours spent reading on the porch. A funny thing happened when he truly began to enjoy his life: he finally realized outrageous sums of money weren't making him any happier. He's focusing more on reconstructive surgeries now, and only does house calls once a week—which he will drop entirely when I move to LA this spring. I still haven't persuaded him to go back to pediatrics, but we have many years ahead.

Drew assures me he's going to propose any day now, but she's also convinced Six is still going to settle down with her, so I'd venture to say foresight isn't her strength.

My mother leads us to a pew. "It's a shame Hayes couldn't make it," she sighs. "I really wanted to see what he got you for Christmas."

"I already got my present." He's agreed to take two weeks off to do Operation Smile next summer, which is all I asked for. Baby steps.

She rolls her eyes. "I'd have asked for jewelry if I were you." But there's a hint of a smile on her face and she nudges me with her elbow before she turns to hug my niece.

The service begins. All the little shepherds and angels come forward and Kaitlin scrambles from my lap to her mom's, at one point standing straight up and shouting, "I can't see!" just as the wise men approach.

Hayes would laugh if he were here, and then he'd remind me that we won't have kids unless I can promise they'll be better behaved than Kaitlin. Given that she's now lying in the aisle and chanting "boring, boring, boring" at the top of her lungs, it feels like a reasonable demand.

Communion begins, and my mother leans over and asks me to go get the car. "It's been snowing the whole time," she says. "I'm worried about my leg on the way back."

I'm not sure why she can't ask Alex to do this, but with a sigh, I grab my coat and purse and walk outside.

I stop on the top step and take it all in—the lights in the trees, the fresh blanket of snow, the velvet sky, wishing Hayes could see it. It really is beautiful. *There will be other years*, I tell myself.

"You're sure you'll be able to give all this up?" asks a voice from the darkness.

Hayes. Standing just a few feet to my left.

I launch myself at him, my throat swelling with the urge to cry, hugging him, kissing him, inhaling him in a way he's come to expect. "You're here?!"

His arms band tight around me. It's only been a week since I saw him last, but it's a long time for us. And he knows exactly how unbearable it's been because I've told him so, every single night. "Of course," he says, burying his face into my hair. "I wasn't about to miss our first Christmas together."

"But *how*? You were still texting me from the airport two hours ago."

"Yes. I just didn't mention the airport was in Dallas," he says, "although I was sure your mother wouldn't be able to keep it a secret."

"I missed you," I tell him, laying my head against his chest. I squeeze him tighter, breathing in the smell of his soap and skin. I want him home and undressed. I wonder how much time we have before my family gets back.

"This is pretty spectacular," he says, nodding at the street stretched out before us. "A rather nice place to propose, even."

I freeze and pull back just enough to see if he's joking. His eyes are earnest, a little worried. And then he reaches into the pocket of his coat and withdraws a black velvet box.

He swallows. "I've never done this part before. I'm...surprisingly anxious."

His hair has fallen over his forehead. I reach up and brush it to the side. "I think you have nothing to worry about."

He catches my hand. "I've been in love with you, I think, since the day I saw you reading in the rain as you walked into work," he says. He presses the box to my palm and covers it with his own. His eyes hold mine, and there's urgency there, as if nothing in the world matters more than my answer. He swallows. "Marry me. *Please* marry me."

I want to tease him about the fact that he's finally said *please*, but I can't. That he wants something this much, and that the thing is me, is nothing short of a miracle. "Yes," I finally whisper. His face breaks into a wide, relieved smile, and he tugs me against him.

"You're sure?" he asks. "You haven't even seen the ring yet."

"It doesn't matter what the ring looks like," I reply.

"Jonathan said the diamond was too big," he says. "I suggested you quite like big things."

I laugh shakily. "Did you really just allude to your dick in a marriage proposal?"

"You already said yes," he says with a quick grin, as he pulls my mouth to his. "You can't take it back."

I don't plan to.

THE END

ACKNOWLEDGMENTS

I fell in love with Tali and Hayes from their very first conversation, and I wanted their story to be perfect. In order to get it there, I leaned on a billion people, so bear with me here.

First, the professionals: T Bird London and Silently Correcting Your Grammar read earlier, different versions of this book, followed by Laverne Clark, who edited it. Then I had the good fortune to discover the wonder that is Sali Benbow-Powers and had her give me a developmental edit on what was *supposedly* a finished product. You're really not supposed to get a developmental edit AFTER the book is done, but I'm so, so grateful I did because she is amazing, and I will never publish a book without her again. It was then proofread by Julie Deaton, and I had to have my lovely, eagle-eyed friend Janis Ferguson give it a final glance before it went forth into the world. Lori Jackson took care of the gorgeous cover and Valentine PR has done a spectacular job of letting the world know this book exists. Thanks so much to all of you!

A deepest, most heartfelt thank you to my beta readers: Shannon Vick Alley, Kimberly Ann, Tricia Coan, Katie Foster Meyer, Laura Steuart, Jill Sullender, Erin Thompson and Jen Wilson Owens, with a special shout-out to Katie and Jen, who read approximately 10,000 versions of this book and still managed to maintain their enthusiasm for it. Thanks also to author Jami Albright for taking time out of her very busy career to read this and assure me I was on the right track.

Finally, thanks to my friends and family for supporting me during this agonizingly long process. I promise I'll never waste a full year on a book again, for all our sakes.

**Sand, sea and stuck . . . with your
ex-boyfriend's grumpy brother in paradise**

Meet Drew and Joshua today.

Available now.

PIATKUS

It's all fun and games until your work nemesis tells you to beg.

You don't want to miss meeting Ben Tate . . .

Available now.

PIATKUS

Some people marry the
enemy in Vegas . . .

Keeley managed to get knocked up by him too.

Available now.

PIATKUS